PRELUDE OF LIES

VICTORIA SMITH

SOUL MATE PUBLISHING

New York

PRELUDE OF LIES

Copyright©2015

VICTORIA SMITH

Cover Design by Syneca Featherstone.

This book is a work of fiction. The names, characters, places, and incidents are the products of the author's imagination or are used fictitiously. Any resemblance to actual events, business establishments, locales, or persons, living or dead, is entirely coincidental.

Published in the United States of America by
Soul Mate Publishing
P.O. Box 24
Macedon, New York, 14502

ISBN: 978-1-68291-132-7

ebook ISBN: 978-1-61935-909-3

www.SoulMatePublishing.com

The publisher does not have any control over and does not assume any responsibility for author or third-party websites or their content.

For my Momma…

Kristine!

Enjoy. V.

Acknowledgements

Thanks to my momma for never giving up on this book or me. Sharing this with you was one of my greatest joys. I hope you're watching from heaven! Thanks to That Man, Those Kids, Bootsquad, and the rest of my crazy family for always supporting me. I don't know what I'd do without you!

CHAPTER 1

Sydney squinted in the darkness. Nothing moved. There wasn't even a paw print in the muddy ground. She'd seen the wounded dog, or she wouldn't be out here. The pitiful, whining gray animal had disappeared, exactly like it had this morning when she'd seen it limping into the woods.

Her heart hurt for the dog. She turned and stopped at the door of the cabin as movement to her left caught her eye. Cold air seeped through her sweatshirt and her breath came out a foggy white cloud. Her pulse increased as she watched a vague circle of light skitter across the still bare trees, stopping to rest in a pothole in the middle of the mostly mud, supposed-to-be-gravel drive.

She shook her head. This was not paranormal stuff. What she saw was a flashlight, and a dying one at that, not an orb or whatever bullshit Daisy spouted off about spirit forms and hauntings. Someone was definitely messing with them.

Still. The odd light spurred her into the cabin, irrational fear causing her to turn the lock and lean against the aged wood.

"No luck?" Daisy's head snapped up at Sydney's quick entrance.

"Gone again. Wounded animals are not . . ." Sydney took a deep breath, trying to shake off the unease.

"The spirits are back." Daisy stepped away from the window, batteries in one hand and a tape recorder in the other. "I'm going to try to talk to them."

"I don't think you should. There's something out there, but not spirits. And it's cold. Really cold." Sydney doused the lamp, ignoring Daisy's impatient shriek, and peeked through the dusty curtain where her sister stared.

"No way. The thermometer says it's fifty degrees." Daisy moved the curtain back farther and shouldered Sydney away from the window.

Fine. Sydney experienced the cold, she knew it was real. "I could see my breath. That thermometer's, like, forty years old and someone *is* out there. On private property in the middle of the night." She grabbed the rifle from the pegs beside the door.

"Not someone, an orb. Look. It's so pretty." Daisy's voice took on a singsong quality as she pressed her face to the grimy glass for a better view.

"Bullshit." Against her will and trembling with irritation, Sydney went to peer over her sister's shoulder, amazed at how the light played over the limbs with slow precision before zipping to the next tree. "Vile Violet probably put Jace up to scaring us. That jackass."

"There's the dog again. Is that blood? Oh, Syd, he's so skinny. We have to help him."

Sydney grabbed the high-powered flashlight and the rifle. So she was a sucker for wounded animals. Maybe trying to help the dog was a bad idea, especially since someone was out there. Had to be Jace. Her anxiety faded.

"Okay." She grabbed a half-eaten sandwich left from their dinner. "We'll try to catch him one more time tonight. If we can't, we'll call someone tomorrow."

"You are not going out there." Daisy tried to take the flashlight. "I mean, not without me."

Releasing the flashlight into her sister's hand, Sydney checked the rifle and opened the door. The baseball-sized light continued to skitter over the sparse stand of trees dividing campsites, despite the fact that they stood in front of its apparent point of origin.

The dog was gone. A puddle of reddish thick liquid left on the ground where it had laid. Sydney opened the foil and waved the food around, hoping to entice the animal into the clearing.

"It's an orb. See? We're not blocking the source." Daisy stepped forward. "Feel that? Cold spots can also come from spirits. They suck energy out of the air around them to try and materialize."

Sure. Right. That made perfect sense. "Turn the flashlight on and check behind us. The dog could be behind those bushes. As for the light, I'm betting The Vileness sent Jace." Sydney was going to kick his ass when they flushed him out.

"Didn't you charge this?" Daisy flicked the button back and forth a bunch of times. The light didn't cooperate.

"Worked fine a minute ago." Sydney shrugged and handed her the flashlight she'd stuck in her back pocket. "Try this one. The batteries are new."

"Nope. Look."

Sydney turned her attention back to the random light. The circular shape had grown, the center swirling with frenetic movement.

"This won't work, Jace," Sydney shouted, clenching her fists at her sides.

"Syd, it's not Jace. The energy sucked the life out of our flashlights. That's why it's bigger. This area has to have a high level of paranormal activity. Maybe the dog is a ghost. Maybe he died here."

Sydney wanted to vomit at Daisy's awestruck tone. "Right. That's why there's blood here. I don't think ghost dogs bleed, Daisy. The dog is real and Jace is trying to scare us." And if he was trying to use that poor animal to get to them, he'd be sorrier than he'd ever been in his life.

Daisy's eyes widened as she grabbed Sydney's arm. "Watch."

The light stopped on a branch before gradually descending to the base of the tree. The glowing circle hovered over the exposed roots before brightening and moving away so fast, Sydney almost didn't see it.

Except she did and there wasn't an explanation. Well, there might be, depending on Jace's determination. Who knew what he'd do in his quest to take over the campground for his beloved, evil grandmother. The flashlight came to life, blinding her for a moment. Sydney took it and scanned the property. Nothing, not even the wounded dog, showed up in the beam.

Satisfied whoever put on the little freak show had left, Sydney grabbed the light from Daisy and turned it off, allowing her eyes to adjust to the darkness.

"Wait. I told you there was something at the pond." Daisy took a step forward.

Wispy clouds hovered over the center of the water. The clouds swirled and moved, as if in a complicated dance. It was beautiful. And just fog.

"I'm going over." Daisy held up the tape recorder.

"You are not. That's fog." Honestly, if she clanked chains in the middle of the night, Daisy would be convinced some tormented soul inhabited their cabin.

Daisy believed everything, even stuff that was so fake a five-year-old wouldn't accept. She was like a supernatural sponge and disregarded scientific explanations no matter what. After growing up with her sister, the amateur ghost hunter, and listening to tale upon tale of ghosts and spirits, Sydney couldn't stomach the subject. At all.

Not that she didn't believe. She'd had her share of unexplainable situations throughout her life. Sydney swore Gramps was with her sometimes. The smell of his aftershave would surround her and she could almost hear his raspy laugh. She didn't know what the difference was. Gramps visits comforted, but Daisy's ghost obsession left her cold.

"I want to help them. They only need to be told it's okay to move on. Sometimes they don't know because their death might have been traumatic or unexpected. The spirits are trapped in the time they died." Daisy moved out of Sydney's grasp.

"No way. Not with Jace and his cronies snooping around. It's not safe. He'll do whatever he can to make us leave. What would Gramps say if we let that happen?" She didn't doubt Jace's grandmother would concoct underhanded and dangerous plots to get them to sign over Brookside.

Daisy shrugged her off, her attention focused on the water and the clouds hovering at the surface. Sydney watched with her for a minute, guilty for being such a bitch about her sister's favorite subject. The clouds did resemble figures, dancing at some long-ago ball.

When one of the clouds stopped and seemed to point a long wispy arm their way, a chill filled Sydney and she gently put her hand on Daisy's shoulder, not wanting her to know how shaky her insides were. "Come on."

Daisy followed, constantly turning toward the pond as they walked. She didn't speak and Sydney's guilt ratcheted up a notch.

Back in the cabin, Sydney locked the door, checked the safety on the rifle and put it back on the pegs. Fitting the charging plug into the back of the spotlight, she refused to think anything had happened to the battery except a bad charge. The wiring in the cabins wasn't up to code, another thing that needed to be fixed before reopening the campground.

"Don't even think about going back out there." She glared at Daisy.

Daisy put her camera down. "Like usual, you're afraid of things you don't need to be afraid of. All I want is a few pictures to send to my friend. You need to relax and open yourself up to new possibilities a lot more. And I'm not only talking about the ghosts."

"Knock it off. This isn't about me and my beliefs, or my social life not measuring up. Quit acting like I'm telling you what to do. Be logical. This place hasn't been open in five years. It's not safe in the daytime, let alone when you can't see where you're going. I don't want you to get hurt, by nature or Jace." Sydney took a deep breath, trying to quell her irritation. Why did Daisy always bring up Sydney's choices and lack of social life?

"Fine. Whatever." Daisy turned to the window, effectively shutting Sydney out.

"Daisy, please. I can't do this without you. I know you don't want to be here. Hell, I'm not sure I want to be here, but we promised Gramps. As soon as we beat Vile Violet at this stupid game of hers, you can go. No questions asked." And Sydney hoped Daisy changed her mind in the end.

"Why did he marry her, Syd? Gramps did everything she wanted and she was so mean. It's stupid." Daisy faced her, her hand still on the window.

"I know. I wish I knew why Gramps did the things he did. Marrying Violet, the bizarre stipulations he let her put on our ownership of Brookside, he had to have reasons. We just might not ever know." Unless they could find Gramps' journals, though reading his personal thoughts wasn't something she really wanted to do. Her chest ached. She missed him so much. "Beating The Vileness is all that matters right now."

Daisy stepped away from the window and Sydney wondered if she'd given up on wanting to go outside. "She didn't used to be so mean. At first we thought she was good for Gramps. Remember?"

"Not that we had much chance to get to know her." Sydney shrugged, hoping Daisy would drop the subject.

Vile Violet had banned them from hanging out at Brookside shortly after she married their grandfather and it still hurt.

"Why are we even here? We're not going to beat her. The will favors her and so did the judge. She probably paid him off. She has the money and resources to stop us. She's going to win. Let's just sell and get out while we can. Let her build her stupid casino. What difference does it make to us?" Daisy fingered her camera, no conviction in her words.

"Don't talk like that," Sydney warned, knowing Daisy only spouted off in frustration, but also maybe a little afraid because she'd been having similar thoughts lately.

"I know. I'm sorry. Trying to reopen this place is just so overwhelming. Our cash is low. We can't afford to hire help and even if we can open by our June deadline, what do we have to offer guests? I mean, except for a grand case of poison ivy and more mosquito bites than they can scratch?" Daisy spread her arms wide and let out a frustrated sigh.

Daisy *was* right. Their task was enormous, but Sydney wasn't about to give up yet. She needed to do this for Gramps, for Daisy, and for herself. Why else would she quit her high-paying job, leave her condo and move into the middle of the tick-infested woods to run a campground? She and Daisy promised Gramps they'd reopen, and they would.

"We're going to do this, Daisy. We have to." They had no choice and they both knew it, despite the griping and complaining. Unwilling to argue, Sydney got up and banged her bedroom door behind her.

Daisy watched Sydney slam the door, guilt almost making her change her mind about going outside again. No matter what Sydney thought or chose to ignore, spirits did roam the campground. Daisy watched the balls of light from the window as she tried to decide how to make her sister believe. The injured, disappearing dog, the lights, the ghostly figures on the pond and the strange noises from the bathhouse neither of them liked to use. Unfortunately, she wasn't qualified to prove anything, but she knew someone who was.

In her heart, Daisy knew Brookside was where she needed to be. She couldn't escape the feeling that something big was about to happen and she felt guilty for her negative thoughts. Wanting to be here was an entirely different story. Grabbing her camera, she opened the front door, hoping Sydney didn't hear the loud creak and mentally adding a can of "anti-squeak" to her list of things they needed as she shut the door as gently as possible. Thoughts raced through her head as she tried to find the positives in this situation.

When she couldn't, she hunkered down beside a tree and waited for the spirits she knew would come.

Sydney woke to the smell of coffee. The room seemed brighter than normal. Daisy waved through the window, scrubbing the panes with a concentrated expression that told Sydney she hadn't slept much.

With a groan, she rolled over, her body protesting the physical labor they'd done since they arrived. Yesterday, they'd spent the entire day untangling years of poison ivy from the power boxes. When they arrived the day before, they'd used every moment of daylight making the cabin habitable.

The door opened and Daisy bounded in, her bright smile in contrast with the dark circles under her eyes. "So, I've been thinking."

"Obviously." Sydney forced a pleasant smile, even though she cringed inside. Somehow, she knew Daisy's thinking didn't bode well for her. "It looks great in here. What's on your mind?"

"Well. I watched the pond for a long time and took some pictures. There is something out there. Not Jace. Spirits. Lots of them. You need to see what I captured. And I wonder if maybe we should call a paranormal investigator? I know a few people who might be willing to come out and see what we've got here." Daisy stared out the window and Sydney wondered what she had up her sleeve.

She wasn't even going to bitch at her for going outside last night, even though she wanted to. Daisy was a grown woman and Sydney had no right to treat her like a little kid.

"Do you really think someone's going to come and watch weird lights and funky fog?" Sydney got out of bed with a groan. Daisy would be relentless until they'd fully discussed Daisy's idea.

"There's more than that and you know it. What about the moans in the bathhouse and that dog? Syd, he just disappeared. If you'd only admit weird stuff's going on around here, we might be able to communicate with the spirits."

"With dead people? I'm sorry, but there has to be an explanation for the strange things we've seen. Your friends would only be disappointed. Not to mention we can't afford another expense. We have enough waiting to suck up the little money we do have." Sydney walked away, Daisy on her heels.

"That's my point. These guys try to find reasons to explain the strange things. Their first effort is to debunk supposed paranormal activity. They're very cautious about saying a place is haunted. Like you, only they actually believe in spirits and paranormal activity. They won't charge us. They're good friends. They'll do it as a favor to me. I've helped them on cases without pay many times. Can I call them?" She bounced on the balls of her feet, her smile wide.

Daisy would know she had a great argument. Anything that didn't spend the little bit of available cash would work for Sydney. Still, the thought filled her with dread.

"And what if they say this place is haunted? What then? What does it change?" Sydney fought to control her negativity. This was the first time Daisy had acted like she wanted anything to do with the campground restoration.

"There are a lot of people who seek out encounters with ghosts and spirits. We find out which areas have higher paranormal activity and we charge extra for those sites. We can plan ghost tours and other activities to cater to the people who want to be scared. I mean, as long as the spirits aren't malicious. We might attract more guests. Like a marketing gimmick." Daisy's slick talk made Sydney's head spin.

"So we're going to capitalize on the dead? Don't you think that'll piss them off?" Sydney cringed. She didn't want a bunch of angry spirits hanging around and she didn't want to annoy the spirits she knew were here, despite what she told Daisy about the lights and fog.

"Just think about it. Please?"

"Okay. I will." What else was she supposed to say? Ghost tours were popular in neighboring formerly Civil War occupied towns, but were they plausible for Brookside? Thankfully her cell rang, cutting off the conversation.

Sydney picked up the phone without checking the caller ID. As soon as Jace's voice came over the line, she wanted to pitch the phone into the middle of Daisy's haunted pond. Damn Vile Violet for setting her grandson on them. Since the reading of the will, Jace had been relentless in his quest to help his grandmother take over Brookside.

Jace Levine was going to drive her insane. And she'd never even met him.

"What did you say?" How she wished he stood in front of her so she could deck him.

"I said, we should meet for lunch. Grandmother wants me to go over the terms of sale. Maybe we can come to some kind of compromise that suits you and your sister since you're hell bent on going against your original agreement." His suave, condescending tone grated on her nerves.

"There are no terms of sale. Your grandmother is trying to bully us. We have until June." She paced the tiny front porch of the cabin, wishing her cell signal would dissipate as it so often did out here.

"Grandmother has filled me in on the basics. How about you tell me the rest over lunch? You have a verbal agreement to sell to her. Her contractors are waiting to break ground. The project can't move forward until the paperwork is complete and every day progress is stalled means money out of her pocket. Surely, you know how much that costs? What kind of businesswoman are you?" If she could just reach through the phone, grab his throat, and cut off his arrogant words with her bare hands.

"Listen to me very carefully, Jace. I will not tell you this again. I made no agreement with your grandmother beyond the stipulations in my grandfather's will. I will not willingly give up rights to this property. Brookside belongs to my family. You are not my family. Vile Violet is not my family. This place was my grandfather's dream and I intend to honor him by making Brookside better than it was. Leave us alone and quit trying to scare us."

"What did you call my grandmother?" His words were low, but laced with venom.

"Go to hell and take your grandmother with you." She thought about smashing her phone, but instead threw her head back and let out a screech that echoed through the woods.

"Did you really call her Vile Violet to her grandson?" Sydney grinned at Daisy's smirk.

"I guess I did. He's such an asshole. I swear if I ever run into him I'm going to bust his lip. Violet told him we made a verbal agreement of sale."

"Give him a black eye for me, too. I called Marshal. When should I tell him to come?"

Sydney pressed her fingers to her eyes. "Who's Marshal?"

"My friend. The paranormal investigator?" Daisy's "duh" tone made Sydney wish the ends of her fingers were pointed, then she could poke her own eyes out. She'd be blind and wouldn't have to deal with any of this silly crap.

Didn't she tell Daisy she'd think about it? Why had she so foolishly agreed to even consider the idea? Sydney pressed harder, little white stars erupting behind her eyelids. She deserved to be blind. Taking a few deep breaths, she finally sighed. What was the worst that could happen? Besides, having the extra people around might help keep Jace in check.

"I'll tell you what, let's get this place cleaned up a little better, have either a cabin or actual campsites your friends can use, better bathroom facilities, and we'll go for it. I can't imagine letting anyone traipse through the woods right now. This place isn't safe and we can't afford a lawsuit." She sighed, resigned.

"Yay. Thank you for not saying no." Daisy hugged her.

"It's going to be a while. The other cabins aren't inhabitable and the campsites are a mess." Sydney hated to burst her bubble.

"Not as long as you think. Remember Tucker? The guy I dated a few months ago?"

Sydney nodded. She remembered. She didn't know for sure, but was reasonably certain Tucker had broken Daisy's heart.

"He called me, said he needs to train some guys on new equipment before landscaping season starts and wanted to know if he could use the campground."

"That makes no sense." Sydney started toward the bathhouse, trying to wrap her head around why Tucker would want to come here. Daisy rushed to catch up with her.

"That's what I told him. He said this is how he does things. He finds a property in need of work and does whatever the owners want for the cost of material, just to train his guys and make sure the equipment is working properly before the beginning of his season." Daisy avoided meeting Sydney's eyes. Interesting.

"I'm surprised he doesn't have a waiting list then." Sydney figured Tucker probably wanted something else from Daisy, but kept that to herself.

Sydney had always liked Tucker, especially when she found out how he combined hard work with helping out troubled kids. He and Daisy had been a good match. Sydney didn't think she'd ever seen her sister happier.

"Well, he does, but his regular crew is starting a huge job not far from here. This way he can go back and forth between locations. He gets to train his summer help and still make a profit. The bulk of the work will be done on weekends until school is out, but he'll have his new, out-of-school crew here throughout the week until he feels they're ready for bigger jobs. He'll be here in the morning to do a walk through and maybe get started. That is, unless you want me to call him and tell him no." Daisy seemed like she didn't know what she wanted Sydney to say and Sydney couldn't help but wonder why Daisy and Tucker had stopped dating.

"He's going to let us tell him what we want? Everything we want?" The idea sounded great. A little too great. Sydney stopped at the bench in front of the bathhouse.

"Absolutely. Anything we want. They'll take care of all the poison ivy. All we pay for is materials. Fuel, any special rental equipment, plants, and mulch. It's perfect."

Even though those costs could break their already shaky bank, Sydney couldn't say no. It would take her and Daisy months of constant work to clear just the campsites and they definitely didn't have that much time. June was only a few weeks away.

"Okay then. Excellent. That's the best news we've had since we signed those papers." The thought of someone else trimming, weeding, and dealing with the mess of poison ivy was a dream. Maybe they'd open on time after all.

Her happy moment didn't last long enough. The low, spooky moan coming from the bathhouse froze the smile on her face and turned her stomach with dread.

CHAPTER 2

The next morning, Daisy avoided the creepy bathhouse. They'd endured that sad moaning nearly all night. There was nothing in the stalls. They'd even called the sheriff to come and check things out. He'd found nothing. Sydney had expected a tape recorder, something to explain how Jace was trying to scare them, but nothing. Daisy was certain it was paranormal. There was no doubt in her mind. Maybe the constant noise would encourage Sydney to allow Marshal to come soon.

She stopped at the edge of the clearing and watched Tucker work, her emotions as tangled as the vines growing everywhere. Damn, he was gorgeous. And nice and generous and romantic. And a jerk. He had a smile that reminded her how good things had been between them. Before he ditched her. Why had she allowed him to come to Brookside again? And now he was coming to talk to her. Ugh.

"We'll finish this section of poison today. Thank you so much for letting us start so soon and for allowing us to experiment here. My new guys are shaping up already. Well, most of them." He stood so close she could smell him, a mixture of grass, sweat, earth, and bug spray. Why did that turn her on?

Stepping back, she glanced over his shoulder as one of the crew ran screaming out of the woods, wildly swiping at his head. Watching the new workers had been almost comical, except for the tractor that now sat on the bottom of the pond. Even that had been amusing considering no one had gotten hurt.

"You think?" She couldn't help but laugh as the teenager with the bug issue shivered and stomped.

"Trust me. Their progress is impressive. That kid there, the one you're laughing at, started out this morning certain he wouldn't last an hour. He's a smart kid, graduated at the top of his class, but has never been outside the city. Now he's covered with mosquito bites and had an interesting encounter with a snake, but he's still here. I heard him tell his brother that the woods felt like home to him." The pride in Tucker's voice was obvious. Daisy's heart softened. Why did he have to be so admirable?

Tucker's work with troubled teens and young men previously moving in the wrong direction amazed her. "I'm sorry. I forgot how much these kids have missed."

"Don't be sorry. Their antics amuse me, too. I can't let them know how much." He smiled again. The twin dimples made her want to jump his bones right in the middle of the clearing and forget he broke her heart.

She had to change the subject. "Sydney wants to do a barbeque for the crew when you're done. Let me know when you think that might be."

"Three weeks. Unless it rains, or something else bad happens. We'll get the tractor out of the pond first thing. My brother's bringing a crane. We'll probably be here at sun up. I'd say we'll try to keep the noise down, but . . ."

Daisy laughed. "Bring me a vanilla cappuccino and I promise not to bitch. Oh, and you'd better bring Syd one, too."

"Yes, ma'am." Tucker saluted and went back to his workers, leaving her with a heart full of painful memories and an overheated libido. She watched him as he clasped the shoulder of the kid with the bug issue and directed him back into the stand of trees.

With distance between them, the blood returned to her brain along with the pain of losing him. She wanted to hate him, but couldn't. Not wanting to dwell on Tucker, she went to find Sydney. Maybe she'd let her bring Marshal in tonight. She really didn't need Sydney's permission. Gramps left Brookside to them equally but Sydney had always been their leader. Daisy usually went along with her sister because she was right, sometimes.

Sydney considered Daisy's paranormal beliefs a bunch of crap. If you couldn't see it, touch it or explain it, according to Sydney, it didn't exist. Sometimes, Daisy liked to drive her nuts by spouting off urban legends and old ghost stories as fact, swearing they were true and pushing her sister into annoyance. That was a little mean, so she usually only did it when Sydney drove her nuts, like lately. Really, all Daisy wanted was for Sydney to relax a little.

Daisy occasionally hated the free spirit side of her own personality. She spent her teenage years trying to override nature by dressing like the other kids and attempting more cerebral pursuits. There was no way she wanted to turn out like her mother, a woman who'd never bothered with her daughter and had saddled with the most hideous name.

Starshine. What the hell kind of name was that? What the hell kind of woman drops her eight-day-old kid off for the weekend and then never comes back?

Sydney always made her feel like she belonged, even before Sydney's parents adopted her and allowed her to use her middle name, Daisy. Sydney's shared rage at Nadine made Daisy feel normal. She couldn't have a better sister.

When Daisy finally caught up with her, Sydney stood on the dinky porch in front of their shared cabin. Something was wrong. Hoping Jace hadn't called back and threatened them again, she hustled the remaining steps, nearly tripping over a rock.

"What's the matter?" Anxiety made her shaky as she stared at her sister's pale face and wide eyes.

"I, uh, I was in, um, Cabin B and there was . . ." Sydney stopped and stared into the woods.

"What a snake? A rat? What happened? Are you okay? Did you get bit?" She rubbed Sydney's arms, her cold skin alarming.

"I don't know. There was something. Someone there."

"Jace? Is he still here? I'll kick his ass."

Sydney shook her head. "Not Jace."

She took a deep breath and Daisy waited for her to compose herself even though the pause could kill her.

"I was in Cabin B, trying to clean so your friends can come. I opened the windows in the bunk room and the window slammed shut. Twice. Until I propped it. I know that was just the window."

Daisy rolled her eyes. Sydney had an explanation for everything. "Something else happened?"

"Lots of something else. The temperature dropped by, like, twenty degrees. I heard voices, female voices, calling out. It sounded like someone was running around the front room. When I went out, no one was there. And then, then, someone hurt me." Sydney turned and raised her T-shirt, the red handprint on her lower back raised in an angry-looking welt. "I swear there was no one around. I was in the bunk room. My back was to the wall. The window shut again and opened four times in a row." Sydney shook, tears streaming down her face.

Daisy gathered her in a hug and tried to soothe her. "I believe you." She tried to hide her excitement that her instinct had been right. Sydney had never believed her. Hell, sometimes *she* didn't believe herself.

"Can your friends come tonight?" Sydney's shaky voice broke her heart.

"I'll call Marshal as soon as you're okay." Daisy patted her back, hating to see her sister so upset.

Sydney straightened and took a deep breath. Daisy swore she watched each piece of Sydney's careful control slip back into place.

"I'm fine. I picked up sandwiches from the deli when I went for supplies." Like nothing had happened. If the welts on Sydney's back didn't attest to her experience, Daisy would have trouble believing her sister had admitted to an unexplainable encounter.

"Great. You use our bathroom. I'll take the bathhouse. I'm going to shower and call Marshal. Give me twenty minutes." She grabbed her bag of toiletries, a towel, and her tie-dyed sweat suit and dialed Marshal's number as she went to the creepy-as-hell bathhouse.

Marshal answered on the first ring with a sexy hello.

Daisy wished she could muster up enough attraction for the man who would only ever be a friend, no matter that he shared her passion for the paranormal and was drop-dead gorgeous.

"Can you come tonight? My sister had an experience and she's a little freaked."

"Your sister admitted that?" Daisy knew she had probably told him far too much about Sydney. Hopefully, none of her rants would come back to bite her in the ass.

"She's got a welt on her back as proof. If you hurry, you might get to see it before she wills it away."

"I can be there in two hours. We're ready. Things are somewhat slow around here, so we hoped you'd get your sister to change her mind about when to come. I don't have a full crew, but we'll manage."

"How many guys? The tent areas are kind of rough yet. The cabin where my sister had her experience sleeps eight. Things are primitive at best around here. You'll need air mattresses, sleeping bags, towels, that kind of stuff. Just so you remember."

"I remember. Already packed and ready to go. Four and a guy that's tagging along. He's an author and a major skeptic. He's working on a book debunking paranormal investigators. I'd love to give him a reason to change his opinions. Don't get me wrong, he's a nice guy, but his attitude sometimes gets in the way. Especially since our last case was pretty damned lame."

"He'll probably get along great with Sydney."

"I was just thinking that. Are you sure you don't want to marry me?" He laughed.

Daisy knew he was teasing. He felt the same way she did.

"I will if you ever work up the guts to ask me proper-like." See you in two." She thumbed off the call and took a deep breath before entering the substandard and spooky bathing facilities.

Daisy had spent too much time in this bathhouse, and the other one, today. The list of what they needed to do seemed to grow and she wasn't sure they'd be able to salvage the worn out buildings. The toilets were outdated and needed replacing. The tiles in the showers were disgusting or missing and only one sink out of six remained. And the moaning from the stall on the end was enough to make hair stand on end, even in the bright daylight.

At least the sewer systems passed inspection this morning. She said a silent thanks to Gramps for investing in a quality system his last year in business as she hurried through her routine without venturing past the first shower stall. Thankfully they hadn't heard the moaning since early this morning.

Headlights scanned the cabin windows not quite two hours later. Marshal was as punctual as usual. A van and an SUV pulled in with a sleek black sports car at the rear. Daisy figured that was probably the pain-in-the-ass guy Marshal talked about. She didn't think she wanted to meet him, probably because he gave Marshal such a hard time. Sydney would most likely find an instant ally.

Marshal jumped out of the first van and she rushed to hug him, Sydney trailing behind like she was going to a funeral. Marshal smelled too good and looked far too fine. If the bright red face and speechlessness of her sister was any indication, Sydney noticed at least one of Marshal's crew. In a big way. Daisy just couldn't figure out which one.

After hugging Dave, Eric, and Ron and introducing Sydney, who now seemed like she'd swallowed a bee, Daisy held her hand out to the only person she didn't know.

"Daisy Brooks. Good to meet you." He had a nice face, except for the scowl.

"Graham Winston. Didn't know this would be old home week. I'm sure whatever we find here is going to be *real* reliable." He released her hand quickly, as if she was dirty. She decided right then she didn't like him much.

He turned to Marshal. "How will I know this scene isn't something all of you cooked up to prove my opinions are wrong? You all are very well acquainted."

Sydney stepped forward, and Daisy hid a smile. She knew that expression, the one her sister used when someone was being unfairly judged. There went any ideas she might have had about hooking her sister up with the snotty man.

"I can assure you, Mr. Winston, this scene, as you put it, is a group of people who just happen to enjoy working together. I would not allow them on the property if I felt their intentions were anything but professional."

Marshal winked after Sydney turned away with the keys to Cabin B in her hand. Daisy didn't miss the interest in Graham's eyes, either. Might turn out to be an interesting couple of days around the old campground.

Sydney hid her fear well as she unlocked the cabin door and moved to the side for Marshal and his crew to enter. Sydney couldn't fool her though, and Daisy grabbed her hand on the way inside. Marshal's eyes lit up as he scanned the room. She gasped and so did Sydney.

"What the hell?" Daisy said a little louder than intended.

"This place was spotless when I left." Sydney raised her chin, daring anyone to argue.

"Excellent." Marshal studied the paper products strewn over the floor. Since they weren't sure how the water system inspection was going to turn out, they'd agreed on disposable plates to save the little water they knew they had available.

Two packages of paper plates lay on the floor, and another had been opened and strewn around like someone had played a game of indoor Frisbee. Napkins littered the windowsills and an entire roll of toilet paper had been strung around the room.

"This wasn't spirits." Marshal picked up an empty beer can from the counter. "Unless you left this behind?" He turned to Sydney.

"Not my brand. And no, it wasn't here before." Sydney visibly relaxed and released Daisy's hand. "We're having some trouble with a few individuals who believe this property should belong to them."

Marshal checked his watch. "Let's get this cleaned up and settle in for the night. In the morning, I'd like to interview both of you. We'll hook up the equipment tomorrow."

"Syd, go to bed. You look like hell. I'll help with the cleanup. Besides, you've already done it once." Daisy gave her a gentle push toward the door.

Sydney nodded and left the cabin. The fact that she hadn't argued worried Daisy. Marshal watched Sydney with barely veiled interest. Daisy was pretty sure sparks would fly before he realized Sydney wasn't the woman for him.

"I'd like to interview you as well. And your sister. But not at the same time." Graham's irritated demeanor seemed absent.

Daisy nodded, though she didn't want to. She hoped the guy had an open mind, even if he never changed it. Maybe after seeing Marshal's crew in action on a legitimate case he'd start to appreciate paranormal investigators. After helping clean up the cabin, she told Marshal to check out the pond and went to make sure Sydney was okay. Marshal wanted to talk to Sydney about her experience tonight, but was satisfied with the pictures Daisy convinced Sydney to let her take.

Their days started too early lately. Usually they were both sound asleep by now. And tomorrow would start even earlier, thanks to Tucker and his crew. Daisy shoved thoughts of Tucker out of her overflowing brain and locked the cabin door behind her.

Sydney sat at the table, a bottle of water in front of her and a pensive expression. "Is this okay? Are we doing the right thing?"

"There's no right or wrong to it. This is our property and our decision. We'll know if something underhanded is going on here and with Marshal's crew around, we'll have protection from Jace and Violet. Marshal said they'll definitely watch out for us. I didn't get a chance to tell him everything, but Marshal gets the picture. He's a good guy and he's excited to investigate here." She sat down, wishing for her bed, as uncomfortable as it was. "That Graham is kind of interesting. Cute, in an arrogant kind of way."

"He's a jackass." Sydney flicked her water bottle.

"Yeah, but kind of a cute jackass." Why did she find it necessary to hook Sydney up with Graham? She didn't like the guy much either.

"I didn't notice." That thoughtful expression meant something.

"Who did you notice?" She studied Sydney.

"No one."

"Oh please. They're all handsome in their own way. Just maybe not the highly-polished material you prefer."

"Considering how long it's been since I've had sex, I'm surprised I didn't think the arrogant bastard was hot."

Sydney laughed, her face bright red, but a sparkle finally was back in her eyes. "Too bad none of them are my type."

"There's a type for hot sex? Go for it, pick one and do him with no regrets. Tell him straight up that you're not interested in anything more than a few nights between the sheets." Uh-oh. She should have kept quiet. Sydney's eyebrows raised and that motherly disapproving glare she saved for Daisy's wild times appeared.

Daisy waited for the questions. Sydney would want to know how many of Marshal's crew she'd slept with. Before Daisy got her back up and prepared to defend herself, Sydney's expression softened and she sighed.

"Sure. I wish. I'm not as ballsy as you. Just once, I wish I could. One night of fantastic sex with a stranger and no guilt afterward. That's a fantasy. I could never do that." Sydney put her head down and groaned.

"You have to be true to yourself. Don't beat yourself up because you're not a slut like me." Not quite a laugh because she wondered if that was really how her sister viewed her.

"You're not a slut. Far from it. I think I'm a prude."

"You are not. We're quite a pair, aren't we? Sitting here discussing our sex lives with a cabin full of prime candidates just a few feet away. If those guys weren't like my brothers I'd consider finding a warm place to snuggle."

"What about Tucker? He did a whole lot of watching you and flirting today."

Daisy didn't want to talk about Tucker, but it wasn't Sydney's fault things had turned out the way they did.

"Tucker is sweet, romantic, and wonderful. Too bad his ex-girlfriend turned up pregnant about two months after we started dating. He went back to her. To do the right thing." She tried to ignore the stabbing pain in her heart by peeling the label off of Sydney's water bottle.

"Oh, honey. I'm so sorry. Why didn't you tell me?" Sydney grabbed her hand and squeezed.

"I wanted to, but it was easier to be bitter. I knew you'd make me realize how much he meant to me and I didn't want to admit that. I don't know. It seemed like one more way I screwed up. I guess I felt like a jerk."

"For what? How did you screw that up? Because you still like the guy and he did the right thing? He'd be a jerk if he didn't and so would you, no matter what the rest of civilization does. What kind of an example would he be for those kids he works with?"

"I know. I would have broken things off with him if he would have told her to pound sand or questioned his role as the baby's father. It just sucks, you know? I haven't been with anyone since him. I just can't bring myself to get involved, even for simple sex." Ouch. That hurt to admit. Sydney was probably the only person who understood though.

She tugged her forward and hugged her across the table. "I know. I'm sorry you had to deal with it alone. Maybe you can have some closure with Tucker now."

"Maybe. I don't know." Daisy fought the tears climbing her throat. She would not cry for Tucker. Ever.

"There's got to be a reason Tucker's here."

Daisy didn't know what to say. She cared and she didn't.

"Doesn't matter. I'm okay, Syd. Really." Daisy ripped the label the rest of the way off of Sydney's water bottle, knowing Sydney would see right through her lie. Hopefully, she'd let the subject drop for now.

Silence loomed for a few minutes. Finally, thank goodness, Sydney stood and stretched. "If you're sure you're okay, I think I'm going to bed." Sydney yawned.

"I'm fine. Honest. I've been dealing with this thing for months now. The question is are you okay?"

Sydney nodded. "I'm too tired to even think about ghosts. Or sex."

CHAPTER 3

Okay, so only part of that was true. Sydney definitely was too tired to have sex, but not to think about it. Unless of course, Marshal knocked on her window and then she'd have to let him in.

Hopefully, Daisy didn't notice her reaction to Marshal. Sydney thought all the fluids had drained out of her body as soon as she caught sight of him. Damn, but the man was beautiful. The black T-shirt showed off every muscle. There couldn't be an ounce of fat on him.

She cringed. Letting Daisy know she lusted after one of her best friends wasn't a good idea. She'd been too chicken to ask about him for fear the question would give her away. This was one of those times she'd love to have Daisy's attitude about sex. A couple of nights in Marshal's bed would be enough. More than that would give her complications she didn't need or want.

Too bad she was too scared to act on the impulse.

She could dream about him. At least that would keep her mind off what happened in the same cabin where the guys now slept. Forcing the experience out of her weary mind, she settled in and tried to picture Marshal without his shirt.

The next morning, her fantasy came true as she followed the overgrown path back to the cabin after her walk. Too bad she hadn't kept her head up so she could have watched him come toward her. As usual, her attention was on the ever-growing list of things that needed taken care of before they could even think of opening the campground, and she ran right into him.

At first, she thought she'd bumped into a tree. Stunned, she stayed still, wondering if trees really put out that much heat.

"Sorry. Are you okay?" Husky voice, warm, solid chest. Holy shit.

She tried to compose herself, slyly bringing her hand up to her chin to make sure she wasn't drooling. His chest was directly in front of her and she didn't want to stare. His eyes were no help, they had the same effect on her. She was an idiot and now he would know as well.

"I'm fine." She almost asked if he was okay, but figured she'd have done little damage to him even if she tried. "Sorry. Wasn't paying attention."

"Me either. Trying to get in a run and come up with a schedule." He held up a notebook similar to hers.

"Same here. There's a lot to do." She managed to relax and met his eyes. The warmth there did little for the carnal urges she'd had since meeting him, but she liked the tiny crinkles around his eyes.

"If my team being here is holding you up, we can come back another time. I do believe you both are safe here, for the most part." His smile melted her insides.

"Actually, no. I might not completely believe in what you do, but I'll be grateful to have some answers." *And the protection you provide*. She almost said that last part, but decided against it. She didn't want him to think that was the only reason she'd agreed to this investigation.

"Fair enough. Did Daisy mention I need to interview you about what happened yesterday?"

"She did. Just tell me when." Sydney didn't really want to talk about that ever again, but the truth was, she needed answers.

"After breakfast? I'd like you to be a part of the investigation tonight, if you're up to it. Maybe if you see how we operate, you'll have a better understanding of what we do." Did he seem nervous?

"I hoped I could. No matter what my sister says, I am not closed minded and unreachable." Why was she so defensive? Why did she care what he thought? What had Daisy told him?

"She didn't say exactly that, but she did tell me how she works at getting under your skin by exaggerating pretty much any story out there." He winked and her lower limbs dissolved.

"That brat." Sydney couldn't help but smile. "I had a feeling, but she's always so serious about the subject. I thought for sure she had cracked up."

"That's what she says about you."

Sydney quelled the brief flare of irritation and smiled.

"I'll see you after breakfast." He gave her a half-salute. She couldn't resist the urge to turn and watch him walk away.

His broad back and gray running shorts were enough to make a blind woman drool. She couldn't stop watching and wondered what Daisy would say if she caught her. Yikes. She needed to get a grip and bury the uncharacteristic itch.

She had her libido under control by the time she arrived at the cabin. Except Graham stood on the porch, and all the thoughts about imaginary hot sex with Marshal evaporated as irritation filled the spaces.

"Can I help you?"

"I was hoping I could help you," he said.

The effort it took to not roll her eyes almost zapped her strength. Somehow, she managed to remain polite.

"With what?" She had a feeling she wasn't going to like anything that came out of his mouth.

"I think this whole ghost hunting crap is bunk. From what I understand, you share a similar view of the situation. I thought we might put our heads together and see if these 'top-notch investigators' can spot a ruse, or if they're as dumb as I think they are." He brushed at a fly that continuously landed on his expensive-looking running jacket.

His irritation at the persistent insect amused her, but she tried not to show it. She allowed his words to sink in, stunned. Angry, that he assumed because of her skeptical view, she'd be a party to his scheme.

"So, regardless of the fact that you're researching paranormal activity for a book that pays your bills, you want to mess with the odds and arrange the outcome? I may be a skeptic, but I am not so sealed off that I can't accept the possibility of paranormal activity. Just because I happen to disregard the stories, doesn't mean they can't be true." She was an inch from his nose, barely able to see the shock on his face.

"So, is that a no?"

"Of course it's a no. And don't think I'm going to keep your secret. Marshal and his team will know you want to trick them. You obviously formed a wrong opinion of me." She backed off, putting some distance between them.

"Obviously. Never mind. Without help, there's no way. I would like to interview you, if you would be so kind?" From the scowl on his face, Sydney figured he knew he screwed up.

For a brief second, she felt for the guy. She knew all too well what it was like to be surrounded by die hard believers unwilling to see the hard evidence or logical possibilities. From what Marshal said, most of that had been faked by her sister to irritate her, so now she wasn't quite sure what her sister believed.

"Tell you what, if, by the end of this investigation, you

can find a shred of an open mind, I'll give you an interview. Start treating my sister's friends like professionals. I would imagine you hate to be treated like anything less?" Sydney moved past him. "And FYI, don't wear cologne out here. The flies love it. So do the mosquitoes." She banged the door closed behind her as she left Graham standing on the porch.

Daisy applauded as she shut the door. "Well said. Did you know I was in here?"

"No. I thought you were with Tucker. You thought I said all that for your benefit?" Sydney leaned against the door.

"Kind of." Guilt washed over Daisy's face and glanced at the floor.

"The guy is the biggest asshole I've ever met, except for Jace. I hate that superior attitude bullshit. Did you hear what he wanted me to do?" She wanted to kick something.

"He's a jerk. I'll let Marshal know, or maybe you should tell him yourself." Daisy grinned.

"Maybe I will. I'm supposed to meet with him in a little while and tell him what happened yesterday." Her face burned, but she had to know. "Can I ask you something?"

"I knew it. You have the hots for Marshal. Excellent. Seriously, there is not now, and never was, anything between us. He's a great guy. Sometimes I wish I felt more for him, but there's no spark. He's like my brother. And he's all yours."

"I'm not sure I want him." And she wasn't. At least not long term. God, what was wrong with her? Was she seriously considering following her sister's advice?

"Well, just in case you do, I give you my blessing. As if you need it." Daisy laughed.

Somehow, that didn't make her feel any better. "Don't mention any of this to Marshal. God, I feel like a teenager. The next thing you know I'll have a zit."

"Sister's honor." Daisy hooked her pinky and Sydney joined hers in their symbolic act of promise.

"Heard Graham propositioned you." Marshal motioned to the chair across from him. Too bad he insisted the question and answer session be done in this freaky cabin. She didn't feel good in here and told him so.

"That's not uncommon. We'll try to help you find out what's going on and figure out how to deal with it." His words were soothing even though Sydney figured he used the speech often.

"Why do you let Graham tag along? He thinks you guys are nuts and wants to sabotage you."

"To be honest, I don't know. Except to say that underneath all that arrogant machismo, he's a decent guy. I think he put on an act for you, to see if he could get a different angle on the story." Marshal leaned back on the chair, his T-shirt stretching over his stomach and chest. Sydney forgot to breathe.

"Why are you defending him? What's he got on you that you don't want out?" She'd meant the question as a joke, but when Marshal's expression glazed over, she figured she'd hit a nerve. Interesting.

Marshal shook his head as if he took the statement like the joking she'd meant, but the unmistakable current of tension told a different story. She allowed him to change the subject and recounted the events of yesterday afternoon.

"So where were you when it touched you?"

They were standing in the bunk room. She pointed to the wall closest to a neatly made up bunk.

That bed had to be Graham's. All the other beds were a mess of sleeping bags, clothes and personal items. "You moved the bed. I was here." She pointed at a spot near the head of the immaculate lower bunk.

"We had to. The rain dripped in there. Poor Graham was getting wet. I couldn't sleep with him whining above me." He cringed a little as if he knew telling her the cabin leaked would overload her already-packed repair list.

"Oh. I didn't realize it rained last night. Sorry." She ignored that the neat bed belonged to him because she wasn't sure what it made her feel. As she turned to show him where she'd stood yesterday, icy-cold tendrils wrapped around her. Her breath came out as a fog and she shivered.

Marshal held up a piece of equipment around her, circling her as he shook his head and grinned. Finally, the freeze lifted. Her shaking did not.

"Is there anyone here who'd like to speak?" he asked over and over with pauses like someone would actually answer, moving the tiny tape recorder in a slow sweep around the room.

He patted her shoulder as he passed. "Let's go." He motioned, allowing her to exit first.

She re-seated herself at the table, waiting as Marshal grabbed a briefcase and sat down. The smile on his face was a testament to his love for his job. "Want to hear what we recorded last night?"

He moved a laptop to the center of the table.

Sydney nodded, not sure if she really did. Snoring and shuffling blared through the speakers and Marshal fast forwarded the recording.

"I'm here. Where are you?" The female voice sounded disjointed, and the hair on Sydney's neck stood.

"Margaret?" The response seemed to come from farther away.

"That's pretty much it. There's a more, but we ran out of time to clean up the track." Marshal still grinned.

"Creepy. I thought you weren't going to set up equipment last night." She hadn't meant for that to come accusing. She didn't care what he did.

"We weren't. Until we were getting our beds ready and the window opened and closed by itself. Twice. So we turned on a camera and a recorder. The video shows the window opening one more time, we think. We haven't had much time to analyze it. Dave thinks there's a shadow. Usually it takes us days to go over all the information."

"Why days?" She had to admit the process intrigued her.

"We check and double-check. Sometimes triple-check. Listening, a second at a time, to eight hours of usually nothing is a bit draining." He marked the CDR they'd just made with the date and put it in a plastic case.

"I can imagine. Can we listen to that?" She pointed at the disc.

"Do you want to?"

"Why not? What made the room so cold?" She waited as he inserted the disc.

"You want me to say a spirit, but the truth is I don't know for sure. The temperature changed. There might be a cave underneath and a draft came through the floor. Say there is a cave, ice chunks are breaking loose, and getting caught somewhere a few feet down? Hard to say. Okay, it's ready." He pressed 'play' and she leaned forward.

He asked the same question he had when they were in the bunkroom, the silent space in between felt like hours. No wonder it took them a few days to go over the evidence. Just when she thought she'd die of boredom, Marshal got an answer to his question.

"Margaret? I'm here. Where are you?" the same voice from the recording they'd just made whispered.

Sydney figured her shock showed by the smile on Marshal's face. The recorder had stayed on the table between them the whole time. There was no way he could have altered the evidence.

"Did I say creepy already?"

"I know. Are you still willing to sit with me tonight?"

Why did his simple question sound like an invitation for sex? Was that just her, or was he flirting?

"I'll do it as long as you don't scare me on purpose." And she was flirting right back. She was pathetic.

"I would never do that. Now tell me what you know about this ground." He flipped his notebook open.

"My grandfather's. He passed it to Daisy and me when he died, with the stipulation that we give the campground business at least five years before selling. His evil second wife somehow managed to get the lawyer to add that we have until this season to open for business and then she kept the rights tied up until last week."

"Ah. Something tells me there's bad blood," he said.

"Not just bad, poison."

"We'll go there in a minute. Why did your grandfather insist you re-open the campground?"

"I'm not sure. He wanted Daisy and I to continue with the family legacy, I think. As much as he bent to Violet's demands on everything else, he stayed firm about this place for the most part. Daisy and I spent every summer here, and a lot of the off season, too. He taught us everything from how to run the campground to how to dredge the pond. He wanted us to carry on the tradition. He said that constantly. The property has belonged to a Brook's son for about three hundred years."

"Why didn't your dad take over? That seems to be the pattern."

"Dad is some kind of weird throwback. As much as he loved coming here, he's deathly allergic to bee stings, mosquito bites, and poison ivy. Gramps used to just shake his head and say something messed with the DNA. Dad's the only one in the family with those allergies. Daisy and I can roll around naked in any kind of poison and never get a bump. So could Gramps."

His eyebrow rose. "Do you and Daisy often roll around naked in poison? I'd like to see that."

"Shut up. That's not what I meant." Her face felt hot.

There were those sexy eye crinkles again. Damn.

"Anyway. We were the only Brooks's left. Gramps knew we loved the place. He made sure we did. Two months after the wedding, Vile Violet proclaimed that we weren't welcome here again. She wanted Gramps to turn Brookside into a casino."

"Ouch. Obviously, he didn't want that."

"No. In fact, I think that was what gave him his first heart attack about a year after they were married. The business went downhill with his health, a slow decline. I think he wore himself down trying to keep her happy and make sure he kept Brookside viable for us. She was and is so adamant that this town needs a casino. That's where we are right now. Most of the town wants the campground, others think a casino would be a great idea."

"How long was the campground closed?" Marshal asked.

"About five years. Gramps wanted Daisy and I to take over after his third heart attack, but Violet convinced him we needed to live our own lives before being stuck here. She admitted that when she contested the will. She was right, but Daisy and I would have come had we known how bad things had gotten around here."

"Were there ever any reports of paranormal activity that you can remember?" His pen poised over the notebook.

"You mean freaky shit?"

"Yeah. Freaky shit."

"Well, Daisy and I used to think we saw stuff all the time, but the older we got the less we thought that. I don't remember much with the guests. Wait. A couple rented one of these cabins the last summer I was here. It was late afternoon and the lady was alone. She said there was a man in the room and when she screamed, he vanished. Gramps thought she might have had too much to drink. He said she smelled of liquor. I guess that's not what you mean." Sydney didn't want to tell him anymore than that. Her current experience had to be enough. Dredging up the past wasn't something she wanted to do.

"It's exactly what I'm talking about. You don't happen to remember which cabin?" Marshal's hope nearly unglued her careful composure.

"I don't, but I can find out. I have all of Gramps' business files and the guest logs he insisted on."

"Wonderful. Do you know any of the area history?"

"Only that the woods were supposedly occupied during the Civil War. We're far enough from Gettysburg that I rarely see mention of the area. I'm not sure any battles were fought here. There's also talk that this area was part of the Trail of Tears. I haven't verified that."

"I assume Vile Violet is your step-grandmother?" He wrote the name, including *Vile* in his notebook. Maybe she shouldn't call her that anymore.

"Yes. She's wicked to us, but to be fair, she treats her family well. I don't know why she hates Daisy and I so much."

"I know it's none of my business, but what kind of rules did she put on you and Daisy re-opening the campground?" Marshal asked.

"Well, she took us to court after the reading of the will. And after tying our inheritance up for over a year, the judge approved her new conditions, as if she hadn't made Gramps agree to enough before he died. We have to pass a weekly progress inspection, have to live onsite, and Daisy and I both have to be here at least until we open. I think she did that because everyone knows Daisy has no interest in being here. Gramps left us enough money to be successful, but she managed to find a way to keep us from accessing most of the funds until after we reopen. We're working on a shoestring budget. And then there are the terms of sale, including the money we lose if we have to sell to her . . ." She pressed her fingers to her temples. Her head hurt just thinking about it, but she gave him the rest of the lowdown anyway.

"That's kind of brutal. So every week after Memorial Day, you lose ten grand if you decide to sell? And you have to sell to Violet if you quit before the five-year mark?"

"Gramps agreed to most of the terms before he died. I think that was his way of challenging us and making sure we gave running Brookside a fair chance. Violet has first rights. That's what doesn't make sense. If we sell before May, the price is fair. Why would they try to get us to sell now?"

"Maybe they're only trying to make things difficult for you to delay your opening. Who's Jace?"

"Violet's grandson. I've never met him, but he's a major ass." She never wanted to talk to him again.

"Does he know we're here?" Marshal scribbled in the margin of the page.

"He has to. Why else would the cabin be trashed and a beer can left behind?" She tried to ignore the male influence on the cabin. A pair of orange boxer shorts hung on the bathroom doorknob. Why hadn't she seen them before?

"Maybe you should meet with him? Find out exactly what he and his grandmother are up to."

She turned toward Marshal, her back to the boxers. "I'll break his teeth if I see his face."

Though, Sydney had to admit, she'd thought about calling a meeting with Jace. Maybe she could appeal to his logic and make him understand how important honoring Gramps was to her and Daisy.

"Understood. I'm not telling you what to do, just a suggestion from a neutral party." Marshal had a funny twist on his mouth, like maybe he thought he'd overstepped his boundary.

"No problem. Do you need me for anything else?" She pushed her chair back and stood. Halting at the devilish grin he now wore. His eyes made her think of sex and so did the little quirk of his mouth.

Marshal shook his head. "We'll set the equipment up a few hours before dusk. I want to start with the pond and the bathhouse tonight. You do realize it's going to take us a long time to cover the whole place?"

"Yeah, Daisy explained how you operate. Why the pond first? I figured you'd start with this creepy as hell cabin."

"The tractor is gone now. The pond was disturbed. Sometimes renovations and that kind of stuff will draw the spirits out. We run equipment in here constantly. Take a nap and bring your open mind." He stood and went with her to the door. His nearness made it difficult to remember what he'd said.

Sydney thought about turning around and pushing him back into the cabin and locking the door behind them. She laughed at her stupid self. Like she'd ever have the guts.

As she went toward her cabin, faint laughter met her ears. At first, she thought Daisy had finally lost the crappy mood she had earlier, until the eerie sound surrounded her along with a rush of cold air.

CHAPTER 4

Daisy watched Graham do laps around the bathhouse. He seemed distracted and talked to himself.

Curiosity getting the better of her, she stopped and leaned against the wall. Graham faltered as he approached, reaching his hand to his side and pulling out a tape recorder. Holding the device up, he stopped in front of her.

"Brainstorming."

Daisy nodded. Her roommate in college was a writer. As she waited for him to turn off the machine, she tried to figure out why Graham made her sister so crazy. Was it because he was truly a jerk, or maybe her sister was far too attracted and used her anger as a shield?

"You make my sister nuts. Why?" Why bother sidestepping what she wanted to know?

"I don't do it on purpose. Well, okay, maybe I do. She's fun angry and I had to find out if she was willing to give Marshal a chance without interfering." He leaned against the wall beside her.

"Why? I thought you and Marshal were at odds?" Something else was going on here.

"No. It's a good way to get a better feel for how people will react to paranormal activity. I am a skeptic, but more like Marshal. I write ghost stories. Some based on real events. I've definitely seen some things that add to the old muse, but I'm not saying I believe in this stuff. I am really looking forward to this investigation, though. Did Marshal tell you about the cabin last night?"

She shook her head, confused and interested. Why was

she seeing a different side of him? Was he playing her? But why? The way his eyes lit up when he described the cold air and voices only confused her more. She wanted to hate him as much as her sister did, but couldn't find it. What she did feel worried her.

Graham was handsome, in a perfect *GQ* kind of way. Not her type, so why did her stomach flip when he leaned forward in his excitement? For a brief moment, she could only think of kissing him. Sydney would have a heart attack.

And then there was Tucker. Flirting and making outrageous comments. She wanted to ask him about the baby, but every time she opened her mouth, one of the crew appeared. Who would have thought their quiet campground life would suddenly fill up with more testosterone than either of them could handle? She wondered how Sydney managed her interview with Marshal. Daisy wished Sydney would get over herself and jump Marshal's bones. Maybe Daisy should do the same with Graham.

Daisy held the extension cord for Marshal as he connected the equipment. Setup was always exciting and she realized how much she'd missed working with these guys.

"Sorry I didn't make it over to talk to you this morning." She gave him the slack he requested and moved forward.

"No problem. Your sister gave me a lot of information. She's not like I pictured." He didn't look up, and Daisy wished she could see his face.

"How did you picture her?" Good, he straightened and turned toward her.

"I don't know. Stern, bitchy, and ugly. One of those tight-bunned, gray-flannel-suit wearing matronly types. And fat, too." He grinned and bent to wind the cord around the base of the tree so no one accidentally unplugged the setup.

She grimaced. "That's quite a bad image. I guess I only

told you the frustrating stuff. She's definitely not any of those things."

"Definitely not. No matter what she says to you, she has an open mind and she's interested in what we're doing."

"Maybe her opinions changed after her experience in the cabin? She's fair. Her personal beliefs don't affect how she treats people."

"Are you saying she's only being nice?"

"Maybe. I don't think so. She is nice. Except where Graham is concerned. Why didn't you tell me you two are in cahoots?" She should kick him for lying.

Marshal shrugged. "He wanted to see what happened and since it kind of helped with the investigation I let him."

"Why?"

"He's my brother. Well, half-brother. We grew up together. Until his mom left my dad when I was sixteen. I hadn't seen him for a long time. We kept in touch, but not often, you know? He's a good guy. Kind of prissy, always was."

"Prissy is Sydney's type." Oops. She shouldn't have said that. Marshal seemed a little shocked and disappointed. "She hates him, though."

Marshal didn't say anything. When was she going to learn to keep her mouth shut? She'd probably just blown Sydney's chances with Marshal.

"Lights out in ten." Dave breezed by, taking his job seriously as usual.

"We're ready." Marshal stepped around her.

Somehow, she managed to be paired with Graham for the first shift. They were only supposed to keep an eye on the computer monitors set up in the empty cabin and take care of troubleshooting. In two hours, they'd switch jobs with another team and head out with one of the other crew members and see what they could record.

This part was boring, watching the others record their impressions and experiences. At least their conversation wasn't being recorded like everyone else's. She'd made sure she told Sydney that before her shift started with Marshal.

Graham filed his fingernails in an irritating pattern. She'd love to see him with two-day growth on his face and zero hair gel. A pair of jeans and no shirt. She wondered if he worked out or if that fantasy would disappoint in real life.

She liked him and she didn't. He was cute, too fancy, and hard to read. Daisy didn't think she was seeing the real him.

"So. Is your sister still pissed at me?"

Her fantasy deflated. She tried not to be disappointed and remembered Graham was more Sydney's type.

"Definitely. She doesn't appreciate the deceit. She's pissed at Marshal, too, if that makes you feel any better."

"I think she's madder at me. She hates me." Was he pouting?

"You're probably right. She does hate you." She watched the monitors, hoping something interesting would happen soon.

Graham seemed to want to say something, but when the silence stretched, she figured he either chickened out or decided he was talking to the wrong sister. Daisy didn't know why that hurt. It wasn't like she was interested in Graham except to think about what he'd look like dirty and naked.

Ten minutes later, Daisy wished she'd been able to sleep when she tried to nap earlier. Concentrating on the equipment was putting her into zombie mode.

"Hey." One of the radios crackled to life. "What is that?"

Daisy leaned forward, watching the video of what Sydney said was fog. Figures swirled on the surface of the water.

"Can you hear that?" Marshal whispered.

The faint sounds of music drifted through the speaker.

"Something's going on at the pond." Graham leaned forward and she almost drowned in the masculine smell of his aftershave.

"Are they really dancing?" Sydney's whisper.

Daisy watched the wispy outlines on the screen, convinced they were dancing. But, then, maybe not. "They're not dancing. They're ice skating. See?" She pointed as one of the smaller shapes fell, sliding on imaginary ice.

"What's with the music then?" Graham's concentration stayed on the screen. "They're in tune with it."

Daisy didn't answer. If he stayed in his position nearly over top her much longer she was going to lick his neck. He didn't smell like a priss, he smelled like a man. And, God help her, she liked it.

Sydney watched from the edge of the pond, trying to stay out of the way. The vision in front of her was incredible. The water at the edge of the pond, not two feet from her, appeared frozen solid, but she wasn't cold. The misty figures swirled and skated. They had no distinguishable features she could see, but their disembodied laughter echoed through the odd silence surrounding them.

She glanced over at Marshal, his excitement visible, and suppressed the urge to smile along with him. Her attraction had to be kept to herself. It was bad enough Daisy knew she thought Marshal was drool-worthy. The last thing she needed was for him to figure out he made her knees weak.

Sydney had thought long and hard about what she wanted to do when she was supposed to be resting up for tonight. As much as she'd love to break free and do something outrageous, she wouldn't. She'd done that once and the result had been disaster. It didn't matter that she'd only been sixteen and delusional about love and relationships. She hadn't been thinking short-term when she agreed to park with Duff. She hadn't been thinking, period. When Duff said he loved her and wanted to marry her, she'd willingly opened her legs, dreaming about the future through his awkward lovemaking.

Hell, what had she known?

Maybe the pregnancy scare and the terrible rumors Duff

had tried to spread about her were responsible for her attitudes about sex with no consequences. When she'd told Duff her suspicions, he denied they'd been together. Then, he told the rest of the football team he'd tried because she'd come on so strong, but that she'd ended up being too afraid. The team had made a bet on who could get her to follow through.

Lucky for her, Daisy had overheard some of the conversation and Sydney had turned down every one of them when they'd asked her out. And every other guy, too. She couldn't take the chance they knew the things Duff said about her.

She hadn't had sex again until her sophomore year of college. He was gentle and thorough and she'd come away with a new appreciation for lovemaking even though the relationship had only lasted two months more, until he changed majors and transferred to a bigger school. Sydney hadn't been as heartbroken as she should have been. Maybe that was because he'd changed her life a little and the change was good.

Her attention snapped back to the present, she blinked when she realized the winter time illusion had faded. Marshal came toward her, his expression a mixture of joy and seduction. She didn't think her impression, at least of the seduction part, was on, but it didn't matter.

"That was incredible."

She waited. Would he take the scene at face value or try to find an explanation? "What now?"

"We study the footage. See if there's evidence of this being manufactured and go from there." He touched her arm and pointed to the bathhouse.

Sydney nodded, suppressing a groan at the bathhouse stake out. She hated that building and as soon as they had the money, planned to have it razed and a better facility built. Maybe her hatred stemmed from the way she and Daisy were punished when they misbehaved. Any time they stepped out of line, Gramps made them clean this bathroom three times a day for a week. She'd probably cleaned this bathroom for a total of two years. If not more. Daisy had way more time in.

Before she had a chance to voice her opinions on sitting in the dank stalls and waiting for spirits, her cell phone vibrated with a voicemail. She knew the message wouldn't be one she wanted to hear. Still, she pressed in the code for the mailbox and moved away from the recording equipment surrounding her on all sides.

"Listen, I don't know what you two are up to, but we have to talk. Grandmother is losing a lot of money waiting for you to find your sense of honor. You made a deal with her. You won't get a higher price, if that's what you think. Your grandfather would be so disappointed in you."

Tears filled her eyes as she saved the message and turned off the phone. Would Gramps be disappointed in them? Damn Jace. How dare he? What did he know of Gramps and his wishes?

Marshal didn't ask. So much for what she thought was the beginning of a friendship. She tried not to let his disinterest bother her. He was working and probably felt uncomfortable.

The rest of the night passed in complete boredom. By three, Sydney yawned so frequently, Marshal sent her to bed with a wiggle of his eyebrows and a flirty comment. She crawled under the covers wanting to smack him and every guy in the campground all because of Jace.

The night noises interspersed with an occasional loud burst of laughter. Despite her irritation and the weird laughter she'd heard again on her way back to the cabin, Sydney felt safe. Marshal's crew was in rare form, probably due to the things she knew they did capture.

Marshal planned to leave the equipment up overnight and assigned Dave first watch. Sydney had a feeling it was more of a safety measure than hope of catching any other activity. She turned with a sigh and allowed her mind to wander to places it probably shouldn't. What would it hurt to dream about a night with Marshal? It was better than thinking about Jace's message.

Daisy wished she could hate Graham. They'd spent the past two hours paired with Eric and Ron, who basically ignored them and seemed to be more into each other than their jobs. She wondered if Marshal knew, not that he would care about how much they liked each other, but he'd flip to find out they weren't doing necessary tasks to maintain the company's credibility.

Graham had whispered a commentary on what the men were saying to each other, adding a perverted twist and making it hard for her to not laugh. That was bad enough, but when he touched her back and squeezed to get her attention, she had to hide her reaction or embarrass herself.

Damn. She didn't want to be attracted to him and she didn't want to follow her advice to Sydney. Sure, she'd had a couple of one-night stands, but it had been years. She preferred some commitment, the emotion attached to the sex. Maybe she was only hot and bothered because it had been so long. Maybe she should screw Graham's brains out to teach him a lesson.

Graham leaned against the tree watching Eric and Ron. He caught her assessment and sent her a knowing grin. Damn. Could he read her mind? She hoped not. Otherwise, she was in big trouble.

Sydney's light was out by the time Daisy arrived at their cabin. Daisy peeked in on her to make sure she indeed slept. Truthfully, she wanted to make sure she wasn't holed up somewhere with Marshal having the time of her life.

Images of Graham, alternating with Tucker, filthy and bare-chested haunted her attempts to sleep. She rolled over and reached under the mattress, grabbing the battered journal her adoptive parents gave her when she turned eighteen. Her birth mother's flowing script was neat and funky, the i's dotted with smiley faces or stars.

None of what her mother wrote before she found out she was pregnant made sense to Daisy. She figured the entries were about the band the woman chose, since most of it was a city name, followed by a brief recap of the evening. Her birth mother had definitely been a groupie for some band no one had ever still ever heard of.

The part of the journal around the time of Nadine's pregnancy never mentioned who Daisy's father might be. Only that "he" would be so pleased. Obviously, he wasn't or Daisy would know him. She didn't know what bothered her more—the fact that her mother had been so happy at first and then dumped her, or that her father had not cared that he'd created a child.

She felt like a garbage baby.

Her parents—the ones who loved, accepted, and raised her—should be enough, right? They'd chosen to keep her when they could have easily turned her over to social services. Maybe they'd kept her out of a sense of family duty, but Daisy didn't think so.

Shortly after the adoption papers were final, she'd had trouble sleeping and had gone downstairs for a drink and a hug only to hear her parents discussing how irresponsible her birth mother was. She'd heard her mom say that no matter what she wouldn't give Daisy up, that she couldn't love Daisy more if she'd been her own blood and how she hated her sister for what she'd done.

The words made Daisy happy, and sadder than she'd ever been. She didn't remember her birth mother and Daisy couldn't help but wonder how awful of a child she was for her mother to pawn her off. There had to be a reason. Moms didn't forget to come back for their babies.

Maybe someday she'd get the chance to ask. Logically, she knew sometimes there were no answers and that she'd done nothing wrong. The fault had been with the woman who gave birth to her. But the little girl in her would always wonder.

Daisy didn't seem to be good enough for anyone. Sure, her parents loved, supported, and were proud of her but she figured they pretty much had to be. Daisy had never been as good as Sydney at anything—school, sports, or friends.

Sure, she made a great career for herself and she'd continue even if she never left Brookside. She held on to that happy thought, shoving the sadness away. Maybe she'd even open a photography studio at the campground. The possibilities excited her, and she fell asleep rolling ideas around.

CHAPTER 5

Daisy woke to something poking her. She opened one eye to find Sydney sitting on the edge of the bed, her finger ready to jab her again.

"Wake up."

"No."

"Come on. I have something to tell you. I brought you coffee." Sydney pointed to the steaming cup on the bedside table with a smile.

"What is so damned important that you have to wake me at the ass-crack of dawn? I've only been in bed two hours." Two stupid, restless hours.

"For one, Tucker is here and I have gossip for you. Two, we have to meet with the lawyer in an hour, remember? The weekly checks that Vile Violet is making us do?"

"Damn. That's right. What the hell is wrong with that woman? Why do we have to pass her inspections?" she asked with a growl, grabbing the Styrofoam cup. "I feel like a prisoner."

"You and me both. We're doing great here, so no worries. Are you ready to hear what I found out?" Sydney poked her again, erasing her irritation. Daisy sighed. How could she be mad when Sydney was in such a good mood?

"Cut it out. God, you're totally obnoxious this morning. Maybe you should go fuck Marshal so you can work off some of this insane energy and calm the hell down." She sat her cup down and moved over so Sydney had more room. "Okay. Let's hear this gossip."

Sydney hadn't turned red at her crude comment. Why?

"Tucker is not married, nor is he a father. He's not seeing anyone. At all." Sydney stopped, her happy expression fleeting after seeing Daisy's face.

"Oh. So he's single. I guess that's good for him." Why hadn't he called her when he found out there was no baby? She stood, trying to forget she wasn't good enough for him.

"I'm sorry, honey. I didn't think about the fact that it's been months and he didn't call you. I'm so stupid." Sydney grabbed her hand.

"It's not your fault. He's the asshole. Fine. You know what? I don't care. He obviously didn't feel for me what I felt for him so screw him." Daisy didn't know what to do. Her heart was breaking all over again.

"Screw him. Screw them all. Why are there so many men around here anyway?" Sydney had always been quick to take her side, as she'd been for her. That was one thing Daisy adored about her sister.

"I don't know but they can all go to hell." Daisy crossed her arms.

"Here's what we'll do. After this lawyer meeting, let's go into town. We'll get some wine and come back here and drink ourselves smart." Sydney smiled.

"A perfect idea. Let's get this lawyer meeting over with." Thank God for sisters.

"I was kidding, but you know what, that's a great idea." Sydney jumped up.

An hour later, their evil grandmother's somber attorney followed their lawyer through the rusty front gate. She and Sydney had known their lawyer, Albert Love, since they were babies. He'd been a constant visitor at Brookside and they'd grown up with his grandchildren. Al, or Uncle Al, kissed them both on the cheek after the bear hugs, much to the other lawyer's irritation.

"Are these your clients or your girlfriends?" As soon as the question sliced through the air and hit its intended mark, Uncle Al turned quickly, catching the man off guard by shaking a finger in his face.

"Listen, these girls are like my own granddaughters. Shut your mouth and mind your own business. My relationship with them has nothing to do with what we're doing here." He turned back to them with a smile. "Now. Let's see what you've done."

They toured the campsites, now clear of all poison ivy. At Violet's attorney's gasp of surprise, Daisy could have hugged Tucker, even though she wanted to smack him silly. The pond had been dredged and the swampy end planted, along with the beginnings of a fence. Tucker's crew dumped stones for the walkway as the tour group arrived.

"This is great." Uncle Al pointed toward the previously overgrown seating area near the pond. "I can't believe you got that poison down. What a difference a week made. What else have you managed?"

Daisy let Sydney do the talking. She listened as her sister explained the various inspections and results, interjecting where necessary and taking over when they were asked how Tucker and his crew were hired. Hopefully, she hid her disgust with him. And the violent thoughts.

After Sydney explained the estimates and inspections due the coming week, Violet's attorney left, still shaking his head. Uncle Al laughed as the man drove out of the parking lot.

"That guy's a walking corpse. I've known him for forty years and I've yet to see him smile. Even at his daughter's wedding." He stopped and reached into his pocket. "So, I have good news."

Daisy hoped he wasn't going to breech her privacy. She didn't want Sydney to know she'd asked him to help locate her father. She still didn't know why she'd done that, but it'd been six months and nothing had turned up yet. Squashing the thread of hope, she waited.

"Violet might have set the terms for these inspections, but Gramps had enough life in him to counteract her underhanded scheme. Think of it as a reward system for putting up with all the bullshit." He handed the envelope to her, then got into his car.

"Ten thousand dollars?" Daisy passed the check to Sydney.

"Del wanted to make sure you had some financial backing. He knew Violet would make things difficult for you, and she has. These terms were set without her knowledge. Once her time runs out, you'll get the rest of the money that was supposed to come with the place, even if you have to sell. Until then, every time you pass inspection, you'll get a check similar to this." Al leaned out of the car for them to kiss his cheek, then waved goodbye.

Daisy turned to Sydney, both breaking out into a squeal as soon as Al turned his car around.

They returned to the campground, recharged, beautiful and toting several bottles of wine. Not wanting to use Gramps' money for personal indulgences, Daisy sprang for lunch and manicures and Sydney paid for haircuts and wine.

Daisy didn't remember when she'd had so much fun. Their day had been perfect. The gems she'd had glued to the top of her fingernails wouldn't last through their planned campfire, but they were gorgeous now. She didn't care. They'd fought Vile Violet for so long both sisters had neglected to take care of themselves.

They'd told Marshal they wouldn't accompany the crews tonight, much to his disappointment. Daisy looked forward to the evening plans. Sick of cooking over the fire, they'd grabbed take out from Sydney's favorite chain restaurant.

"I'll start the fire. You get the wine." Daisy tossed her purchases onto her bed and changed into jeans and a sweatshirt.

"You got it. Which should we start with?" Sydney unloaded the various bottles of wine.

"You pick. I'll drink anything." She stepped out the door, nearly crashing into Tucker.

"Sure. Make the uneducated wine drinker pick. No complaints if it sucks," Sydney yelled.

"Hey. Heard you had a good inspection." Tucker smiled, and Daisy resisted his charm. Kind of.

"Yep. We're celebrating. Sister night." Hopefully that was enough to let him know he wasn't welcome to hang out and share their campfire. What was he still doing here anyway?

"Nice. Good for you guys. I waited around because I wanted to update you on our status. Sydney said you're in charge of all the landscaping work."

Daisy would kill her. Sydney had done that on purpose, probably hoping to force them together enough to hook up again. Of course, Daisy knew when Sydney told him that, she hadn't known what had happened between them.

"What's up?" She tried to hide her irritation. Tucker didn't need to know how much he'd hurt her.

"We'll probably be another week or two on top of my original estimate. Does that screw you up?"

She got stuck on the word "screw" and took a second longer than she should have to answer him. "Oh. No. That's fine. You're working in the middle section of sites now, right?"

"Yeah. Except we broke one of the mowers. The part's on backorder. Let me know if there's a problem with us taking longer and I'll do my best to get out of your hair sooner. I could probably borrow the equipment." He glanced at the big green tractor parked in one of the bigger RV sites.

"No. You're fine. You won't be in our way." As mad as she was at him, she didn't want him to finish and vanish from her life again.

How stupid was that?

"Great. Listen, call me if anything weird happens. I heard that guy Marshal talking about your granddad's widow. Why didn't you tell me?"

The words were on the tip of her tongue. *Why didn't you tell me you weren't going to be a father? Why didn't you come back to me?*

She swallowed her feelings and shook her head a little too hard. "We're handling things okay. And she's not going to get her way."

Not wanting to explain further, especially when Sydney hovered by the door to give her time to talk to him, she moved to the fire pit and laid her kindling. Sydney finally burst through the screen door with two glasses and a bucket containing ice and two bottles of wine.

"Hi, Tucker. The place looks fantastic. I can't tell you how much we appreciate the hard work your crew is doing." Her words were sincere and Daisy echoed them.

"I'll let you ladies get on with your girl's only evening. Enjoy. We'll be here early again. I make no promises about the noise." His gaze lingered on the wine, the point he made pissing her off.

For an answer, she took her glass from Sydney and downed the whole thing in three swallows. She wiped her mouth with the back of her hand and held the glass out to Sydney. Tucker shook his head and waved as he left, his smile making her want to follow him and demand those answers.

She didn't care. Tucker could think what he wanted. She was nothing to him. His silence these past few months proved that. She watched him as Sydney came to stand beside her.

"To hell with him," Sydney said, handing her a full glass of wine.

"Hell, yes. To hell with him." She drank half before giving it back and bending to light the fire. As the tinder caught, she plopped down in a camp chair and watched the tiny flames dance.

"He's an ass." She didn't look at Sydney.

"You're right. They're all asses." Sydney downed her wine, her attention on the parking area.

Daisy turned to follow her sister's line of vision.

Marshal made his way through the parking area toward the crew's cabin, apparently oblivious to them.

"His is a damn fine ass though." Sydney grinned and reached for the bottle.

"You need to catch up. I'm already one up on you." Daisy lifted her now-empty glass, the little bit of alcohol in her bloodstream relaxing her.

"Okay, but you'll need to get another bottle then. That's the last." Sydney filled her glass to the rim and topped off Daisy's before tossing the bottle in the grass beside them. "One down and it's not even dark yet. Awesome."

When another empty lay in the grass beside the first, Marshal appeared. He gently kicked at the bottles before turning his attention to Sydney and Daisy. Sydney couldn't stop giggling, and Daisy was in the same condition, only a little surlier.

"You guys are drunk." He didn't exactly sound like their mother.

"Damn straight." Sydney finally stood after a failed attempt. "What's it to you?"

"I wanted to talk to you, but I can see this isn't the time." Marshal leaned over, and Sydney grabbed his collar.

"It's sister night. No boys allowed." She tried to push him but failed, knocking herself backward. The only things that stopped her from falling in the fire were Marshal's quick arms.

Damn, but being up against him felt good.

She lost her train of thought and stared up at him, her brain not engaging until Daisy hollered at her.

"We're out of wine. Again. Dammit." The third bottle landed with the others.

"Your turn," she said. Why was she still in Marshal's arms? Did she want him to let her go?

"Fine. Remember, Marshal, no boys allowed. You'd better be gone when I get back." Daisy's threat came out with a slur and a giggle.

"She's drunk." Sydney stared up at him, wondering when they'd had time to drink three bottles of wine. Had they eaten yet?

"And what are you?" Marshal's face was too close and he smelled way too good.

"Stupid." She was not going to kiss him. Not after her and Daisy's conversation of the past who knew how long. "I'm not kissing you. I'm not sleeping with you, ever, no matter how much I want to."

Oh, but she was going to regret that in the morning.

"You're not?" He smiled as if she'd just told him what he was getting for Christmas.

"Nope. And don't you forget it." She swayed a little and he pulled her against him.

"I won't, but you might. Sounds like you're denying what you really want." He grinned and she smacked him lightly.

"You'd better go. Daisy is coming and she'll kick your ass." The last part almost came out backward, as Marshal lowered her into the chair.

"In the morning, I'm going to pretend you never told me that." His warm breath in her ear did incredible things. The only reason she didn't pull his head back down was the thunder on Daisy's face.

"What did you say?" Daisy passed a full glass of wine to her when Marshal finally left.

"Um. I don't know. Oh. I told him I wouldn't sleep with him no matter how much I wanted to. You know what, sis? I don't hate men as much as I thought I did." She leaned back in her chair, content.

"Neither do I." Daisy let out a defeated-sounding sigh. "Neither do I."

Sunlight spilled in the window, and Sydney squinted against the pain in her head. Why was she sleeping in her clothes and why were her hands so dirty? The night came back in fragments, starting where they started and ending with the last bottle of wine. Laughter and the great time she and Daisy had, which was good since she didn't remember the later part of the night.

Still, if you couldn't get drunk and stupid with your sister, who could you do it with?

Except for the headache, better now that her eyes had adjusted to the light, she felt damn good.

Until she remembered Marshal's visit and what she'd said to him. He told her he was going to act like it never happened in the morning. Great. She'd basically challenged him and he was going to ignore it. She didn't know how she felt about that.

Yelling from outside forced her to the window. Daisy and Tucker stood in the middle of a campsite not far from the cabin. Daisy's hands flew wildly, but Sydney couldn't see her face. What was Daisy freaking out about, and should she get involved?

The next thing Sydney knew, Marshal rushed into her bedroom. Last visitor she needed. She hadn't brushed her teeth or her hair yet, and still wore the dirty-kneed jeans from tending the fire last night. Great impression.

"Daisy is reading Tucker the riot act about something."

"Do I need to go?" Sydney tried to see around Marshal's bulk, but failed.

"Not yet. Maybe soon." Marshal stayed at the window. "Stop worrying about your hair. You're beautiful. You were beautiful drunk, you're beautiful now, and you'll be even more beautiful waking up beside me."

"Wha-What?" Did he really say that?

"Sorry. I know I said I wouldn't mention what you said to me last night. I couldn't resist. I feel like you've offered me some sort of challenge and I want to take you up on it."

Oh. My. God.

"What challenge?" Maybe pretending she didn't remember would work.

"Nope. You know exactly what you said to me. What you don't know is what holding you from falling in the fire did to me. Maybe if we take care of this attraction we'll all be able to get some work done."

"I'm not that kind of woman." She wasn't sure what to think.

"I know. You want to be. Just once. Think about it." He moved away from the window. "Daisy's coming. Tucker's following. I'm getting out of here."

"Shit. Me, too." She locked herself in the bathroom as the front door banged shut.

By the time she emerged, Tucker would either be gone, or in Daisy's bed.

Which did she want for her sister? Sydney had no idea even though she thought about it the entire time she showered. Thinking about Daisy's love life was far easier than replaying Marshal's seductive comment. She still wanted him, despite her sober status this morning.

What did that mean?

Daisy wasn't anywhere to be found in their cabin when Sydney returned from the bathroom. Sydney wondered if they'd gone somewhere private, until she saw Daisy at Marshal's cabin. A black truck took up the space behind her car and Sydney rushed outside to find out who had arrived. They were expecting three different contractors for estimates on the bathhouses, but they weren't due to arrive until noon.

Daisy raised her hands in a symbol of frustration as Sydney rounded the corner. "I'm telling you she's not here."

Uh-oh. She should have stayed away.

"Then who is that?" The man gave Daisy a superior glance and turned toward Sydney.

"Good morning. I wanted to talk to you face-to-face since our phone conversations usually end with you swearing and hanging up on me."

Oh. Shit.

He held his hand out. Sydney refused to take it.

"Jace? You have a lot of nerve showing up here. Especially after your nasty little tricks the other night? Did your grandmother put you up to them, or are you trying to stay in her good graces so you get more money when she dies?" Maybe a tad too nasty, but it was better than slapping him.

Confusion crossed his face. "What? Grandmother has nothing to do with my visit. What are you talking about?"

He could not be that stupid. "Duh. What does your Grandmother *not* have to do with this? Go away, Jace. We have nothing to talk about."

Why did he have to be so handsome with his dark hair and blue eyes? And well-dressed? And why did he have a smile that melted her toe nail polish? He was the enemy and she had a headache.

"You always say that and, yet, here I am with unfinished business to discuss with you." The man practically oozed charm. Sydney had to remind herself he worked for Vile Violet or else she would have smiled back.

"See? That's the part you don't get. We have no business with you. This was my grandfather's land. Your grandmother conned my grandfather and now she wants his hard earned heritage to go to her family so it can be turned into a casino. Trust me, that's never going to happen."

"What the hell are you talking about?"

CHAPTER 6

"What? You cannot be that stupid." Sydney quelled the urge to punch him square in his solid chest.

"Grandmother tells me she's made you a fair offer for Brookside and that you verbally accepted her terms. Now you've changed your mind? My grandmother is a powerful woman, Miss Brooks. I don't think you want to make an enemy of her." Jace folded his arms over his chest, though his words were calm and lawyer-like.

Why did this man always make her think violent thoughts? "Your facts are seriously wrong. I suggest you check them. Your grandmother is lying to you. Surely you're a better lawyer than that? I have nothing else to say to you."

The shock on his face almost made her laugh. She might have, if her insides hadn't already incinerated because of her fury. Damn Violet. And damn Jace.

Yeah. That was it.

"Why didn't you tell me?" Daisy faced Tucker. His stunned expression almost made her wish she had approached him a little differently.

Except with his crew constantly around, she hadn't had any choice but to wait until he came out of the bathroom. She'd snagged his arm as he exited, still buckling his belt and whistling.

"What are you talking about?" His irritation rose to the occasion pretty darn quick.

"The baby. Why didn't you tell me there was no baby?

Was what we had so bad?" She wrestled the hurt into anger, wanting answers more than his comfort.

"What? You knew. Jackie told me she told you." He did seem confused. As if that would save him.

"And Jackie never lied? Give me a freaking break, Tucker. She wanted you back bad enough that she faked being pregnant and you believed her? I didn't know until Sydney told me." He could not be that stupid. Could he?

"Okay. So that was stupid. It was no secret though. I can't believe you didn't know." Tucker gave her an accusing stare.

"Why would I care? Obviously you didn't. Obviously I didn't mean enough to you for you to come and tell me yourself. Why are you here, Tucker? To hurt me more?" Daisy almost lost her careful control over the tears.

"I was embarrassed. I felt like a jerk for being so irresponsible, even if the baby was a lie. I'm here for some closure. I can't seem to forget you." His volume lowered and cut Daisy to raw bone.

"Why didn't you just call me? This is stupid, Tucker. A simple phone call. 'Hi, it's Tucker. She's not pregnant. Can we talk? I still want to be with you.' It's as easy as that." Daisy acknowledged the stab of guilt low in her stomach and it didn't feel right. Maybe it wasn't quite that simple.

"Well. The thing is the baby scare really made me think about my life and what I want. You were always adamant about not having children and that was okay with me. Until I thought I was going to be a father. Now. I don't know. I think I would like a family." He didn't meet her eyes.

"Oh. So you need closure from me so you can go out and find someone to have your babies? Because you know how much the thought of turning into my own birth mother scares me and you know I have no desire to repeat her mistakes? You can't even talk to me? You're just going to give up on what was a really great thing? Fine. I gave you everything, Tucker. I told you everything. I trusted you. I can't believe you're even here." She turned to leave.

He caught up with her before she cleared the stand of trees behind the cabins. "Daisy, wait. I'm a jerk. I know that. I came here thinking I could put my feelings for you in perspective and I'm even more confused than when I got here." He looked into her eyes.

She threw her hands up, unable to continue the pointless exchange. She was out of here. He grabbed her arm and she ended up against his chest. His breath brushed her cheek and despite the pain radiating through her, she relaxed as his lips found hers. His kiss tasted like home and she leaned into him, missing him and everything they had together.

"Sorry. I can't. I just need time, Daisy. I don't even know who I am right now." He walked away.

Daisy's head hurt. There had been more yelling in this quiet setting than she could bear and her heart hurt more than it had when Tucker had left her to be a daddy to his nonexistent baby. He didn't want her.

And she didn't cry. Yet.

Sydney's argument with Mr. Fancypants had ended right after Tucker had kissed Daisy. She'd thought about going to help but when she realized Jace purposefully baited her sister, she backed off, hoping Sydney would get the clue on her own. The effect was far different from when Graham pushed her buttons. With Graham, Sydney stayed coherent and logical.

Jace made her speechless.

The whole scene had been pretty amusing, except for the way Marshal slammed things around. Interesting.

Sydney stormed by with one of the Tarzan-like screams she employed when frustrated, her face a mask of rage. Daisy knew better than to follow just yet and set off down the path toward the front gate. Maybe a walk would help her figure out what Tucker had been trying to say.

When she returned, Graham stood by the campfire ring, obviously waiting for her. Daisy wondered if anyone had heard her confront Tucker.

"Why is everyone so crazy here today?" he asked, loud enough for Marshal to hear.

No wonder Sydney always wanted to punch Graham.

Daisy snorted. "Get a life, Graham."

"I'd have one if you'd give me the time of day." This time, he was quiet, his words meant for only her.

"I thought you wanted Sydney." Could this really be happening?

"Get a life, Daisy." He smiled and she saw the sincerity and fear in his eyes.

"Just go out with me once. Let me take you away from this cursed campground and out on the town. We can get to know each other and figure out if there's anything there." Charming.

Shit. What was she going to do?

She liked Graham, and he was damn fine to look at, but a date? Crap. Did she even like him enough to think about it? Tucker obviously didn't want her. Would it be wrong to take care of her own happiness for a change?

"You need to give me some time, Graham. There's a lot going on here and I'm not sure what to do about any of it."

"No problem. I'm not giving up. I think there's something between us we need to explore. Think about it. You know where to find me." He touched her face, leaving her more confused than ever.

Hoping Sydney had calmed down enough to talk, she opened the cabin door and peeked inside. Sydney caught sight of her right away.

"I can't believe the nerve of him, showing up here after everything he's done and then acting so innocent and clueless." Sydney paced around the table in their cabin.

"Don't let him get to you. Violet has him wrapped so tight around her finger. He's as horrible as she is. What did Jace want anyway?" She probably shouldn't have asked that.

"To talk. He wants to know why we're going back on our verbal agreement with Violet. I swear, he acts like he has no idea what's going on here." Sydney shook her head.

"Weird. Another tactic to spy on us, I'm sure." She stood and grabbed the specifications for the contractors. "What are you going to do then?" She already knew the answer and wondered if her sister was being smart.

"I'm going to call him and meet with him. On my terms. Not here, just in case he is spying. I'm going to be nice, polite, and do my best to figure out just what the heck he's up to." Sydney's head hit the table again. "What happened with Tucker? I heard you yelling." Sydney seemed to shake off her encounter with Jace, or at least she pretended to.

"I have no freaking clue. Apparently, this whole project is supposed to help him find closure from me. Apparently, he feels conflicted after thinking he was going to be a father. Apparently, now he's even more confused. Apparently, he now wants to be a father no matter how adamant he was about not bringing anymore children into a world with so many troubled kids already." Now it was Daisy's turn to bonk her head on the table.

"And?"

"Apparently, I have no fucking idea."

Daisy spent the rest of the day repeating herself to contractor after contractor. Sydney had disappeared with a crushing headache after the second man finished telling them that a casino would better serve the community. Daisy had politely thanked him and then crossed his name from the list.

Even if his estimate undercut all the others, she would not hire him. She'd even told him to mail the proposal instead of dropping it off as she'd invited the other companies.

With the extra ten grand from Gramps, they'd be able to do more than they'd thought. Depending on how the next inspection went, they very well could end up in the clear.

Or not.

One of the plumbing contractors had remarked on how terrible their wiring was. The electrician wasn't due for a few more days. And then there was the pool, recreation building and main office to think about.

Daisy tried to concentrate on the website she was designing. Checking for messages from prospective customers and updating their progress on the blog. Hopefully, their tiny web presence would help build a customer base. As soon as they knew an exact opening date, she'd finish the advertising.

Maybe they'd have a full house by opening weekend.

Her hopes crumbled by the time the sun went down.

A thunderstorm rolled through, the first one since she and Sydney had moved in. There'd been light rain, spring rain, but not the torrential downpour that knocked out the electricity and pushed the roof off of Cabin C. Trees fell and the new plantings were under water.

The electricity had gone out with the first flash of lightning and according to the electric company's dispatch, it would be morning until crews could come out and assess their situation. Daisy had no hopes that the problem didn't come from their antiquated system. The generators had come on and then died just as quickly. Outdated and expensive to replace. Daisy sighed.

No power meant Marshal and his crew couldn't film or record tonight. Or process any of the footage from the two nights they'd already filmed. It also meant she couldn't continue to work on the website under battery power, since the satellite dish that had only been installed yesterday crashed to the ground in the wind.

At least Sydney had emerged from her migraine and Daisy had slept through most of the storm. Now there was nothing to do. Unless you were Sydney, then the possibilities were endless as long as Marshal was involved.

Ron and Eric had disappeared in one of the vans at dusk. She didn't even want to think about what they were up to about now. And she still didn't think Marshal had a clue that his best crewmembers were very into each other. Daisy wondered when they were going to tell him and then decided it was none of her business.

Marshal knocked once before entering the cabin. "Let's go."

Daisy stood, wondering what was going on.

"Both of you. Let's go. The wood is wet. There's no power, and I'm starving. Let's get out of here before we go stir crazy. I'm buying."

Daisy jumped up, noticing the purposeful way in which Sydney complied.

Sydney slowly walked in front of Marshal, as if challenging him. Besides the arch of his eyebrow, he said nothing. Oh. This should be an interesting night. Her sister was torn between a man she lusted after and the picture of her ideal mate.

Daisy couldn't wait to see this play out.

Then again, she was in the exact same situation. Tucker or Graham. Sydney would smack her if she even mentioned going out with Graham. Hell, she'd smack herself. They'd promised each other if one of them hated their boyfriend, they'd take that as a sign of impending doom and break things off.

Maybe not logical, but it worked in sister world.

Of course, Sydney liked Tucker and hated Graham.

Daisy liked Marshal and hated Jace.

They were doomed.

She was even more doomed when Graham jumped into the backseat beside her. And worse, Graham wore faded jeans and a T-shirt that showed off every muscle of his chest and arms. He was like a dream and Daisy had a hard time keeping her eyes to herself.

Marshal hadn't mentioned the addition, making them think he was the only one from his crew going along. Then Dave squeezed in and Daisy decided to make the most of the night. She relaxed in her seat, trying not to let Graham's sexy closeness affect her, and told herself she was going to have a good time.

Sydney couldn't believe she'd blindly agreed to go out tonight. Now that Graham, even though he was a pain in her ass, and Dave had piled in the backseat with Daisy.

Sydney relaxed some. The thought of making small talk with Marshal while Daisy observed hadn't sat well.

Daisy would probably have critiqued her methods and given her tips for improving her flirting skills. Somehow, Sydney thought Daisy was going to have her hands full with Graham.

Graham had the hots for Daisy. Sydney didn't know if her sister realized that yet. She certainly wasn't going to tell her. Sydney didn't hate Graham as much as she thought, but he still got on her nerves. Maybe that was because he followed her sister around like a dog in heat and Daisy didn't even notice. The guy was pathetic. At least he was handsome. She'd have put him out of his misery if he'd been any less.

Marshal stopped in front of a local eatery, known for good local talent and killer wings. Not many cars filled the parking lot, which was good. Sydney wasn't thrilled with crowds. Especially crowds in a bar. She liked to actually hear the people she talked with. She knew this place. At least she thought she did as a memory of coming here with Gramps surfaced.

A waitress met them at the door, properly sizing up the three hunks that had accompanied them inside. She winked at Sydney when Marshal urged her forward, placing his hand at the center of her back.

"Pick your seats. You're probably the only customers we'll have tonight. Most everyone is cleaning up after that storm. Trees are down everywhere and power is out in half the county." She waited until they chose, putting menus down in front of them as soon as they adjusted themselves in the oversized booth.

Of course, Sydney ended up thigh to thigh with Marshal.

"We thought it was just us without power." Sydney picked up the menu, but waited for the waitress's response.

"Where are you folks?"

"Brookside Campground." Sydney watched because the reaction from the folks in town always interested her.

"You're Del's girls? Sydney and Daisy? Oh my goodness, how you've grown up. I haven't seen you since your momma put a stop to Del bringing you to a bar for lunch. We need to talk. I can tell you stories about Del that will make your hair curl. You both are even more gorgeous as the last pictures he showed me."

Perfect. Maybe Sydney could find out what prompted Gramps to marry The Vileness. Eventually. She caught Daisy's warning glare and figured asking those kinds of questions the first time probably wasn't a good idea.

"That's right. We'd love to hear your stories about Gramps." Daisy's politeness had an undercurrent of suspicion and Sydney kicked her under the table.

Besides the brief shock that crossed Daisy's face, she gave no indication that the kick hurt, even though Sydney knew it had.

"I'm Kay Peters. You probably don't remember me. Del and I went to high school together. My husband, Ed, and I own this place. We opened about the same time Del took over Brookside. I'm so glad you girls are planning to reopen."

"There's a lot of work that needs to be done first. I don't think we'll measure up to Gramps' standard for a little while yet." Sydney didn't want to say too much, or give away too much information. What if Kay liked Violet?

"You let me know if you need any help. My grandsons are looking for part-time jobs. They're strong boys with a good work ethic." Kay tapped her order pad. "What can I get you all to drink?"

After ordering a round of beers and an ice tea for Dave, Sydney waited until Kay went to the kitchen to grab Daisy's hand. "We could use the extra help, even if it's just on weekends and after school."

"That we could, but we don't know Kay's relationship with The Vileness yet. If we can't find out before we leave tonight, we'll come back and talk to her." Daisy swatted Dave, who'd made a show out of trying to see down her shirt.

Marshal chuckled at their play, the vibration reaching Sydney from where they touched. She had a hard time concentrating on the menu and ignoring him.

Kay reappeared a very short time later with a loaded tray. "Hopefully you all are ready to order? Ed wants to close down the kitchen just in case that storm moves back in like it's supposed to."

"Would it be better if we went someplace else to eat? We don't want to put you out." Sydney hoped her question sounded genuine and not snotty.

"Don't you dare." Kay was offended. Now she'd done it. After a brief and intense stare down, Kay laughed. "Damn, but if you aren't Del through and through. He was as polite and stubborn as you."

Sydney took the statement as the compliment it was intended. They gave their orders, mostly burgers and fries. Except for Graham, who ordered a salad. Wuss.

"Vegetarian?" Daisy asked, her eyebrows raised.

"Not really. I just limit my intake of red meat and processed food." Graham sniffed and turned his head.

She hid her smile, but at the same time, wondered at Daisy's expression. She seemed almost . . . interested. Oh God. Marshal's hand brushed Sydney's leg and he fidgeted in his seat against the wall.

"Do you need me to move?"

"Not that I don't love having you pressed against me, but I'm feeling a little claustrophobic. How about a game of pool before our food comes?"

"Okay, but I'm not very good at pool." Sydney shifted and stood, sending Daisy eyes that hopefully told her to stay quiet. Daisy took the hint and covered her mouth with her hand. Maybe Sydney could get some of her dignity back after last night's stupid comments.

She let Marshal break, watching as he sank two solid balls in rapid succession. He moved to the opposite side of the table and lined up his next shot and Sydney saw her chance.

Leaning forward, she exposed enough cleavage to make her mother screech. "Call your shot."

Marshal looked up, not getting farther than the swell of her breasts.

"Six. Corner." He took a deep breath and scratched.

Grinning, Sydney took over the table, purposefully missing an easy shot. When Marshal went to try the same set up, because she hadn't done anything but put the cue ball back in its original position, she leaned forward again and almost laughed when the shot went wild.

Marshal came to her side of the table, picked up the chalk, and growled in her ear. "You did that on purpose."

She turned innocent eyes on him. "Did what?"

"Quit showing me your boobs."

"I did not. Quit looking." God, she wanted to suck his neck.

"Your shot." He nudged her bottom with his stick.

By the time she lined up the eight ball, Marshal's expression had changed to a glare of suspicion. "You lied."

"About what?" She tried to sound innocent. "Eight ball, side."

"You're a con artist." Marshal shook his head as the ball dove into the pocket.

"I am not. I'm just lucky."

"Yeah, right. How about this . . .?"

Their food arrived, interrupting the challenge she was certain Marshal was about to lay down. Damn.

"After dinner. Rematch. Only with a little wager."

The dare in his eyes was too much to resist.

"You got it."

Kay urged them to stay as she cleared the dishes. "You realize I'm not kicking you out. Ed just wants to get the gas turned off on the grill. You're welcome to stay as long as you like. Actually, you probably should. The TV's beeping with a severe weather alert, telling everyone to stay put unless traveling is an emergency."

Good. She and Marshal could play their game of pool.

Daisy played with Graham at the next table. Apparently, Graham hadn't immediately figured out that both of them had a gift for billiards. From the time they were old enough to see the top of the table, Gramps taught them respect for the game and their opponent and when not to bet. She and Daisy had made a little extra pocket money during college. Sydney hated to admit it was far more than necessary and that they'd scammed their share of drooling drunks.

Daisy winked as she lined up her shot and barely sent the cue ball six inches. Graham was in trouble and didn't even know it yet. Sydney wondered about the terms of their bet, but, then again, considering the way Daisy flirted, maybe she didn't really want to know. Marshal ordered her another beer, setting it on the high table beside the cue sticks.

"Thanks. Don't think alcohol is going to make a difference in my game. It won't. I could drink you under the table and still win." Uh-oh. Those were big words for someone who hadn't played, or drank like that in several years.

"I know you can outdrink me. I saw the pile of wine bottles this morning. You should be in bed and moaning."

Holy shit. Did he just say that? In bed and moaning?

He winked, and she shook her head. "You have no idea who you're up against."

"Neither do you."

Oh. Sydney hadn't thought of that. The last time she bet on pool she was in college, playing with boys who were more hormones than experience. Marshal was a man. The testosterone was still there, but so were years of experience.

"How old are you?"

"Thirty-six. You?"

"Thirty." Yep. She'd underestimated him.

"Ready to hear the terms of the game?" He cornered her by the high table, not exactly touching her, but not doing anything to settle her libido either.

"Bring it on." She straightened and locked eyes with him. No way would she let him know the dirty thoughts running through her head.

"One kiss for each ball I miss." He seemed very satisfied with himself. His terms would prevent her from any more cleavage shows, well, unless she liked his terms.

She probably would. But she couldn't let him know that.

"Okay." She didn't blink.

"What are your terms?" He stepped a bit closer.

"Let's play even. Same bet. Just to keep things interesting." What had she just done? Now if she missed, and she would eventually, he'd think she'd done it on purpose. Where was her brain?

Probably in her pants, or in his pants, or anywhere but in her head. Maybe it was time to rethink her "sex for fun" stance? Did she even know what she was getting into?

"Fine. The thing is, I collect when we get back to the campground. These bozos would love that kind of a show, so let's keep this private." Marshal whispered in her ear, the warmth penetrating every female part of her and turning her knees into mush.

She nodded. She didn't want to give a peep show either, but the thought of kissing him in total privacy changed the whole thing. How many balls could she miss and not seem like she'd done it on purpose?

She stood with her back against Daisy as Marshal sank yet another ball. So far, the score was dead even. Too bad for her. Daisy leaned her head back and smiled.

"How's it going?" She moved, watching Graham, or so Sydney thought.

"Just peachy. How about you?" Sydney had a feeling they'd made a similar bet.

"Eh. I'm losing, and by that, I mean I'm winning. Which is essentially losing." She laughed.

Sydney nodded. She knew exactly what she meant. The only problem was, Sydney didn't much care for Graham and she didn't think Daisy should get involved with him. No matter how different—translation: damn sexy—he was in faded jeans and a black T-shirt.

He still did nothing for her. On the other hand, the few buttons undone on Marshal's dark-blue shirt made her itch to slip her hands inside and feel the muscles she'd only vaguely viewed the day she crashed into him.

Thunder rolled overhead and the lights flashed. Kay arrived on the scene with candles for the tables surrounding them and a lantern at the bar. And another round of beers.

"I'm glad you all have a designated driver," she said, nodding toward Dave who was busy with a stack of papers at their table. "Also glad to see you're having fun." She winked at Sydney and handed her a beer.

Sydney accepted with a smile. She liked Kay, no matter how cautious Daisy seemed about the woman. If Kay was really Gramps' pal then she couldn't like Violet. She was dying to ask Kay's opinion and pick her brain over why Gramps married such a woman, but that would have to wait.

Kay obviously didn't do well with storms, based on the screech she let out when lightning cracked close by, and the way she nervously buzzed around the restaurant re-doing chores. When she passed again, Sydney stopped her. Marshal had the pool table tied up and it would probably be ages until she got to play again. If she ever did. Stupid bet. You'd think he'd miss on purpose just to collect. The jerk.

"Is there anything I can help you with?" Sydney felt like a sponge for having a good time when Kay worked her tail off.

"No. Storms make me nervous and I need to keep busy or go nuts."

Kay patted her arm.

"Would it help if we left?" She really didn't want to take advantage of the hospitality offered.

"You'll do no such thing. It's terrible out there and you are absolutely not in the way here. Ed and I want you to stay or you wouldn't still be here." The passion and kindness in her eyes made Sydney shut up about leaving.

"Thank you. We appreciate you letting us hang out. We'd be bumping into walls at the campground." Marshal stopped at her shoulder, his close proximity making her want to lean into him. Or maybe that was the beer.

"Did Del ever tell you some of the stories about the

campground? Why am I asking? Of course he did." Kay laughed, a choked sound due to the clap of thunder.

"What stories?" Daisy moved in to listen.

"The ghost stories. He never told you? We always laughed about it. Del said he didn't have time for such things. He did an open mind though. He'd never say spirits didn't exist, but he'd never say they did either." Kay warmed to her subject.

"Sounds like an inherited trait." Marshal's breath brushed her cheek. She kept quiet, not sure what he meant by that. Had he seen through her mask of indifference?

"We'd swap tales and then be too scared to move." Kay leaned against the pool table.

"What do you mean?" Marshal asked, his interest obvious.

"There are at least two ghosts here in the bar. Friendly. Or at least I think so. Nothing bad has ever happened. In fact, one night as I was leaving out the back door, I heard a male voice plain as day say, 'Check the front door.' Sure enough, I'd left the door unlocked. Another time, I was in the kitchen, alone and I heard noise out here. I started out to inform whoever was here that we weren't open yet, not thinking about the fact that I hadn't yet unlocked the front door. The kitchen door shut and locked on me. I couldn't get out. I saw someone trying to break into the cash register." She pointed to a window Sydney hadn't noticed.

"Those are good spirits," Daisy said, her interest in Kay's story obvious.

"Do you want to know exactly who's here?" Marshal was nearly jumping up and down, like a kid with an ice cream cone. Oh, to get him to look at her like that.

"I don't know. Why?" Kay moved so she could see Marshal better.

"I run a company called Tyler Investigations . . ."

"I know who you are. I've heard of you. Ed wanted me

to call and ask you to come here."

"Well, I'm here. We're working at the campground. When we're done there, we'll come and set up our equipment. That is, if you want us to?" Marshal's excitement was catching. She could feel the vibes coming off him and they just made her want to get closer.

"Would you? That would be great. But . . ." Kay wrung her hands.

"No charge," Marshal quickly added.

"I don't . . ." Kay wanted to accept Marshal's offer, at least she seemed like she wanted to.

"You don't understand. I don't charge unless it's a corporation."

Kay appeared shocked. "How do you make any money?"

Sydney raised a brow at him. She'd wanted to ask, but had been too chicken. Coming from anyone else the question would have been rude. Somehow, Kay's worry over not being able to pay Marshal made it okay.

"Most of us have other jobs. Dave is a computer consultant. He works mostly from the road." Marshal nodded to Dave, still hunched over a stack of forms, his laptop battery dead.

"I have a rotating crew and with enough notice, I always have enough help. We manage."

"What's your other job?" Sydney asked.

"Would you believe me if I said I work part time as a male stripper?"

"Yeah. I probably would." The thought of him stripping down to a G-string was enticing.

"Too bad. Believe it or not, I own a chain of restaurants. I have the freedom to travel and do this, plus I get to cook when there's nothing going on in the paranormal world."

"You're kidding." Sydney couldn't see him donning a chef's hat and apron.

"You should see what I can do with whipped cream," he

said in a low voice with a wiggle of his eyebrows.

She smacked his arm.

"Ed and I would be grateful if you'd come here and find out about our ghosts," Kay said, and Sydney wondered how much of their flirting she'd heard.

"We'll look forward to it." Marshal's eyes crinkled and Sydney watched as Kay fell victim to his charm.

"What's going on at the campground? I thought Del made most of those stories up." Kay sat on one of the stools.

Sydney kept quiet. Her secret was going to bite her in the ass one day soon.

"I can't believe Gramps knew there was activity there and never told us. I mean, Sydney and I sometimes thought we saw stuff, but Gramps acted like we were just playing." Daisy leaned her cue stick against the table, the games forgotten as they gathered around to hear Kay repeat Gramps' tales.

CHAPTER 7

"Del and I grew up in this town. I guess you knew that. What you don't know is that I had my very first kiss in that campground. Behind one of the bathhouses." Kay's eyes sparkled in memory.

"And who was it that kissed you? Ed?" Sydney had a feeling she already knew the answer.

Kay glanced over her shoulder. "Not Ed. Del. He and I were an item for a while, but realized we were better off as friends. No spark at all. Anyway, Del tricked me into going into the trees by the bathhouse. Of course, I wanted him to kiss me. I didn't expect what happened next."

Sydney knew exactly what trees Kay talked about. They were the same ones where she'd had her first kiss.

"Well. I'd just decided that maybe kissing wasn't for me. I think I was eleven or so. Del had just finished slobbering all over me when a cold wind blew through the trees. The next thing we knew, snow started falling. It was July. We were amazed and thought there was some kind of weather weirdness until we went to find out what was going on. At the entrance, the trees were almost like a little fort, there was a man. Half-dressed, with long dark hair and a bow in his hand. We stopped short when we saw him. He studied us for a few seconds and then went right through us. When we turned, not a bit of snow was anywhere and the temperature had returned to normal."

"Wow." Daisy leaned forward. "Anything else?"

"Lots of stuff. People have been coming in here for years talking about odd experiences in the campground. Let me think and I'll write them down as I remember."

"Excellent." Marshal's face mimicked Daisy's.

"I think Del kept a journal about the strange stuff. If you have his records, you might find it."

Sydney thought about the contents of the box she'd received with the campground records and other family items. Could the journal be inside?

Wait. Why was she getting excited? She wasn't so sure she believed this stuff, even what she'd felt and seen with her own eyes. Now she was as bad as Daisy, believing any story without question.

Marshal's excitement was rubbing off.

Oh. Bad way to compare.

Daisy couldn't believe Gramps never told them about Kay or the ghosts. She hadn't trusted the woman, but her first kiss story had convinced Daisy that if Gramps liked and trusted her than they should, too. She wasn't sure what Sydney thought. Her sister was acting weird.

Having an ally that had the opportunity to listen to people discuss certain things was a benefit. Hopefully, they'd get time to ask if Kay had heard anyone talking trash about the campground. If she had, Kay would have probably already spilled those details by now.

Sydney took a swig out of her beer bottle and sat back, apparently fighting with herself over something. She and Marshal had been pretty cozy during their pool game. Daisy couldn't help but wonder what their stakes were, and if they were the same as hers and Graham's. How she let him talk her into five minutes of total privacy for every ball he missed was beyond her. Apparently, Marshal and Graham were scam artists. So far, neither had missed, which didn't say much for their desire to collect on the debt.

Jackasses.

Ed called for Kay from the kitchen and she rushed away,

assuring their group that this was their nightly routine and no, she didn't need any help.

"Let's play while we still can." Graham tossed her the abandoned stick.

"Your ball." She tried to ignore him as he lined up his shot and thought about playing her sister's cleavage trick.

Except, she didn't have any cleavage.

Damn.

Standing, she stretched, feeling a breeze where her shirt came untucked.

Graham stopped behind her, his voice nearly a whisper. "You did that on purpose. Your shot."

"I did not." Five minutes of total privacy. Oh, what she could do in those brief moments.

She couldn't remember if she'd decided to purposefully miss and add to the time or play fair or let things happen as they may. Playing for time didn't really mean anything, but it sure did a lot for her hormones. Sinking the shot, she moved around the table never missing a ball and ignoring Graham as she went. The table was down to one solid, one stripe and the eight ball.

Graham put his hand on her stick as she lined up the way too easy sink. "If you win, I get one whole night."

"How's that fair?" Her blood heated, as if it could get any hotter.

"What's fair? You made me miss with that sweet tummy show." He growled in her ear, his warm breath making it difficult to concentrate.

"Not my fault. Half a night."

"All or nothing." Graham leaned into her, his face only inches from hers. "I promise to make it worth your while."

Oh shit. She was done for.

Marshal wiggled his eyebrows as he cleared the table of first his balls, and then hers.

"And you called me a con." Sydney didn't know what to think. One minute he teased and flirted and the next, he sank the entire rack, technically losing those promised kisses for each missed ball.

"Let's play again." He racked the table, moving the balls to order.

"Fine. I break." Did she want him to kiss her?

"Let's up the stakes." He reached over her for the chalk.

"No. Our original agreement is fine by me." She kept her tone playful, but wouldn't look at him. Couldn't. He'd see the confusion and hurt on her face and that would be a mistake.

"Whatever, but you're missing out." He leaned back over her arm to replace the blue square.

"Your opinion." She broke, sending four balls home, and chose her mark. "Stripes. Corner."

She didn't pay any attention to him as she sank the next three balls without effort. Two could play at Marshal's little game. She'd clear the board, call them even and forget about his seductive wager.

As she made her shot, the candles and lantern went out.

"That's what I'm talking about. Mischievous, but not nasty," Kay called from the kitchen.

"You missed." Marshal almost gloated after relighting the lantern.

"Not my fault. I get to try again." She held her stick in front of her like a shield.

"Nope. You wouldn't let me shoot again after your boob show. I think Kay's ghost wanted you to miss."

"Don't be ridiculous."

As if in answer, the house lights flickered. Sydney tried to shrug off the feeling that Marshal was right. "Your shot."

If Marshal had acted even a tiny bit superior, she could hate him. He lined up the ball, confident but not cocky, and she couldn't think of a single reason not to like him. During his second shot, the lights flashed again and he missed.

"Guess Kay's ghost isn't only picking on me." She moved past him, sliding her chest across his back though there was plenty of room to go around.

"Oh. Getting bold, aren't we?" Marshal leaned against his stick and she resisted the urge to kick it out from under him. That would be playing gone too far.

"We're even." She met his eyes with confidence.

"Two kisses. In total privacy. Miss again." He poked her with his stick.

"You miss again."

"I might. On purpose."

"Whose turn is it?"

"Yours? Don't forget to miss."

She lined up the shot, the scenarios that rushed through her head making it impossible to concentrate. This little game needed to end before things went too far.

Sinking the rest of the table, she leaned against the side trying not to laugh.

"You didn't miss." He pouted with sexy lips.

"We're still even." How many beers had she consumed to make her this bold?

"That we are." He moved closer, filling her senses and making her crazy.

"In private," she warned him off, not that anyone paid attention.

"The storm's over. The weatherman said there's about two hours before the next band hits. The next bunch of storms is supposed to be the worst yet. Doesn't sound good," Kay called from the kitchen.

"We need to get back, assess the damage, and see if we can prepare for the worst. What if the roof leaked again and your equipment is wet?" Anxiety overrode her sex drive.

"We do need to go. Though the equipment should be fine. We locked it in the van before we left."

That relaxed her a fraction. The last thing she needed was a claim against the insurance for what was probably tens of thousands of dollars of Marshal's ghost-hunting equipment.

Gathering beer bottles, they all pitched in to help Kay clean up. By the time they said their goodbyes, the place sparkled and Kay hugged each of them.

"Come in as soon as you can and let me know how the storm treated Brookside. I'll worry until I hear from you." Kay crushed Sydney in a tight hug.

"I promise."

Kay moved on and Sydney turned to Marshal. "Where's Dave? Did he leave?"

They'd all consumed several more beers than necessary. She'd been so involved in their game that she hadn't paid a bit of attention to Dave. Of course, she got the feeling he preferred it that way.

"Dave's still here."

Dave held the keys up with a wink as he came out the door and Sydney wondered why she'd ever worried about these guys joining them at Brookside. They were wonderful and that wasn't the beer talking.

In fact, Sydney felt fine, only a tiny bit tipsy. Maybe the heated innuendo and sexual bets had rushed the alcohol through her system.

The gates to the campground were lying on the ground. They would have to be repaired first thing in the morning. The last thing they needed was curious folks wandering in to see what they were doing. As the headlights cut through the darkness, she made out several downed trees. Besides the standing water everywhere, the campground seemed okay.

But it was still dark and more rain was expected. A lot more rain.

Lightning streaked the sky as a reminder the storms were coming back and long and low thunder rumbled across the sky. The whole scene—the brief bright view of the campground with the woods dark and looming—freaked her out in a way she couldn't describe easily. Something felt wrong at Brookside and she didn't know why. The campground had never scared her before, even after her horrible experience in that damned spooky cabin and her adventures trying to rescue the still missing and apparently injured dog.

The cabins appeared ominous as Dave stopped in front of the one the guys inhabited. She moved to get out of the vehicle when Daisy touched her arm.

"What is that?" Daisy pointed out the window to Sydney's left.

Four ghostly figures moved through the trees. Like the misty forms they'd watched at the pond. Sydney couldn't make out facial features.

The misty forms stopped at the clearing, the one in front holding his hand up in a signal to wait. He—Sydney assumed the form was male—looked back and forth before taking a step.

Another figure stepped out of the trees and toward them. The new presence was very different from the faceless mist that appeared to be on some type of journey.

A grisly face pressed against the glass of the opposite rear window, and she screamed.

Horror and evil, the mouth opened in a silent scream and eyes of red cast a gruesome glow over the interior of the van. Her fear vanished as she realized she was looking at a mask.

"That's it." Fury prompted her to jump out of the vehicle and rush around to the side where the "creature" teased them. Grabbing the cloth at the neck, she didn't let go. Even when it spun and spurted what some kind of red, thick liquid from the gaping mouth.

"Knock it off, asshole. You're stupid if you think any of us bought your little scheme." She reached and grabbed off what she suspected. A rubber mask.

The bewildered face under the gruesome visage wasn't one she recognized. As Marshal grabbed the guy from the back, twisting his arms behind him and making him grunt, Sydney looked for the rest of the ghostly bunch.

"Where are your friends?" she commanded, her tone hopefully conveying that she'd stand for no bullshit.

"What friends? There's no one with me." Scared. Young. And a little bit of attitude.

"We all saw them. They followed behind you in the woods. They took off when you tried to scare us." Sydney was sure he lied.

"Come on. You have some explaining to do." Marshal dragged him toward the cabin.

"I'll call the sheriff." Daisy moved into the clearing with her cell phone, the only place they seemed to get a decent cell phone signal after dark.

Dave followed Marshal, his expression the same as it'd been all evening, a mixture of boredom and apprehension. Sydney, not for the first time, wondered what his story was. Now alone and still furious, she hoped for a glimpse of the intruder's cohorts.

What she saw wasn't what she expected.

The ghostly figures moved right past her. Their shoulders slumped as if their journey threatened to suck the life out of them. They paid no attention to Sydney, even when she reached out and came up with nothing but air.

Oh.

CHAPTER 8

The sheriff couldn't come right away due to trees blocking several roads, and a whole bunch of emergencies, all of which were more important than their teenager in a scary mask. They were to hold their prisoner and nothing else until he arrived. At least they had electricity. For now. The impending storm was moving in sooner than expected if the lighting and thunder were to be believed. Sydney paced the tiny front porch of Marshal's cabin, not sure what to do.

Her anger got the better of her and she went inside. "Who put you up to this?" She stopped inches from the kid.

"N-No one. I don't know." He appeared scared, but that did nothing to ease her irritation.

"Oh please. Don't lie to me. Start talking or . . ."

Marshal grabbed her arm and moved her away from the scared punk. "You can't threaten him. Take a walk. Now."

Sydney complied. Only because he was right. She was acting like a jerk. Going inside to confront the kid had been stupid. What was wrong with her?

This had to be something Jace cooked up. They'd tried to be careful letting anyone know Marshal and his crew was in residence, but Jace probably found out when he appeared here the other day. She shouldn't be surprised.

She wasn't really. But the nerve of Jace Levine.

Oh, she'd meet with him all right.

Headlights finally swept through the trees marking the arrival of the sheriff. She stepped down to greet him, another of Gramps' lifelong friends.

He hugged her, releasing her with a sympathetic smile. "You girls sure are having the trouble."

"You know it, Frank."

"Everything's going to work out. You'll see. You two will do this and make Del proud. As much as I hate to say it, I think you'll do better than old Del. The community wants Brookside back, not a casino. The people of this town don't want that kind of change and the clients that kind of place would bring."

"We're doing our best." She fought tears.

"I know you are. Most of the whole town is behind you. It'll happen. Now, let's go have a word with your creepy visitor." Frank's heavy shoes echoed through the pre-storm quiet.

Sydney followed, nodding when Daisy held her finger to her lips. Usually their roles were reversed. Sydney was always the cool head. Not this time. Why she'd gotten so worked up over something she was certain had been going on the whole time was beyond her.

"So, young man, why are you here?" Frank opened his notebook after reading the kid his rights.

"I don't have to talk to you." The kid had to be about sixteen.

"No. You don't, but things might go easier on you if you do. And these pretty ladies might not press charges if you cooperate." Frank nodded to where Sydney stood by Daisy.

Sydney took a deep breath in an attempt to calm the rage knotting her stomach. It helped a little, but it wouldn't take much for it to come back.

The kid regarded them for a few seconds before moving his attention to Marshal and Dave. His gaze rested on Daisy before he lowered his head. "Some guy stopped me at the arcade and asked if I wanted to make a hundred bucks."

"What guy?" the sheriff asked calmly.

"He didn't tell me his name. Just said he wanted to play

a practical joke on the people staying here. He said it was all in fun and that they'd laugh. He sounded like he knew everyone here." The kid seemed even younger, and scared. Sydney softened.

"What did he look like?" Frank wrote the description and Sydney was disappointed that it didn't sound the least bit like Jace. Damn.

She wished it was Jace wearing a disguise, but when the kid said the guy was stick skinny and like a skeleton with skin, she knew there was no way.

One of his cronies. Maybe. Damn. Why couldn't it have been Jace? Who else had a vested interest in making them leave the campground?

No one. And that was the problem. It had to be Jace. Or Violet. Her temper rose again, but she tamped it down.

"This guy someone you've seen before?"

Good for Frank. Sydney definitely hadn't thought of that.

"Once or twice. I think he lives in the trailer park off Liberty Road. His daughter, April, is in my class."

"Last name."

"Jones."

"You friends with her?"

"Kind of. She's quiet. Doesn't really talk to anyone. Just sort of there. She only started school after Christmas. I don't know where she came from." The kid shuffled his feet a little, but met Frank's eyes.

"Who are her friends at school?" Sydney wasn't sure why Frank asked about the teenager. Unless it was to find someone he could ask about her family.

"She doesn't have any that I know of. I've never seen her in the halls with anyone. She's always got her face in a book."

"That's sad," Sydney commented.

"I never thought about it, but you're right." The kid looked at Sydney and for a minute she thought he was playing her to make sure they didn't press charges. When she saw no deception in his eyes, she nodded.

"Well, Mr. Jackson, I'll take you home." Frank closed his notebook.

"Am I in trouble?" he asked Frank, his eyes on her and Daisy.

"Don't know yet. I need to verify your story and then the rest will be up to the property owners." Frank waited for the kid to adjust his huge cloak.

"I am sorry. I hope you can believe me. I thought this whole thing was a joke. The guy made me think you all were friends and that you'd laugh. If I would've known, I wouldn't have taken his money. This place is really creepy after dark." He held a wad of cash out toward Daisy.

"Keep the money. As long as Sheriff Frank feels you're as much a victim as we are, there won't be charges." Daisy looked at Sydney and she nodded. "And make friends with April. She's new and probably lost. She could probably use a friend."

"I'll be in touch." Frank smiled and touched the brim of his hat as he escorted their teenage spook out the door.

"Do you think Jace paid that guy to do the job and he passed it on to the kid?" Daisy stood at the window and watched Frank leave.

"Could be. I can't believe we're not supposed to mention this to Jace." Sydney went to the door.

"Let Frank do his job," Marshal said, his attention out the side window.

"I never said I wasn't going to. I always listen to Frank."

Daisy snorted. "Yeah. Always. Except for when he tells you not to call him any more about the stray animals you've found wandering the campground. And when he told you not to try to stop the state workers from spraying that section of highway that borders this land."

She waited. Surely, Daisy's stories would bring more questions than she cared to answer. Except they didn't.

"Guess what, though? Frank is retiring in a few weeks. He promised to let the department know our situation and that they better look out for us. I'm sad," Daisy said.

"No. That stinks." She sighed. "I'm going in." She walked away, hearing Marshal approach even though she didn't turn around. Unlocking the cabin door, she went in but left the door open.

"Did you come to collect?"

Marshal leaned against the door frame, his bulk nearly filling the space. "Not tonight. You're too stressed. How'd you know that ghoul was a fake?"

"Don't tell me you didn't." She had a hard time believing that. Especially since he'd pegged the first night destruction of his cabin as a prank.

"I knew. I saw him sneak up to the car from behind us. I just wondered how you figured it out."

"Ghosts, no matter how scary, probably don't have hickeys on their necks. The makeup job was pretty poor. I guess for what he thought he was doing, it was pretty darn good, especially for a kid."

"That it was. I didn't see the hickey until you ripped his mask off. That wasn't what I wanted to ask you though." Marshal didn't move and she wondered if he meant what he said about not collecting on their bet tonight.

"What then?" She sat at the table.

"Before he showed up and after. You saw them, all of them, didn't you?"

She knew what he talked about, but didn't understand why he questioned her and asked him. Hadn't everyone seen the ghostly trio?

"We all saw them at the beginning. The second time Dave didn't. Daisy didn't either. She watched you from inside and called me over when you reached out. She couldn't see what you tried to touch and neither could I then."

"They were there. I couldn't touch them. Three men, their shoulders sagged like they were defeated. I felt their misery, felt that their journey held a lot of pain and sorrow." Why was she accepting her experience so readily?

"I wonder . . ." Marshal shifted but didn't leave his spot. "You said you thought the Trail of Tears may have traveled through here. I think you might be right."

"Oh." Sydney stood, then sat quickly. "That's the impression I had. I don't know how to explain it. But I could feel different things. Anger, pain, regret, betrayal. There was a lot of helplessness and worry. One of the travelers buried his wife a few hours before. Oh."

How would she know that?

Marshal only stared. "For someone who spouts off disbelief of the paranormal, you have a deep understanding. People who can absorb the emotional energy of the spirits around them are rare. I would have never guessed."

"Neither would I, because that's not true. It was just an impression I had. Kind of like seeing the sky and knowing it's probably going to rain."

"Exactly. What about in the cabin? What did you feel then?" Marshal finally sat down across from her.

"Scared."

"Besides that. What went through your mind?" He grabbed her hand, the warmth there offering some comfort for her chaotic mind.

"Frustration, and not my own. It was different somehow. Desperate. Like someone I loved was lost. I was sad. I figured the feeling was because of Gramps and how much I miss him. They left, but not on purpose and there was no peace. What?"

Marshal smiled. "You're gifted. No wonder you yell so

loud about not believing. What you can do scares the hell out of you. Can you talk to them?"

How had he figured her out so rapidly? She didn't know what to say. Or think. Should she continue denying the truth, or allow him to see the depth of what she'd tried so hard to hide from everyone? Including herself?

"I haven't tried for a long time. In fact, I thought all of this had left me. Until we came back here."

"What happened in the bathhouse that you hate so much?" Marshal leaned forward, clearly interested.

Sydney didn't think he meant her extended janitorial duties.

"Suicide. She's a young woman. She has bruises all over her body. She smells like liquor and vomit. She died in the last shower stall. The one with the broken tiles. Her wrists are slit wide open. When I see her, I can see the brief moments before she used the blade and then she's dead. She took a whole bunch of pills and washed them down with booze before cutting herself." She shivered at the disturbing image.

"You tried to talk to her." Marshal rubbed her palm with his thumb.

"She doesn't hear me. I tell her it's over. That she should follow the path, but her eyes are blank and nothing ever changes. I read something once about the hell people who commit suicide have to endure before they can move on to a better place. Do you think that's true?"

She shook her head. "There's no way to know."

"How did you know my feelings on the bathhouse?" She hadn't told him anything.

"I didn't, except by how anxious you became when we went there."

"Did you catch her on film?"

"We haven't reviewed the footage yet. We have two nights of video and audio from inside to go over. The first night we taped in the bathhouse Ron said someone pinched him when he cleared the equipment. That's why we went back. Can you go through your grandfather's records and see if there's information on that woman? And try to find the journal?" Marshal glanced around the cabin as if the boxes of files were easily accessible.

"Tomorrow. I have to find them. The only journals I've found have been only business transactions." She stood and stretched with a deep yawn.

"Good enough." He wrapped his arms around her. The hug felt way too good. "For what it's worth, you're not a freak. Just an anomaly, and a damn cute one."

He lowered his head and brushed her lips with his. Sydney's exhausted system rushed to life and she leaned into him, taking what he offered and giving back the same.

The door banged open, breaking the precious moment and the promise in Marshal's kiss. She was going to kill Daisy.

"That one doesn't count." Marshal released her, shooting Daisy an exasperated look on his way by.

"What's wrong?" Sydney waited, but Daisy said nothing.

Giving up, she went to her room and grabbed her pajamas. Daisy followed.

"Graham is such an asshole." Daisy plopped down on the bed with a sigh.

"I thought you two were getting along great. At least you were at Kay's. What happened?"

"We were. We even had a bet. He was all hot for me and flirty. Until we got back here. He got a phone call and has ignored me ever since. What if he's married?" Daisy flopped down on the bed in an exasperated movement.

"Find out. If he is, we'll take turns kicking his ass all the way back to his hometown."

"He can't be," Daisy almost wailed.

"He could, and if he is, then you don't have to choose between him and Tucker. It's a bonus."

"That would mean I let a married man feel me up." She shuddered.

"Doesn't count. He didn't tell you. You didn't know. And you still don't," Sydney pointed out, confused by Daisy's erratic behavior.

Eventually she was going to have to tell Daisy the only secret she'd ever kept from her. After all the hiding and spouting off nonsense about Daisy's beliefs and ghost stories, Sydney thought she'd better have ample room to run or else get her hair yanked out like the fights they had as pre-teens.

Right now was not that time though. Daisy practically breathed fire at the notion that Graham could be married. Her reaction was unusual and only meant her sister was falling for her less-than-ideal vision of a mate.

"I'll kill him," Daisy screamed into the mattress before rolling over and scooting off the bed. "I'm going to go clean something. Good night."

Drained, Sydney crawled under the covers and closed her eyes tight. Was she really the freak she'd always thought? She'd rejected all of this stuff so long ago. For a while, she'd poured her experiences into her journal to get them out of her head since no one wanted to hear what she had to say.

Journal. Gramps had kept a journal of stuff that happened at the campground. Could she have inherited this weird gift from him? What about Daisy, did she have the same abilities? Was that why he insisted they run the campground? Did he take care of the wandering spirits that roamed these woods?

A chill moved across her, but she refused to open her eyes. Ever since she'd come back to Brookside the experiences had started again. The first night she'd felt the breeze, she'd opened her eyes to find an elderly woman standing beside her bed.

Sydney couldn't deal with the sleep interruption tonight. She would not open her eyes.

Then, she did.

After scrubbing the bathroom in candlelight, Daisy punched the pillow wishing it was Graham's head. They'd had a blast at Kay's, but ever since coming back to the campground their little group had come unglued. Maybe this place was as cursed as some seemed to think.

Sydney was acting weird. Weirder than normal, she should say. Maybe it was that Sydney was going against her morals and beliefs to have a little fun for the first time in her life. Yeah, right. As if she'd act on her hormones. Daisy saw Marshal's frustrated expression as he'd left their cabin. Of course, some of that could be related to her earlier-than-expected arrival.

Daisy could understand that being the reason if she'd looked out the window and found her sister dry humping a tree. But the woman had been reaching into thin air with total amazement when they'd arrived back at the campground and that crazy shit had happened, like she'd taken a hallucinogenic drug or something. Truthfully, the scene had freaked Daisy out and she thought about making an appointment with her psychiatrist friend for Sydney. Maybe the stress of trying to get this place open was taking its toll.

Lightning lit her tiny room, casting weird shadows. She was exhausted, but furious, and didn't know if she'd be able to fall asleep. Especially with Graham's sexual descriptions rolling around in her thoughts. Still, she drifted, shoving the negatives of the evening to the back of her head. She concentrated on how good it felt pressed up against Graham, and all of the naughtily wonderful things he'd promised.

Oh. If he would only make good on the things he'd whispered into her ear. Graham might be a little too prissy for her, but he sure knew how to give a girl a fantasy.

She let herself get lost in the thoughts, until something heavy crashed outside the cabin window.

CHAPTER 9

Daisy rushed out of bed, bumping into Sydney at the door.

"What the hell was that?" Sydney didn't appear to have slept yet either. Maybe they needed to have a talk that didn't include bitching about men.

"Probably more bad news." That was all Daisy could think of, too. Good things never happened during a storm.

Daisy grabbed the flashlight and opened the front door, only to be yanked back by Sydney.

"You'll get soaked. Here." She handed her a poncho and Daisy slipped it over her head, impatient. She waited until Sydney copied her movements, keeping silent at the irony of Sydney's bright yellow poncho. Wasn't it just yesterday Sydney insisted Daisy was more the brightly colored one of their duo?

Daisy shined the light in the direction of the crash and almost burst into tears. Cabin C was demolished. A huge tree now lay through the center of the building, the walls tilting in, toward the hole the tree created, the blue tarp Tucker's crew had put up to cover the hole in the roof now waving in the wind.

"Do you realize how far this storm has set us back?" Thank goodness, serious Sydney seemed to be back. "We won't pass Violet's inspection next week. God only knows if we'll be able to open in time to stop her."

And they would lose the stash of cash Gramps had wanted them to have.

Damn.

The guys circled the damage, shaking their heads in sympathy.

"Come on. There's nothing we can do out here but get wet." Sydney grabbed her arm and tugged, urging her back inside before Graham had a chance to catch up with them.

Daisy wiped the moisture from her eyes and followed, positive she'd never find sleep.

The next morning, the sun shone brightly and still Daisy woke with an ominous feeling. She could hear Sydney in the kitchen area, softly humming to herself. They'd survived the storm, but who knew what damage awaited them in the aftermath?

When did she turn into such a prophet of doom?

Climbing out of bed, she dressed and joined Sydney, just as the strong, dark coffee finished trickling into the pot.

"You look like hell. Didn't you sleep?" Sydney turned, her hair still wet.

"Only about an hour. What got you up so early?" She plopped down at the table, not sure if she should take a shower or wait until the day ended and she was sure to need another.

"Tucker. He got here before first light. I think he was disappointed that I came out and not you." Sydney laughed, but Daisy didn't share her joke.

"Too bad for him." Why was she in such a foul mood? Well, besides the cabin disaster?

"Tucker brought this for you. It's from Uncle Al." Sydney passed her a large envelope, the end sealed with Al's trademark clear snowman-covered Christmas tape. "Something you want to talk about?"

A family code. If the tape was on, the contents were private. She and Sydney learned to respect the boundary, though sometimes the curiosity killed them. Like she figured it was doing to Sydney now.

"I'll let you know." She took the envelope and stood.

Sydney stopped her with a cup of coffee and a one-armed hug. "I'm here."

Nodding, Daisy closed her bedroom door and tossed the envelope on the bed. Did she really want to know what was inside?

She must, or she wouldn't have asked Al to find out.

Her father. Her parents.

Why should she care about the people who'd created her and then abandoned her? Dropping to the bed, Daisy ripped off the silly tape and slid the contents out.

Her mother was alive, though not in the best of shape mentally. Her visits to an outpatient mental facility were listed, the details of her extended visits not included. Daisy couldn't help but wonder if the drugs had done that to her mother, or if mental illness ran in her blood.

The man listed as her father lived in town. This town. He was recently widowed and worked as a mechanic in a local garage. Daisy had probably talked to him when she'd gotten gas a few days ago. Not that she'd remember. Not that she believed the man was really her father.

Now that she had the facts, she still didn't have the answers. Maybe it was time to talk to the parents who raised her and see if they would tell her anything.

She picked up her phone, pleased she had a signal. Even though she and Sydney used the same cellular carrier, and had identical phones, they each found signals in different locations, at different times. Another weird and baffling Brookside Campground mystery.

Dialing home, she waited. Her mom would be up this early. The call would probably put her into cardiac arrest though. As expected, her adoptive mother answered with a concerned hello. Daisy immediately told her all was well, wondering if she should even bother with the questions she needed to ask.

"Then what's wrong? This is early for you." Though still worried, her mom sounded a bit more relaxed. "You guys make out okay with the storms?"

"I don't know yet. Not really. It was rough. We lost one of the cabins. Tucker is here with his crew and I can hear the chainsaws already." She hesitated.

"What's wrong, honey?"

Thank goodness for mother's intuition. Daisy had almost chickened out and made the call all about the severe storms.

"I had Uncle Al investigate stuff on my parents." She paused, wondering how her mom would take the news.

"I wondered when you would." The understanding nearly undid Daisy. "What do you want to know?"

Daisy swallowed. "Most of what I want to know they have to answer for. Like why. I guess I want to know what my mother was really like."

"Nadine was the star of the show." The words were a bit sarcastic, but still affectionate. "My sister was destined for greatness and fame. She sang, danced, and had a flair for the theater. And she was nice. Probably the kindest, most compassionate person ever. Your gramps loved her. Said she would be the one to take our family to fame. She broke his heart, I think. He took us both in when I met your dad. He treated Nadine like a daughter, like he did me. I couldn't figure out why he was so kind. He accepted both of us like his own children. Families are weird like that, though."

That made Daisy smile and cry. "So what happened to her?"

"She got mixed up with the wrong people. People who thought greatness came from inside of a pill or liquor bottle. Everything changed after she realized it was easier to ignore our childhood than deal with it. I know I've only eluded to what we went through and I'm sorry for that. Maybe one day I will tell you and Sydney what happened to us as children." Mom sniffled.

"You don't ever have to. It's okay." Her heart was already broken from the few things her mom had said. She was almost scared to know.

"Thanks, honey. We'll see. Anyway. My Nadine was gone once she started hanging out with those people. I was devastated that my big sister had left me. In her place was a wicked, nasty person who didn't care about herself, much less anyone else. We didn't speak for years. Then, one day, she called. I thought I finally got my constant prayer—my sister back. She'd cleaned herself up, gone through rehab and was in her last semester of college. I was so proud. After that, we talked almost every day."

Daisy knew there was a big "but" coming soon.

"She was the maid of honor in our wedding. It was a very special day for me, and for her, too. She was healthy and acted like she had when we were girls. We knew Gramps before I knew your father. We grew up not far from the campground and both had jobs there as teenagers. In fact, your grandfather introduced me to your dad. He said he knew we were destined to be together. He was such a great support to Nadine and me."

"This doesn't end well," Daisy managed.

"For me it does. But for Nadine . . . you know it doesn't. We vacationed together at the campground the summer after your dad and I's wedding. We all had a great time."

"And?"

"She'd met a man while in town. Said he was with a band and they needed a female singer. Nadine saw fame and fortune. She went to meet him on Wednesday and I didn't see her again until she dropped you at my door. Seems we both conceived that weekend. Only she never bothered to let me know I was going to be an aunt." Her mom sniffed.

Daisy wasn't the only one her birth mother had hurt. She'd never thought about how her mom figured into the equation. Now she felt like a jerk for bringing the subject up.

"When she dropped you off, she seemed clean. So did you. She swore she hadn't touched a single vice while pregnant. But motherhood was trying for her, especially since she hadn't heard from your father since the night she told him about you. I had no reason to doubt her. Okay. I had a lot of reasons to doubt, but I wanted to believe her. Her story about who fathered you changed four times in the short period of time she was there."

"Oh. I think I know the rest." Daisy's heart sank and she wiped tears from her cheeks.

"No. You don't. Six months after she dropped you off, she tried to take you back. Things were different. She was different. Drunk, or something, and with the worst group of guys I've ever seen in my life. I didn't even want them in my house. They all made such a fuss over you, saying how pretty you were and how awesome it would be to have you with them, but so very creepy. There was no way you were going anywhere with them."

"You never told me that."

"I know I didn't. It was awful. I couldn't let you go with her. They all stank of booze and cigarettes. You know me, I never judge people by the surface appearance, but that gang, well, they embodied evil. I told her she couldn't take you. I just knew they were up to no good. I made up some story about you being sick and needing medicine, medical tests, and doctor visits. She handed you back to me and left without asking what was wrong with you. She called me once a week after that, usually in the middle of the night. Telling me what town and what band was playing, always a message. I didn't speak to her again until we tracked her down and made her sign the adoption papers."

"Did she ask about me when she called?" Why was that important? And why had she actually asked?

"I'm sorry, honey. Usually she just wanted to borrow money or wanted the phone number of someone who owed her a favor. Usually, she wanted to talk to Gramps, but I quit forwarding the messages when she got too weird and cumbersome. Gramps could never say no to Nadine and I didn't want him to have to deal with her constant demands for the money she needed to feed her habit." Daisy had never thought about that. Had never realized that technically she wasn't even blood related to Gramps. And yet, he'd stuck by her, helped her, given her half ownership to the thing that had mattered most to him. He'd loved her through his dying years. Hell, he'd even stuck by her drug-addicted mother, even though there had been no blood to obligate him.

"Oh. What did she say when she signed the papers?" Why was she torturing herself?

"Nothing. She asked if there was any money in it for her. We told her no, that we'd need the money to take care of you and that if she was lucky we wouldn't sue her for support. That was all it took to get her to sign her rights over. We showed her your picture, but she didn't even look. I'm sorry, honey. I know you hoped for a fairy tale, but there isn't one here. Your mom got mixed up in bad stuff and it ruined her. All I can tell her is that she isn't the same person I grew up with and I'm sad. Sad for you and sad for me."

Daisy realized just how many bad memories she'd dredged up for the person who loved her no matter what. "I'm sorry. I never meant to cause you pain."

"No. You need to know. I understand. What are you going to do? I assume you know where she is?"

"Kind of. The information Al gave me says father works in town as a mechanic." Would she see him?

"Remember he may not really be your father, but follow your heart and do what feels right. You can't go wrong that way. And remember, I'm going to be here no matter what. We all are. I'm sure you already know that if you've shared this with Sydney."

"I haven't. I will. You will always be my momma. I just need to figure this out. I'm not doing it to hurt you. I just want to know why. Why she got rid of me? Was I such an awful child that I drove her back to drugs?" She hadn't meant to say that.

"Oh my. God. No, honey. You brought so much joy into our lives. I can't imagine ever not having you. You're my baby girl. You always will be." Her mother didn't bother to hide her tears.

Daisy's face was covered in tears, too. "Thank you. I'll let you know what I find out. If I do anything. We have so much to handle here. I might have no choice but to wait."

"Things happen for a reason. Remember that."

"I always do. Love you, Momma." Daisy waited until her mother hung up before closing the line.

So much to think about. She felt like she was losing her formerly solid grip on reality. A reality that included the occasional indulgence in fairy tales and ghost hunting, but a pretty good way to live.

Maybe this campground was to blame for all the questions and unsettled emotions. Maybe the ground really was cursed by ancient spirits and demons. In the past, she'd always felt at home here. Like the minute she stepped on the grounds all her troubles slipped away, or at least to proper places, leaving her with the sense that everything was going to be okay.

What changed, and when did it change? Was it the stress of preparing the campground for opening while dealing with Vile Violet's threats and stipulations? Was it the men running around, each with an offer of companionship and sexual promise? Or was she going crazy, as her mother obviously had?

Daisy leaned back onto the pillows and closed her eyes as the thoughts assaulted her sleep-deprived mind. When were things going to be okay? When was she going to find the answers she needed and why did she keep dreaming of two different men, each with a happy future?

Sydney tried to be quiet when she opened Daisy's door. She'd heard the muffled sound of conversation and figured Daisy talked to their mom. And she assumed the secrecy had something to do with Daisy's parents.

She understood. But still felt left out.

Daisy would talk to her when she had things in perspective. She always did. Sydney couldn't help noticing the change in her sister since they'd come back to Brookside. Daisy was always cheerful and full of hope, and now, not so much. She seemed to have taken on Sydney's serious side, and now Sydney was the one watching out the window for spirits.

Daisy slept curled on her left side, almost in a fetal position, her cell phone and the big mysterious envelope beside her. She seemed so peaceful. Sydney didn't have the heart to disturb her even though contractors were stacked up outside waiting for their attention.

She'd handle the day and they'd worked things out later. Her poor sister. Not only was she dealing with the total change in her life, she had to be thinking about her birth mother and wondering. Maybe that was what this was about. She gently closed Daisy's door and organized what needed to be done in both her mind and on the notepad that was her constant companion.

Her cell phone rang on her way to meet the electrician. She glanced at the number and cursed. Damn. Jace. Like she needed to talk to him this morning.

Sydney debated for a few seconds, listening to the notes of her jazzy ring tone. Finally, she answered, doing her best to keep her tone semi-pleasant.

"I wasn't sure you'd answer." Jace sounded different.

"Busy. What can I help you with?" Good job of being nice. Now if she could only keep it up.

"You're not the same this morning."

"Same to you. Listen, if you just called to harass me I'll take a rain check."

"I called to ask you to lunch. I think there are some things we need to clear up. I know you said we have nothing to discuss but after going through this file my grandmother keeps sticking under my nose, I've decided there are some things you need to know." Something about his tone made Sydney stop.

Now that was a switch. Had he just used a note of disdain in reference to his beloved grandmother? Lunch was definitely going to happen. Except one glance at the downed trees and demolished cabin, she didn't think that day would be today.

"The storms left a lot of clean up. What about Thursday?" She wanted to hear what he had to say, but wasn't counting on him being completely honest. He could be yanking her chain just to get her away from the campground and stop their forward momentum toward re-opening.

"I figured as much. Two options. I pick up something and meet you there. You have to eat. Or we do dinner. Again, eating is crucial." His insistence piqued her interest.

"I'll tell you what. Let me take care of my morning appointments and I'll call you back. I don't want to commit when I don't know what's required of me around here today."

He agreed, his pleasant regard intriguing. Sydney would definitely see what she could do about meeting him today. With her luck, the request would end up as a trick, but she'd make sure Uncle Al knew if it was. That way, if they didn't open on time, maybe they could get the judge to give them some leeway for nasty tricks and rotten interference.

Besides, Al thought her meeting with him was a good idea. She didn't know why, but figured if her legal counsel advised her to work things out this way, there was probably a reason. And she'd definitely ask Uncle Al about that reason when she talked to him.

After giving the contractor a brief rundown of what they wanted in the bathhouses, she left him to do his measuring and met up with the electrician. Thankfully, the guy had some brains and was already checking out their system.

He smiled when she approached. His shaved head and solid build caused her stomach to flip. If she was going to have a one-night stand, this Mr. Clean look-alike was the man for the job. Until she saw his wedding band. Sydney was more relieved than she thought she'd be. Like she needed the stress of another man in her life.

"Your wiring is a mess." His friendly tone erased the fear that he'd seen her checking him out.

"Great. That makes my day."

"Not as bad as you probably think. This section is in need of new outlets and wiring." He pointed to the oldest group of campsites. Then to the area that included the office and what would be her and Daisy's house.

"The rest is fine. You'll want to replace the receptacles in the sites and you have a few options with that. Your service is up to date and except for that old section, you'll pass inspection for opening." He smiled and Sydney reminded herself he was obviously married.

"Excellent. How difficult will it be to add to this? We have two hundred more acres we'll eventually want to utilize."

"I'd recommend new service. When you're ready it won't be a problem."

"Okay. Hit me with the bad news. How long and how much?" She should have asked that first, but it was good to know what they'd need when they were ready to expand.

He passed her a proposal, the numbers not as shocking as she imagined. "That's just for the campsites. I'll do separate figures for the house and office."

She should have never gotten her hopes up.

After showing the electrician the buildings, she waited while he went over the structures. The office was relatively simple, at least she thought. Most of the space was supposed to be a gift shop. Private bathrooms for staff were next to a kitchenette and a conference room. The office area had an open floor plan so it would feel accessible to customers at all times. As long as the wiring could handle the computer systems, they'd worry about rearranging the building in a few years, providing they were in the black. The house was a different story. Thanks to Violet and her refusal to live there, it had sat empty for far longer than the campground. Sydney had always loved Gramps' place. He managed to keep the house and garden showplace-worthy while running the campground at full capacity during their childhood was too much for her to fathom. The house was what she always compared with every other living space, except now everything was sad and terrible.

Weeds choked the sidewalk, taller ones covering the windows. Some critter had used the antique chair as a nest. Dead birds and several chipmunks died on the wood floors, dark stains spread out to outline their long-gone bodies. The stench wasn't too bad right now, but on a hot day, she couldn't imagine.

She and Daisy hadn't even considered moving in to the house or spending money to fix it up. At this point, restoration was going to cost a fortune and that didn't include new appliances. The furniture was a total loss, but that didn't matter since she and Daisy both had full sets in storage. Still, the destruction saddened her more than anything.

She showed the electrician the breaker box and went outside, unable to bear the condition of Gramps' house. The man returned a few minutes later, shaking his head and wiping spider webs from his snug jeans.

"What's the damage?" Sydney crunched numbers in her head.

"You won't believe me." He reviewed the paper on his clipboard.

"Try me." She tried to see what he'd written.

"The house needs nothing. New service was nearly complete. The entire house is updated. All I have to do is run a line to the new box and unhook from the old one. Same with the office." He quoted a price that made her want to jump up and hug him.

"Wait. That's too easy. You're telling me this house and the office are good to go?" Did she dare believe him? What did he have to gain by lying?

"Absolutely. I'll have to confirm because I was relatively new back then, but I have a vague memory. The owner should remember. I'll let you know."

Gramps had used this company or she wouldn't have called them. She wanted to work with the same people he trusted. She'd obviously been right to do that.

"Thanks. When can you start?"

"Next Monday. I already fixed the problem with your power going out, a squirrel- or chipmunk-damaged wire. I'll give you a call if the day changes. If you don't hear from me, I'll be here Monday morning." He handed her his business card before shaking her hand.

"Excellent."

Considerably lighter, she checked her watch. She had time for lunch. Dialing Jace's number, she tried to squash her excitement. She was only happy about the electricity, not about having lunch with her nemesis.

Yeah. That was it.

CHAPTER 10

An hour later, showered and trying to look her best, despite the mud surrounding her everywhere she went, Sydney left Daisy a note and headed for the restaurant. She tried to pick out Jace's car in Kay's parking lot. She'd seen his fancy truck the other day, so she should be able to recognize it.

When her scan turned up nothing but a beat-up old pickup truck with a new-looking pop-up camper attached, she figured he ran late. Good. Now she'd have a little time to talk to Kay.

Kay greeted her at the door with a smile. "Your lunch date is at your table."

Sydney leaned in and whispered, "He's not my date. It's a legal matter."

"Shame. He's damn fine. Cuter than your ghost hunter and hot enough to make this old lady sweat." Kay kept her voice at the same whisper Sydney used.

With a sigh, she moved around those naughty pool tables. Jace saw her and stood, holding his hand out and giving her a welcoming smile.

"I'm glad you came." Damn. He was cute. Not cute, sexy as hell. And in jeans and a well-worn denim shirt, too.

"Have you been here before?" His office had to be quite a drive from town.

"Not enough and not for a long time."

She didn't ask what he meant, but got the impression there was more to what he didn't say.

"How'd your morning go?" Was he trying to be nice, or nosy?

"Far better than I expected." She didn't elaborate, though she could see he wanted her to tell all.

"Good. Listen, I wanted to talk to you about . . ."

Kay appeared with a tray of drinks. Her favorite diet soda and what had to be an iced tea for Jace.

"Have you decided yet?"

After a quick glance at the menu, she ordered the same burger she'd had during the storm. Kay seemed to sense she'd interrupted an important conversation and left with a wink.

"You were saying?" she prodded. Really, her impatience was too much.

"Okay. Grandmother is asking a lot of weird questions. She keeps calling to find out what I've done about 'our little campground problem', as she calls it. My caseload has been heavy and even though I kept telling her I didn't have time to deal with her drama and that I'm not her attorney, she insisted I help her settle this sale with you even though she has her own lawyer. It's really not my place to be involved."

Again with the nearly derisive tone concerning Violet. Interesting.

"Now that I've cleared my backlog and am officially on vacation, I had no choice but to check out her *important matter*. I spent the weekend going over everything and I'm here to tell you my grandmother is trying to take Brookside from you."

Was he serious?

"You didn't know?" How could that be?

"Of course not. Grandmother asked me to talk to you about the deal you made concerning the campground. She said you agreed to sell. I had no idea about the will. I had no idea what she'd done, that she'd lied. No wonder you wanted to stab me in the eyes."

"Violet said she contested the will because you wanted the campground. We were told you felt Gramps owed you some inheritance and that she was only acting in your best interest." Could he be serious?

"Bullshit. I liked your grandfather a lot. He was a great guy and treated me very well. Spent more time with me than Grandmother ever did. Of course, he talked about you and Daisy all the time. He missed you so much. He seemed to think marrying grandmother is what kept you away."

"Why did he then?" Had she really asked that? Crap. She didn't care. Not really. Jealousy that Jace had the time with Gramps that should have been hers made her stomach bleed. How was that fair? She didn't care how much Gramps had spoken of her and Daisy to Jace, she wanted that precious he had experienced.

And it would never happen.

"You know, I've never been able to figure out why. I even asked him, not long before he passed. He said the reasons were private and someday everything would make sense."

"Are you telling me you've had nothing to do with the trouble at the campground?" Her patience thinned, probably because of her resentment.

"I'm not saying that. Unfortunately, I followed Grandmother's instructions twice. Believe me when I say she won't use me again. I thought I was negotiating a business transaction. That's why I came out there and called you. And that's what I get for acting without all the facts."

"No. Not that stuff." Was he yanking her chain?

"What are you talking about?" He really did seem confused.

"The flashlights and noises in the middle of the night? The destruction in the cabin? The graffiti in the bathhouse? The kid dressed up like Halloween? He said a guy paid him a hundred bucks to prank us." Shit. She wasn't supposed to tell him that.

Jace sat back. Either he was a good actor, or he really had no clue. "No. That does sound like Grandmother on a mission though. I'll talk to her. It'll stop, if I tell her she stands to lose any option she has on the land, she'll quit."

"She will lose her option to the land." Sydney pulled herself up and met his eyes. "Daisy and I will open on time."

"Good. I don't think folks around here want a casino. I know I don't. Besides, the land is yours. I wish I knew why she wants it so badly. It's not like she's desperate for cash."

He said good? What the heck was going on?

"What kind of acting do you do?" Snotty, but she was not going to let him take her for a ride.

"What? Oh. Listen. I know you don't trust me. You have no reason to, but you will. I promise you I'm not involved in this. Many of my responses to you stemmed from being told you made a promise to Grandmother and were trying to back out. This weekend, I made the connection. Actually, that's not true. The first time I came to the campground I knew something was wrong. Grandmother told me you'd promised to sell her the land." He leaned back as Kay placed their food.

As Kay sat her plate down she winked and Sydney pretended not to see. She was confused enough without Kay's strange expressions.

"I never promised that. How is it that you missed all the legal stuff? Where were you at the reading of the will?" Really, his explanation didn't make enough sense. And why had she never met him before?

"I didn't know. Gramps passed his gift to me before he died and I wasn't called to the reading. Grandmother kept everything else to herself. I've been too busy to care."

"What was his gift to you?"

"I'd rather not say."

Oh. She'd find out, not because she feared he had something she wanted. Why then? Because she was nosy and would be able to understand how Gramps viewed him by what he imparted on him before he died.

"Where does this leave us?" She picked up a fry, using it as a pointer.

"The legal stuff is tight. I don't see a way around her stipulations. She had every right to set them since Gramps agreed. There was no prenup. I think this is a compromise, one I don't believe she thought you'd be able to honor. I understand Gramps built some cash into the deal? You pass your weekly inspection and you move forward?"

"Right. Something no one bothered to tell us. That's not going to happen this week. The storm caused too much damage and I have two days and not enough hands to get the cleanup done," she explained to Tucker and his crew.

"Don't give up just yet. Did I mention I'm on vacation?" He smiled, and she felt the movement of his lips to her toes.

"What are you suggesting?" Was he really planning on helping? What would Daisy say?

"Maybe Grandmother will understand how serious I am if I'm part of the crew."

"So you're doing this to teach your grandmother a lesson?" Worked for her, but could he be serious?

"Yeah and maybe because I'd like to spend more time with you." He met her eyes. She was in huge trouble.

"Ha. Don't you live in York? That's a long drive every day." Was she really going to accept his offer? What did she have to lose? If he proved to be anything but a help, she'd send him packing.

"I wasn't planning on going back and forth every day." His eyes held something Sydney didn't think she could even try to figure out right now.

"You will unless you want to sleep in a tent."

"Did you see that camper in the parking lot?" He grinned as if he'd just won an award. "Mine."

Sydney sighed. Daisy was going to kill her.

She was right. Daisy stood on the front porch of their cabin, her eyebrows practically fused together. She was furious. Sydney didn't think it was only because of the truck that followed her into the campground.

Jace stopped at the site where the funky lights had been all over the trees. He waved at Daisy as he got out of the truck. She wasn't happy in the least.

"What did you do?" Daisy's voice was low.

Sydney shrugged. "He's on our side. Apparently, Violet lied to him." She explained as quickly as she could – before Daisy went over and smacked Jace.

"And you're trusting his word? Unbelievable. You let me sleep when there's tons of work to be done around here, then you go off to meet him without telling a soul where you've gone? Do you know how worried I was?" Daisy paced, ready to unleash her beast on Jace.

"Whoa. Listen, Mom. You obviously needed the sleep. I handled the contractors and I left you a note. And I figure we'll keep a close eye on him. If he's lying, then at least we've gotten some work out of him. We need the help, Daisy."

"I know. Don't keep too close of an eye on him. Marshal won't appreciate that." Daisy cocked an eyebrow.

Sydney stepped back, anger erasing the feeling she'd done something good by allowing Jace to appease his guilty conscious.

"Marshal does not own me. I make my own decisions and there's nothing going on between Jace and me. Or Marshal and me for that fact." Her words were quiet, but Daisy heard.

"You led him on. Maybe nothing's happened yet, but until Jace showed up, it was going to. Marshal's my friend, Syd, don't hurt him." She turned and went inside the cabin.

Sydney followed, guilt eating her insides.

"I'm not trying to hurt him. The thing is, I don't know what the hell I'm doing. Up until this morning, I hated Jace. Now I don't know." Great. She was doomed.

"Just be careful."

"You know what? I don't have time to play this game of who's a better match for me. We have a campground to open, and not much time. Neither one of us have time to go all soft over a pair of tight jeans. We're not here to find love."

Daisy paused for a few seconds. "You know what? You're right. Absolutely right. Good. We don't need these stinking men. Let's get busy." Daisy breezed past her, the sound of her work boots echoing through the cabin.

Sydney sat down at the table and dropped her head to the scratched wood. What was happening? Daisy was hiding something big and painful. She wanted Sydney to be with Marshal, but Sydney didn't know if she should even be thinking about the opposite sex right now. Maybe she should forget this campground idea and get a bunch of cats. Or find a convent that would take her as a reformed virgin.

Daisy kicked at the stones along the path. One pinged off the side of Jace's camper, but she ignored his startled expression. From the way he wrestled with the canvas, he obviously didn't know what to do with that brand-spanking new camper. There was no way she was helping him. What the hell was wrong with Sydney?

Jace was the enemy.

All that shit Sydney told her about his time with Gramps felt like a hot knife in her heart. Jace had taken what should have been hers and Sydney's. So what if it wasn't his fault?

He still had their grandpa all to himself when Gramps needed his only granddaughters. Damn. That hurt. A lot.

She kicked a bigger rock, not caring that Tucker and his crew had just finished raking new stones into the path. She didn't want to talk to Tucker either.

Or Graham.

Everyone seemed to think they knew what she wanted. She was tired of being told what to do and how she should feel. After arguing with Tucker again this afternoon about the ticking of his biological clock, she almost told him his services weren't appreciated any longer.

Thankfully, she'd managed to walk away without cutting off her nose to spite her face. The argument stemmed more from hurt feelings than the job Tucker was doing. She was mad because he'd ignored her this morning and because of the things he'd said about wanting children. Jerk.

Graham had made a derogatory comment about Sydney when Daisy couldn't find her. She'd given him the death glare and left, even though he'd tried his best to apologize for his rude behavior. She didn't care. No one talked about her sister like that. Except for maybe her.

This whole thing with her birth parents had her on edge. She didn't know if she wanted to pursue this any farther, or if she should just leave the search alone. Her father supposedly lived and worked just a few miles from here. What would he do if she showed up and announced herself as his love child?

Soon she'd have to talk to Sydney. Not yet. Getting the information straight in her head was required before that happened. Sydney would want to take action, and Daisy had to decide if action was what she wanted. She pulled the gloves out of her back pocket and shoved them on, concentrating on the weeds nearly obliterating the door to the office. If the building was in decent shape, they might pass inspection this week.

Daisy looked over at Gramps' house. They'd agreed the house would be last on their list. The oversized cabin they were in would suffice until they had the money to do a little repair and renovation. She was pleased that the house would need a little less than they thought. Melancholy washed over her. Summers spent running the path between the house and the office, fishing in the pond and begging Gramps to put a pool in.

Now that pool was going to give her a whole head full of gray hair. The cost to fix it was twice as much as they'd budgeted. She hadn't told Sydney that yet. Daisy sighed and yanked at the weeds with determination. Her head might be cluttered and confused, but she'd put the unease to good use.

Hours later, her back had taken all the abuse it could handle. Daisy needed a shower. And Tucker waited for her on the cabin porch. Great. Daisy shoved her gloves back into her pocket, wondering how bad she looked after the hours spent weeding.

"You don't want us to clean up around the office?"

Oh. So that was it. He was hurt that she'd removed all the weeds herself.

"What? I can't help?" She was too defensive.

"I didn't mean that. It's just when we talked the office wasn't mentioned. I guess my real question is why?" He didn't respond to her obnoxious tone.

Daisy sighed. The hours spent doing physical labor had taken the edge off her mood. "We didn't know if we'd be able to use the building, but it's good to go. We were going to rent a trailer to use as the office, but now we don't have to." She sounded stupid.

"Excellent. I have four guys that need experience with creating pond gardens. What do you think of a set up in the flowerbeds? I have supplies left from another job. It wouldn't be very big, so the cost would be minimal. And we might be able to use some of the old stuff around here."

She blinked. "Okay."

Maybe the sun had fried her brain.

"The storm damage is cleaned up. Well, except for the tree in the cabin. Sydney said to leave it for now. We still have a lot to do here before we start our summer schedule."

That's right. Tucker would be gone soon.

Would anything change between them? Did she want it to? How could she take a chance with him again when he was certain he wanted children and she was certain she did not?

She nodded and waited for him to move. He gently grabbed her arm, stopping beside her.

"I never meant to hurt you." He touched her face and she couldn't stop the tear that escaped her careful composure.

The next thing she knew she was in his arms. His familiar kiss drew her in and the comfort bolstered her spirit. When he moved away, she glanced up, confused and impressed.

"I don't want to hurt you again. I just don't know what I want." He released her and left.

Daisy watched him until he disappeared. As she turned, Graham stood against the cabin he shared with Marshal. He stared at her for a few minutes before turning around and leaving, too.

She started toward her and Sydney's cabin, letting out one of Sydney's primal screams.

God. She was a screw-up.

CHAPTER 11

Daisy tossed and turned, trying to get comfortable on the lumpy mattress. She stopped wrestling with the blankets when she heard voices through the interior wall. For a minute, she thought Marshal or Jace had snuck into Sydney's room. Except the voices were female.

She rose, trying to be quiet and stuck her ear against the wall. Sydney spoke to someone in a pleasant, patient voice.

Definitely not Jace or Marshal.

"There's nothing to be afraid of. Your family is waiting for you." Sydney. Quiet and soothing.

Daisy could use those kinds of words herself.

"Yes. I'm sure. You've been trapped here too long. It's time." Why hadn't Daisy heard the answer that should have come between Sydney's words?

Confused, she debated for a minute before deciding the time for secrets had passed. She'd tell Sydney hers, and hope Sydney would do the same.

Softly, she knocked once on Sydney's door before opening it without waiting for an answer. Sydney sat up in bed, the sheets around her waist. An odd glow filled the room and Daisy looked around for the light source.

"What's wrong?" Sydney glanced over Daisy's shoulder to the empty corner.

"Lots of stuff. What's going on in here? I heard you talking to someone." That wasn't how she'd planned to ask. She'd wanted her sister to tell her because she wanted to.

"You first. What happened this morning?" Sydney patted the bed beside her and Daisy scooted in next to her.

"I asked Uncle Al to find out information on my birth parents." She waited, knowing how Sydney would react but curious just the same.

Instead of the anger she expected, Sydney nodded and smiled. "I wondered when you would."

"I didn't think you'd understand."

"I do. It's hard though. I don't want to think about it and I don't want to see you get hurt." Sydney leaned against her.

"Knowing isn't going to change anything." Why was she comforting Sydney?

"I know. I know you need answers."

"I know where the guy they say is my father works." Daisy told her everything.

"What do you want to do? Do you want to meet him?" Sydney's patience almost freaked her out.

"I don't know yet." She didn't, but wished she did.

"How about we check him out first? You don't have to tell him who you are. We'll see what we think. That is, if you want me along." This was very unlike Sydney. She took charge and that was that. She didn't ask first, but apologized often afterward.

"Let me think about it. Your turn. What's going on in here? Are you cracking up and talking to yourself now?" She tried to sound light, but failed.

Truthfully, she was a bit worried about her sister's recent judgment. Daisy wondered what the number for the psychiatric hospital was and how quickly they could get the men in white coats out here to pick up her clearly deranged sister.

"You won't believe me." Sydney again looked to the corner of the room and Daisy realized the weird light seemed to originate there. *Oh.*

"Try me." She adjusted the pillows and leaned back.

"Well, I'm a fraud. Remember when we used to pretend we saw ghosts? Well, I really could. I thought you did, too, but when I realized you couldn't, I stopped saying anything. Then, it all went away. And then we came back here . . ." Sydney went on to tell a terrific tale of how she could see and talk to spirits when they were kids and then again now.

"You're not serious." If Sydney wasn't teasing, and Daisy didn't think she was, the story made sense on so many levels and caused a touch of regret for the way Daisy teased her.

"I rejected the whole thing after our last summer here. Actually, I think I denied the ability for so long I believed my rants. Believed everything I ever said to you about there being no such thing as spirits. I would dream odd dreams of people talking to me, begging me to help because no one else could hear them. In the cabin, when I was touched, it all came back. I knew what he wanted, why he had to get my attention. It scared me spitless and I didn't want it. I am visited every night by people looking for the way to peace. I try, but I don't think I'm doing the right things."

"I wondered why you accepted Marshal and his crew so readily. And here I figured you just thought Marshal was sexy and wanted in his pants."

Sydney smiled and shrugged. "After talking to Kay, I think Gramps had similar experiences. I need to find his journal."

"That journal is nowhere, we've searched. Gramps probably hid it in some abyss or something. That would be so like him. And even if we do find it, would we be able to decipher what it says? His way with words was something else." Daisy shook her head. "Have you told Marshal?"

"He knows, but . . . this is hard for even me to believe. Sometimes I want to give it back and forget everything. Even this campground. What happened to my normal life?"

"You mean the life where you stayed home every weekend wondering what was wrong with you? Where you busted your ass for a boss who ignored you and tried to take credit for your ideas? You hated your job."

"I know. I did. I think I planned my career wrong." Sydney shook her head.

"You worked at the wrong place. That's all. You're a great accountant."

"You only say that because I do your taxes for free." Sydney laughed and sobbed at the same time.

Daisy laughed. "Well, yeah. No. You're dedicated and you enjoy the work. It's not about what you do. Your skills will come in handy around here."

"Yeah, I can open a tax season business to pay the electric bill in the off season." Sydney's sarcastic tone didn't sit well. Though she did have a point.

"You might have to, but that wasn't what I meant. Neither one of us would have been able to quit our jobs and take over this nightmare if it wasn't for you. So now you have another skill."

Sydney leaned against the pillows and yawned. "I haven't had a full night's sleep since the cabin. It's like some kind of portal opened and spirits from everywhere are coming for help. Do you think Gramps dealt with this?"

"I don't know. Okay. We need to set some ground rules then. No more waking you and entering your private space at any hour. I assume you did something about Suicide Sally in the bathhouse?"

"How did you know about her?" Sydney studied her and Daisy realized what she'd given away.

"I saw her. She's kind of hard to miss."

"She finally realized I could see her. I don't think she understood the finality of suicide. She was waiting for her lover to rescue her, thinking that seeing her bleeding would make him realize what he would lose, but I don't think she understands."

Daisy shook her head. "That's too sad."

"At least she's listening to me now. Who knows how long it'll be until what I say makes sense to her. If it ever does. It's almost like she enjoys being a tortured soul. Like a dead drama queen." Sydney yawned again and rearranged the blankets. "What are we going to do?"

"Sleep and figure the rest out later." Daisy leaned over and kissed her forehead before getting up. As she opened the door, a spectral form appeared in her path. Daisy took a step back until Sydney's dilemma reminded her of what her sister was dealing with. This could not continue.

"She's sleeping. You are not to wake her this night, or any other. Tell them she is not to be bothered until she tells you. She will help you all, but not now."

She didn't know if the message got through. The figure stood at the door as if debating. If her speech didn't work, Sydney would have to tell them.

Finally, the vague shape moved away.

How weird were they? Stuck in some kind of alternate reality with ghosts and a falling down campground. And too many men to choose from. And an evil step-grandmother.

Were they living in some kind of fairy tale land? And if so, which prince was her true Prince Charming?

"Stupid." Crawling under the covers, Daisy tried to forget the images of Graham and Tucker on white horses, dueling for her honor and love.

Daisy woke before the sun. Her dreams had mimicked her final thoughts before drifting off. If anything, she was even more confused than before she talked to Sydney. After a shower, she fought with the ancient coffee pot, finally giving up and adding a new one to her list of things to buy when they went on a supply run.

Tucker's crew arrived as she searched for the jar of instant caffeine she thought Sydney brought with her. She watched from the window as they unloaded out of the trucks and stretched, most seemed like they'd prefer to be still under the covers like her. A soft knock sounded at the door while she organized her tasks for the day. It would be Tucker and she didn't know if she really wanted to talk to him this early.

She opened the door anyway. He held out a tray with two large cups of coffee and that smile that made her forget her name. "Peace offering."

"Thanks." She opened the door so he could come inside but he shook his head. "Another delivery from Al."

He held out another yellow envelope, holding on tightly when she tried to take it. "Is there anything I can help with?"

Damn. Why did he have to seem so concerned?

"Nah. Just some copies of stuff for our records." She lied. And judging by Tucker's face, he knew.

"If you say so. You know where I am if you need me." He released the envelope and closed the door behind him.

Daisy sat at the table, no longer needing or wanting to hide her turmoil from Sydney. Uncle Al had written a short note at the top of a fax.

Your mother is actively searching for you. She found out about your inheritance. Be cautious. Her intentions can't be good. I'll be out tomorrow with the inspector. Love, U.A.

Great. It wasn't bad enough that her mother dumped her and went off to do her own thing without care one for her daughter's well-being. Now Daisy might have to deal with her whether she wanted to or not.

Damn.

How would her mother appearing affect what she and Sydney tried to do? Pushing aside the paranoid questions, she decided to stop this head on.

An hour later, she'd forced the still sleeping awake and demanded a group meeting. Everyone showed, including Jace and Tucker's entire crew. She'd had no worries about

Marshal and his bunch. They were used to her occasionally bossy outbursts.

"I won't keep you. I know everyone is busy. I have a personal situation that I need some help with." She explained the details, watching Sydney's anger grow. "If a woman shows up here don't tell her a thing. Just call me and keep her in the parking lot. I'll handle her."

Feeling in control, she accepted the support as each person went back to work. Marshal stopped her, his eyes sleepy and unreadable. "I need to talk to you then. We went over all of the footage last night. You wouldn't believe some of it. I want to go out again tonight. Are you in?"

"I'll be there." Daisy figured he probably wanted to grill her on Sydney's odd behavior as well.

"After lunch. Bring Sydney, she'll want to see too." He one-armed hugged her and she assumed he headed back to bed.

There went her assumption that he worried about Sydney's choice to bring Jace here. Maybe she'd read too much into their relationship. Maybe they only flirted and nothing else grew under the surface like she thought, or hoped.

"What are you going to say to her?" Sydney fell in step with her on her way to clean the office.

"I'll figure that out when she gets here. Right now I'm thinking, 'Go to hell.'" And she was. But she wanted some answers first.

"Good for you." As always, Sydney knew when to leave things alone.

They walked the rest of the way in silence. Daisy dreaded the job ahead, but if the office was in top shape by the time Al came with the inspectors, maybe they'd pass even though their progress had been minimal this week, thanks to the storms.

Of course, the electric work wouldn't start for a few more days. They'd finally chosen a contractor for the bathhouse remodel and construction was due to start tomorrow morning. Probably enough to pass inspection, but neither she nor Sydney wanted to take any chances.

Sydney opened the door and stepped back with a scream. Daisy added her scream to her sister's, unsure if they should run. Graham showed up while the screams still split the air. He put an arm around each of them and looked inside, a shudder going through him as he gently urged them away.

A deer hung on the wall, each hoof spread out and tied with barbed wire. The head hung by only sinew and blood still dripped onto the floor. The same blood that seemed to be on every surface in the room. Including the 'Get Out' that was written on the wall next to the deer's nearly severed head.

"Who would do this?" Daisy had a few ideas. One of them had put up his camper the previous afternoon.

"I was in here with the electrician yesterday." Sydney choked out, not quite in tears, but not calm either.

"I'd say someone came in after you. Did you lock the door?" Graham forced them to take a step.

"There isn't a working lock."

Graham urged them to a rickety bench. "We need to call the sheriff. That's a threat if I ever saw one."

He grabbed his walkie-talkie, but didn't use it because every guy in camp now ran up the path toward them. Daisy let Graham explain and watched each take a turn at viewing the grisly visage. Sydney stayed mostly silent, wrapping her arms around her upper body in a clear signal of "hands off."

Even her prime suspect seemed dazed and concerned. Either he was a good actor or he truly had nothing to do with the scene. She counted on the first choice.

The deputy sheriff finally arrived. He documented the evidence, and shook his head. "Maybe something will turn up on the carcass. Get a lock for this door. Anyone could have done this."

"Seriously, you know as well as we do that not *anyone* did this." Sydney stepped toward the red-faced deputy, her frustration evident. "Where in the hell is your boss?"

Daisy moved away, not wanting to be in the path of her sister's temper. Jace blocked Daisy's exit.

"You think I murdered an innocent animal and mutilated its body just to scare you?" he asked, though no anger showed in his eyes.

"I'm not as gullible as Sydney. You have a reason for wanting to be on the property. I know what that reason is, so you can cause more destruction and fear and take control of the property for your dear, sweet Grandmother." Her words tasted like poison. She didn't care.

"Doesn't the fact that your sister accepted my offer of help mean anything to you?" His demeanor hadn't changed.

"I think my sister agreed because she wanted to keep an eye on you. To prove your motives are less than noble."

"Then why would I do something like this my first night here? Wouldn't I wait and see where my efforts would have more impact and cost more to repair? Wouldn't I strike to hurt your memories of your grandfather and break your will?" His ice-cold tone jarred the anger into fear.

"You are a devious bastard." She clenched her jaw to keep her volume low.

"Am I? Have I done anything like that? Didn't your sister tell you how Grandmother played me?"

Daisy could only stare at him. Could he be for real? "My trust is something you'll need to earn. I'll be watching you. Hurt my sister or this land and you will feel my wrath." She was impressed he accepting her vicious threat without flinching.

"Fair enough. I don't plan on doing either."

Sydney leaned against the side of the building, her face a mask of calm control.

"Well?" Daisy positioned herself beside her, surveying the activity in the parking area.

"We can't touch the office until they're done gathering evidence. There's dissention on whether this was bored teenagers or a malicious act. With everything the sheriff knows, he's still not willing to accuse Violet of masterminding everything that's happened."

"Could Jace find out?" As much as she hated to think it, Jace could prove his intentions by providing them some answers straight from his darling grandmother.

"I'll ask." Sydney glanced at her, the unspoken proof they both required from their newest guest unmentioned.

"He is very cute." Daisy tried to find that anger she'd used to bully him, but she was too weary.

"That he is. I don't think he did this. I'm not sure he could manage. He looks fit, but his hands are too soft. Does that make sense?"

"Actually, yeah. Okay. I'll get off his back for now." Daisy leaned her head on Sydney's shoulder. "Are we going to be able to even do this?"

"That's the thinking this stunt was meant to bring out. Yes. We are going to open the campground. We both know we can. The only thing that's against us is time and Vile Violet."

"Two very big things." Worry, and the fear of failure threatened to overwhelm her.

Since they could do nothing until the investigating crew released the office, they went to see Marshal. He opened the door, shirtless and barefoot, and Daisy swore Sydney had a little heart attack. Daisy explained the situation at the cabin, not realizing Marshal hadn't been around to offer comfort when they screamed.

"Okay. Let me put a shirt on and I'll show you." He went to the bedroom and Daisy reached over to Sydney's mouth, pretending to wipe drool from her chin.

Sydney turned to her with wide eyes. "Oh. My. God."

"Yeah." Even Daisy was impressed. Marshal must have started working out, he was much more defined than the last time she'd seen him shirtless. And back then, he'd been something to gawk at. She almost wanted to change places with Sydney.

Marshal returned and before Sydney found her normal breathing pattern, had the equipment all set up. He motioned them to the table with an excited smile.

"This is from two nights ago." He pushed a button on the laptop and Daisy strained her ears.

She heard Marshal's stock ghost question and then a brief period of silence before a different voice crackled, sounding distant but not.

"I can't find you. Where are you? Sydney?"

"They called your name?" Daisy stared at Sydney.

"Shh. There's more." Marshal held his hand up.

Sydney didn't appear affected by the use of her name. She leaned forward, her expression passive and unreadable.

"Sydney? Help me. He said you would help us find our way. I can't find you."

Marshal pressed stop. "Do you want to hear it again?"

"No. What else do you have?" Sydney sat back.

Marshal put in a disc and cued up the video from the pond. Everything they'd witnessed was there, including the music she hadn't been sure she heard.

"What do you think?" Daisy turned toward Marshal.

"I don't know. We've taped twice since then and haven't had a repeat. I'm not sure so I'm not commenting." Typical Marshal. "Okay. This is from the woods behind the bathhouse. The area Kay talked about."

Daisy leaned forward, trying to find her bearings through

the video. A figure appeared at the edge of the screen. Marshal pointed and slowed the speed down so they could watch the progression.

"Here." He moved his finger to the other side of the monitor, revealing two shapes. The smaller moved with boundless energy, back and forth.

"That's the dog." Daisy sat forward.

"Shh. Watch."

What she thought was the phantom dog from their very first day here moved toward the camera. Daisy could make out a tail but the rest of the body was a blur, even with the slower speed. Then, nothing. Had she blinked and missed it running away?

"Watch again. The dog just disappears." He rewound, and Daisy knew she hadn't blinked.

"What about the other one?" Sydney asked, her eyes fixed on the screen.

"Here. Don't pay attention to the little one, but watch again." He backed up the video to where the shape had first appeared on the screen.

"There. Now here. Here." Marshal pointed. The figure seemed to disappear and then reappear several feet away from where it started. "Watch."

A face appeared in front of the camera. Marshal paused the footage at the exact moment the image recorded itself.

"Why didn't we see that the first time?" Sydney stared at the vague face with interest.

"Too quick. That image is about a half a mili-second on the timer. See." Marshal backed up and then played the footage at the same speed he'd used for the dog. "In normal speed we would have never seen him. If it weren't for the dog, we'd have missed this. Impressive?"

"Awesome. And your thoughts?"

"No comment. You know I don't give my true thoughts until the end of the investigation."

"You usually don't let clients go with you either," Daisy pointed out. "Or let them see the evidence before you've picked it to death."

"Okay. You're right. No comment."

"Is there more?" Daisy asked, eyeing the stack of CD's beside the computer.

"Yeah. More of that dog thing or whatever it is. This time outside the bathhouse. Let me show you." He went through the stack of CD's.

A knock sounded on the door. Daisy got up to answer, finding the deputy sheriff on the other side.

"The building's all yours again. Sorry for the delay. I had some of my guys clean up the worst of the blood. I figured it was the least we could do for acting like assholes. Plus, we talked to Frank. He never told us what to expect out here before he left for Florida."

Daisy hugged him, even though she didn't know if that was appropriate. She didn't care. He'd just made their afternoon easier and she was kind of mad at Frank for not filling the new guys in. Not that it mattered now.

"Go. Get busy. I think the guys have the CD in the van." Marshal stood, obviously aware how important getting the office ready was for their inspection.

Sydney appeared a little dazed. Daisy started to ask, but she shook her head. What had happened those few minutes her back was turned?

Interesting.

They were a pair. Each stuck between two men and no clear choice for either. Of course, neither of her choices had made a move except for Tucker and his hormonally raged kiss. Graham had stayed out of her way and though his lack of attention hurt, she couldn't say she really cared. Maybe she should adapt and follow her sister's advice and just ignore them both. Sydney was right. They had a campground to open.

CHAPTER 12

Sydney tried her best to ignore Daisy's curious stares. Pretending to concentrate on scrubbing the wood floors in the cabin, she'd successfully sidestepped having to discuss what happened in Marshal's cabin.

God, but the man could kiss.

Seeing him without a shirt had totally clouded her sense and hormones. She'd spent most of the time daydreaming instead of focusing on the images and figures his crew had caught during their nighttime wanderings.

She already knew this place was haunted. Marshal wasn't going to tell them anything new, but the verification from someone trusted in the field could only help Daisy's master plan for the campground. Heavy boots sounded behind her. Not recognizing the gait as Daisy's she turned to find Jace. He smiled, his jeans covered with paint and his shirt ripped directly over his left nipple. Disheveled, but oh, what a sight. If she kept having to see men in various forms of hotness, her ovaries were going to explode. Daisy came over, obviously not willing to leave her alone with Jace for a second, lest he sprout fangs and drain her of all her blood.

"Good. I have to tell you both something." He seemed worried, a sign that didn't bode well. "My grandmother let a few things slip this morning. Your birth mother knows about your inheritance because my grandmother told her. Apparently, Grandmother is not against using unconventional means to get her way. She also told her there was more cash involved and that she was sure her poor, lonesome daughter would be willing to part with some to have her back in her life. She really talked it up from what I understand. Acted like she was close to you and that you've cried on her shoulder many times because of your childhood."

"That bitch." The words were out before Sydney remembered she stood in front of the bitch's loyal and loving grandson.

"My thought exactly." His agreement surprised her.

"How did she find her? I searched for a whole year before finally finding out where she was." Daisy's anger showed.

"The difference of a bottomless budget. I'm sorry. I know she's my family, but I want you to know I don't think very highly of Grandmother these days. She never used to be so vindictive and mean."

"Why, besides the casino, does she want this property so badly? It's almost like she married Gramps just to get her hands on it." Sydney went back to work as she talked, not willing to take a chance on her laziness earning the evil woman what she so badly desired.

"I thought the same thing. Grandmother never used to be this horrible. I always loved spending time with her. I adored her. I don't know what happened to change her personality. Or else she hid this side."

"We only have one choice. Make sure she doesn't get her hands on this land." Daisy moved back to the windows she scrubbed.

"Amen to that." Sydney dropped her rag in the bucket and stood, unsure of what she should say to Jace.

Sure, there was a chance he was messing with their heads, but the frustration and disappointment she saw in his eyes made her believe him. Maybe she'd be a fool at the end. Until he gave her a reason to stop believing in him, she trusted him. There was something about him that spoke to her soul, and she hated it.

Besides, Jace had already accomplished more in just a few hours than she and Daisy managed all week. The outside of the office had its first coat of paint and he'd helped Tucker's crew remove a nasty nest of snakes from under the front porch.

Not good for the inspectors, those snakes. She and Daisy had stayed inside. Not that she feared the slithering beasts, she just didn't want to touch them or have them go up her pant leg in a desperate attempt to get away from the chaos of moving to new quarters.

She and Daisy had continued scrubbing, each keeping watch at the crack under the door for strays. At least the snakes weren't poisonous. This time.

Two hours later, the office was ready to go. The outside paint was still wet, but the inside sparkled with their efforts. They'd arranged the desks in a way to facilitate easy check-ins and discussed the gift shop they'd open once they acquired the capital.

Sweaty, smelly, and completely worn out, Sydney wondered how she'd stay awake for Marshal's ghost hunting tonight. Her stomach growled and she groaned in response. One bad thing about not having all the conveniences of home yet. Decent meals took foresight and planning even with their microwave and ancient hot plate. Skills Sydney definitely did not possess. And she definitely wasn't in the mood for canned spaghetti tonight.

Apparently, Daisy didn't either. "I'm starved."

"Let's get cleaned up and go to Kay's. It'll be quicker. I could use a break from this place anyway." Sydney stretched.

What she wouldn't give for the Jacuzzi tub she'd given up with her condo. They'd install one in Gramps' cabin for sure.

Kay's face lit up when they came in the door. They'd missed the dinner crowd and only a few patrons were scattered around the restaurant. How they'd managed to get out without the horde of men at the campground was a mystery. Not that they would have minded, but the guys seemed preoccupied.

"Do you two mind if I take my break with you?" Kay asked when she took their orders.

Sydney agreed and Daisy assured Kay they welcomed the company.

Daisy winked as Kay left to put their food order in. "Maybe we can pick her brain."

Kay returned faster than expected. She carried three plates and a huge smile. "Premonition. I had it right, for the most part." She sat their plates down and squeezed in beside Daisy.

"Did you really have a premonition?" Daisy asked with narrowed eyes.

"Well. No. Marshal called and asked if we delivered. We don't, but I made an exception when he told me what happened out there. You guys had quite a day. I asked him what you two wanted and he said you were on your way. I guessed at what you'd want, and I did pretty good, too. I think?"

"Yes. Sneaky. So you took our boys food?" Sydney didn't want to think about what the guys were up to. She hated the thought that one of them could be behind the nonsense today.

"My grandson. The one I told you about that needs a job. Though I'm not sure I want him working out there until you figure out who is trying so hard to scare you." Kay seemed embarrassed.

Sydney reached over and covered the woman's hand with her own. "I don't blame you. Once we get this situation resolved we'd be happy to have him as our first real staff member."

"Don't you dare hire him because he's my grandson. I want him to get the job on his own. He'll go through the process like any other applicant. He's a good worker, but

I believe he feels weighed down by this town. Everyone knows everyone, so it's hard to get a job on your own merits and not because of who your parents and grandparents are. If that makes sense." Kay picked up her burger.

"Perfect sense. You going to be mad at us if he's not suited for the job?" Sydney teased, already knowing Kay's answer.

Kay swatted her arm and laughed. "Absolutely."

They ate in silence. Sydney didn't realize just how starved she was until she finished her burger and scanned the dessert menu.

"What did you two want to ask me? I can see the questions on your faces." Kay pushed her plate away.

Daisy stopped and nodded for Sydney to take charge of the conversation.

"You knew Gramps for a long time. Why do you suppose he really married Violet?" Sydney's stomach responded with a tightening and she wondered if she should have grilled Kay on an empty stomach. What if Kay revealed something that made her want to vomit?

"There was history between them. Violet's family moved here when Del and I were in seventh grade. She was beautiful. Long, blond hair and just gorgeous. She seemed a little standoffish at first but Del had a crush on her. I think she knew, too. Eventually, she joined our little circle and the three of us became the best of friends."

"That's not what I expected." Daisy leaned forward.

"I'm not done yet. In tenth grade, Violet broke Del's heart. They'd gone to the Homecoming dance together. Del was thrilled. He was so in love with her. I don't really know what happened. I never asked, figured Del would tell me in his own time. About a month later, Violet stopped coming to school. I went over to her house to check on her after the third day. Her parents wouldn't say where she'd gone, only that she'd transferred to a new school."

"Creepy. And Gramps never told you what happened?" This didn't make sense.

"Nope. He was devastated and wouldn't talk about Violet at all. He met your Grandma our senior year. She'd moved here from Tucson. The Del I knew came back then. They were deliriously happy, those two. Your gram was the best thing that ever happened to him. Beautiful, but down to earth. When she died, I worried Del would go with her. I think he stayed strong for you two. He always said you had her spirit and nature." Kay patted both of their hands.

Sydney tried hard to remember their Gram. She'd died when Sydney was five after a nasty flu virus that drained her physically and mentally. Sydney's memories were good. She just didn't have many.

"Del was alone for a long time. And then Violet came back. She breezed in here, acted as if no time had passed and that she hadn't hurt us by the way she disappeared. Her first question was about Del. Her husband had passed on the previous year and she said she had to make it up to Del for the way she'd hurt him. And apparently she did."

"Why would he marry her? She was so mean." Daisy flicked her straw.

"Not to him. Or me. Not to anyone until several months after the wedding. Then her moods became erratic and drastic. Del never knew what she'd be like at any time of the day. I can't help but wonder if she's mentally ill. She could be sugar sweet one minute and all claws the next."

"We've only seen the claws, except before they married. I think she knew how we felt. She was so fussy about everything, totally different from Gramps." Daisy tied the straw wrapper into knots. "Do you think Gramps was happy with her?"

"I kept my distance for the most part so I can't say for sure. Del was happy at first. I know that. We were happy for him. It seemed like one of those true romances you usually only hear about. The weirder she acted, the wearier Del appeared. You might find some answers in his journals, if you've found them." Kay checked her watch, and then gathered their plates. "Violet didn't used to be such a terrible person. She was my friend and I'll always have a soft spot for her, just like Del did."

"We weren't trying to be disrespectful." Sydney hoped Kay hadn't thought that.

"You're frustrated and haven't had many good experiences with her. I understand that. And I'm not saying you should change anything. Something happened to her though and it makes me sad." Kay sighed. "Remember we're here for anything you need. If you get sick of staying out there by yourselves, give me a call. We have a nice guest house you're welcome to use. And remember to be careful. Del would haunt me forever if I let anything happen to the two of you."

Kay's last words hung in the air as she went into the kitchen. Sydney couldn't get them out of her head.

"Do you think we could contact Gramps' spirit and ask him about all of this?" Judging by Daisy's face, Sydney was about to be committed to a mental facility.

"Cut it out. That's creepy. It's one thing if spirits are lost but another altogether to purposefully call them from the other side. You don't know what could happen. Instead of Gramps we could summon the devil himself." Daisy shook her head.

"We're already dealing with the devil," Sydney pointed out a little defensively.

"True. Let's not make more trouble for ourselves. The ghosts in the campground aren't the issue. The real problem is flesh and blood people trying to stop us. We still need to know why." Daisy stood. "Where is our bill?"

"I'll get it." Sydney stood and went to the bar where Kay wiped the counter.

Kay greeted her with a smile.

"What's our damage?" She opened her wallet.

"No charge. On the house for keeping an old lady company during her break." Kay had that expression, the one that said she'd take offense if Sydney argued with her. Gramps used to get the same expression when he was too generous with her and Daisy.

"Thank you." Sydney gave Kay a hug across the bar and met up with Daisy in the parking lot.

She still hoped they'd pass inspection tomorrow, but wouldn't bet on it. Having the contracts for the bathhouses and electric work wasn't enough. The office nearly ready probably wasn't either. And considering the storm mess, they were doomed to fail.

Trying to stay positive was becoming increasingly difficult.

Graham met them at the gate. He had the expression of someone who had bad news and didn't like that he was chosen to be the bearer.

"What?" Daisy asked, annoyed.

"You left your cell phone here," he said. "You had a telephone call. Well, a lot of calls. I finally answered after the hundredth time." Graham took a step back, holding up the cell phone Daisy left in the office by accident.

"And?" Daisy reached through the window and took her phone, obviously ignoring how Graham's hand lingered.

"Your mother. She'll be here by morning."

Daisy's expression change from irritation to fury.

"Fuck. Argh. Thank you." Daisy nodded and put her window up, leaving Graham wounded and confused, if his expression was any indication.

Sydney put the window back down. "Thanks, Graham. Don't mind her, she's in shock. Did you hang out here to tell us that when we got back?"

Graham shook his head. "We're working on the office. Come and see."

Sydney put the car in gear and drove toward the office. The lights were out and she had no idea what Graham was talking about.

As she turned off the headlights, the lights around the building blazed on. The paint gleamed, still probably wet, but perfect. Flowers poked out of the gardens and the fountain sputtered before coming to life. Sydney got out of the car and stared in amazement.

Landscape lighting lined the sidewalk, the repaired board sidewalk. The front porch of the office now held two brand new benches and several pots spilling over with beautiful flowers.

The sign was what caught her eye though. Placed right beside the door:

Brookside Campground and Resort.
Sydney and Daisy Brooks, proprietresses.
In loving memory of Del Brooks.

Tears filled Sydney's eyes. Daisy nudged her arm as the door opened and light filled the interior. Following the welcoming glow, she stopped inside the door, moving only to allow Daisy to stand beside her.

Their day's work still intact, the new changes were stunning. Comfortable furniture filled the space they'd designated as the reception and waiting area. Mature potted plants hugged the corners, giving the room a homey feel. The desks now housed everything needed for office work. Framed prints of the campground in earlier years covered the walls and soft music played in the background.

"How? What? Who?" Daisy sputtered behind her.

"We all pitched in." Marshal motioned to the office area. Every man in the campground, including Tucker's crew and Jace, now stood on the porch.

"You guys have had such a rough time of it. We all can't help but feel we've held you back. You've opened your property to us. We wanted to give something back. You don't deserve what's happening around here. We're not leaving until whoever is messing with you is caught."

"You guys are incredible. This is wonderful. Thank you so much." Daisy started down the line, hugging each in turn.

Words escaped Sydney. No one had ever done anything like this for her before. Her hands shook and she didn't know what to say. She finally found her voice as she wiped at her tears. "Ditto."

Following Daisy, she hugged each man. She couldn't help but wonder whose idea this makeover had been and didn't miss the barely concealed animosity between Tucker and Graham.

"The phone lines are in, but it'll be Monday before they're hooked up. The satellite Internet is back in business, too. And the electric work for the office and house is finished." Jace pointed to the lines.

"How did you do that?" Sydney blurted out. "The electrician said Monday."

"Turns out he and I went to school together. When I explained the deal you guys were forced to make, he came out on his own time to take care of this part." Jace grinned.

Sydney couldn't help it, she hugged him tight, not caring what kind of spectacle she made of herself.

Marshal cleared his throat from behind her. "The house . . . the air conditioners work, the dead animals are gone, and we removed all the damaged furniture. It doesn't stink anymore, but I'm afraid you'll probably have to do more repair work than you thought, but you should be able to move in soon."

Sydney hugged him, wondering what Jace would say next. She seemed to be caught between these two trying to outdo each other.

"All the plants you wanted are on order and will be placed early next week. My guys want to do the house painting. All you need to do is pick a color." Tucker smiled, and Sydney watched as Daisy hugged him. "We moved a few jobs back so we can make sure this place is perfect when you open. No problem." Tucker's grin at Daisy's second hug made Graham turn green. Wow.

"The stones for the parking area will be delivered in the morning, hopefully before the inspectors arrive. I talked the guy into throwing in a spreading crew. He was more than willing after hearing your story." Graham glared at Tucker.

The stones had been a huge deal. They hadn't been able to talk the quarry into delivering them for at least another month. Daisy squealed and hugged him, the same tug of war going on for her sister.

"He's also dropping your order for the campsites off. We'll have to spread those though." That earned Graham an extra squeeze.

"You'll be able to work from the house with the wireless Internet we set up."

"We'll replace the faucets in the kitchen."

And on it went. Sydney was stuck in the middle of a childish game of "My dad is bigger than your dad." Interrupting their banter, she thanked them again, the words coming from her heart even though their current behavior irritated her to nearly a screaming level.

"Sydney. We found this in the closet." Marshal pointed to a battered box on the coffee table.

"What closet?" She went to Marshal, an ominous prickle at the back of her neck.

"There was a false front in the bathroom storage. We didn't open it." Marshal sounded a little freaked.

When Sydney read the top of the box, she understood. The frayed and dried edges of the layers of duct tape even deterred her. The message printed on top was kind of frightening.

This box intended for Sydney Brooks. Anyone who tries to reveal the contents will face my wrath, either in life or death.

Yep. Creepy.

Still, Sydney brushed the remaining dust away, melancholy washing over her. Gramps had hidden this box for her.

She hopefully now possessed his journals.

Maybe she also possessed some answers.

CHAPTER 13

Daisy woke early, before the sun and Tucker's arrival. Why was he her first thought every morning? She stretched and tried not to think about Tucker, which wasn't hard when she remembered her mother would also show up this morning. She still had no idea what she'd say to her or how she would react.

Her mother was only interested in the money she thought Daisy inherited. If it wasn't for Violet, none of this would be about to take place. A burning sensation spread from her stomach to her chest. She needed to hang on to that anger.

Something crashed near the office. Fear had her out the door and down the path before she realized the stone delivery Graham arranged had arrived. She turned to go back to the cabin, a creepy chill covering her neck and legs. The temperature was chilly this morning, but this breeze felt like winter.

The fine hairs on her body seemed to stand and she rubbed her arms to try to dispel the chill. The cold air swirled around her, moving from her ankles to her neck and then back. Something brushed her face, like a hand or a feather, and she turned to find nothing. She took a step, her legs heavy and her brain confused. There was a weight on her back, as if she tried to carry someone twice her size. Each step was a chore, but somehow she managed to move her feet in rapid succession, finally running and feeling the pains and weights drop from her body.

What the hell?

Her whole body shook as she kept running. Up until right now, she'd always felt safe here. She'd lurked around the campground at any time of the night and had never been creeped out. It was like she moved with some kind of invisible protection in the past.

Obviously, that protection wasn't present this morning. What if Sydney had helped her guardian cross over and now she'd face the world on her own? Did she even believe that? Catching her breath, she entered the cabin to find Sydney at the table.

"Couldn't sleep. You okay?" Sydney looked up.

"Weirdest thing happened," Daisy said, then explained what she'd experienced, watching the shock and worry on her sister's face.

"We're messing with the environment. Sometimes that incites paranormal activity. You told me that." Sydney shook her head as if she didn't believe she'd repeated those words.

"Yeah. I did. I couldn't see anything, but I sure felt it." She ran her hands over her arms.

"Maybe your conflicting emotions about your mother's impending visit and the inspection have something to do with what happened." Again with the head shake.

"I don't know. Oh shit, Syd. What if she shows up during the inspection?" She banged her head on the table, too hard.

"We'll have one of the guys watch for her. Tucker will probably do it."

"She's my problem."

"Wrong. She's *our* problem. You have to be present for the inspection or we don't pass. Violet probably planned Nadine's arrival. That bitch." Sydney rose and paced around the table.

"I'm sure she did. Okay, fine. Tucker can handle Nadine if she shows and we'll deal with the rest later. No problem. I'll talk to him when he gets here." Daisy tried to sound confident, even though she didn't feel that way.

"Good. Let's get going. We've got an hour before Uncle Al gets here." Sydney disappeared into her room, leaving Daisy alone to try to organize her nerves.

An hour later, Al parked on the newly spread stones in the parking area, surprise on his face. The inspector also appeared surprised, but also a little skeptical. Was he now going to quit being fair?

A third man stepped out of the car and looked around. Daisy had never seen him before and wondered who he was. She glanced at Sydney who shook her head. New rules, probably. New Vile Violet rules. This could not be good.

Al approached, his usual easy manner and friendliness absent. Yet, he winked. "Good Morning, ladies. You know Edgar. This is Peter Green, mediator. Violet feels our relationship has influenced Edgar. She now insists we bring a second opinion inspector each week. We're not to use the same person twice." Al rolled his eyes so only they could see.

Shaking hands with the men, Sydney's smile was pleasant. Most definitely fake. "Shall we get started then? We'd like to show you the office area." Sydney led the way.

Neither man seemed to own a face that didn't border on grumpy. Not even a grimace when they told them about the snakes and the deer. The inspection seemed to take forever. Daisy couldn't help but stare over her shoulder for the ominous presence of her mother. Tucker would alert her if she showed. She needed to keep smiling and trying to hurry this up without seeming like they were trying to hide anything.

Finally back at the car, Edgar's pinched expression was now gone. "You ladies are doing a fantastic job here. Pass."

He ducked and got into the car.

"I only have the before pictures I saw to go on, but the

difference is remarkable. Pass." The mediator returned to his seat and Daisy did her best to keep still.

"Same bonus as last week. You gals are in good shape." Al stepped toward them and lowered his voice as he handed Daisy an envelope. "Violet in two weeks. Just so you know."

Daisy couldn't stop thinking about different things she could do to drive Violet crazy when she showed up for inspection in two weeks. If she dug random holes and covered them with leaves, she could trap the horrible woman. Paint buckets in doorways, the snakes, or maybe the bathhouse that seemed to be a mosquito breeding ground. All were good ideas, but too obvious.

"Get the revenge ideas out of your head. We couldn't get away with any of that stuff." Sydney elbowed her in the ribs.

"What are you, a mind reader now?" Daisy asked.

"I was thinking about taking her out on the pond and showing her the fish we found. Or the caves on the edge of the property." Sydney giggled.

The fish was one of the biggest Daisy had ever seen. She didn't remember the pond ever having such huge fish. Now, they seemed to be awash in hideously huge carp. The caves were the winter resting place of a family of bears. So far, they hadn't bothered them, and Daisy hoped it stayed that way. According to the conservation ranger she talked to, the bears would move on soon.

"You're bad."

"You were thinking the same thing." Sydney waved at the retreating car, her face frozen into a polite smile.

Probably matched hers. "Paint cans, snakes, and the mosquito breeding ground."

"Yeah, but we'll have that done before she arrives." The bathhouse contractor was due to start today.

"Damn. Too bad."

As soon as the car pulled away, Daisy let her shoulders slump. "We did it."

"Not without help." Sydney yawned.

"I know. We're lucky. And we're stupid. Why did we let them talk us into staying up until four for nothing?" She glared at Marshal's cabin, where it remained quiet.

"Because we owe them. Last night was pretty lame, wasn't it? We didn't even see a thing. What's up with that? And then you have an experience this morning." Sydney kicked a rock as they stopped in front of the stones for the campsites.

"Holy shit, this is going to kill us." The enormous pile would take them the rest of the week to spread, even with the extra help.

"Don't look now, but I think Nadine is here." Sydney's gaze went beyond where Daisy stood.

Taking a deep breath, she turned, shocked at the petite woman who trailed after a pissed-off-looking Tucker.

"I tried to call you. No signal." He held up his phone. "She wouldn't wait." Breathless, Tucker stopped in front of her.

Daisy nodded at Tucker with a wry smile, trying to decide if this woman could really be her birth mother. She regarded her with no emotion. Nadine stared back with hard, calculating eyes, her face finally crumpling into the fakest tears Daisy had ever seen.

"Oh, my baby. My baby. I've tried to find you for so long. Oh. You are so beautiful. Come here." Nadine held her arms out.

Daisy stepped back.

"Don't you know me? I'm your momma. I told you I would be back."

Daisy retreated again. "You're not my momma. I have momma and you never were and you never will be her. What do you want?"

At her harsh tone, the woman, her birth mother, stopped the fake crying and glowered at her.

"I was told you were beside yourself missing me and I rushed to see you. What kind of people did I leave you with that you turned into such an ungrateful brat?" Venom dripped from her words.

"You left me with people who love me and taught me how to be a good person. I shudder when I think of what I would have turned into had you not dumped me when I became inconvenient to you. You did me a favor." Daisy held on to the anger she'd found this morning. Gone were the hurt and questions. She could see now that she'd been a very lucky child.

"What do you know about me? How dare you judge me? You have no right." Nadine screamed, shaking her finger in a ridiculous gesture.

"I have every right to judge you. I'm the one and only person who has that right. You abandoned me. Left me to go party and spread your legs for any member of your beloved band that would do you." Daisy kept her tone even and her volume low. "See? I know plenty about you."

"You owe me. I gave up so much when I had you. You ruined my figure and gave me these terrible stretch marks. You wrecked my body."

Sydney stepped forward, but Daisy grabbed her arm.

"I didn't ask to be born. Is Joe Brown really my father? Or just a name you made up?" Daisy held on to Sydney's arm when she tried to take a step forward. She wouldn't stop her, but she'd have to wait until Daisy spoke her mind.

"How dare you? You little slut! How dare you speak to me that way?" Nadine's hands shook as she reached into her pocket for a pack of cigarettes.

"How dare you show up here thinking I'm going to be glad to see you? I would have been glad when I was four, six, or nine, or even sixteen, but not anymore. You are not my mom and you never will be. And how dare you call me a slut? You don't even know me." Daisy stepped back and released Sydney's arm.

"Do you know what I spent to come to you? I heard you needed me so badly. I dropped everything, even quit my job to come and rescue my baby." The fake tears started again, stopping long enough for Nadine to take a drag from her cigarette and blow out the smoke.

"It was nice of you to visit, but you really should be going." Sydney moved toward Nadine, her tone pleasant but firm.

"Who the hell are you? Don't tell me. Nancy's baby girl. Half-owner of this hellhole. I heard all about how you think you're entitled to a bigger cut of the property because you're blood related. Well, let me tell you something . . ."

"Lady, you have no idea what you're talking about. How much did she offer you to come here and cause trouble?" Sydney was now inches from Nadine's face. "Go away."

"I have a right to be a part of my daughter's life. Damn you, move and let me talk to my baby."

"You gave up that right when you signed the adoption papers without even asking how Daisy was doing. Don't come here expecting to be a part of her life. She has family. Family that loves and supports her. I am her family and I will not let you hurt her."

Daisy had to admit, Sydney had an impressive way. Nadine seemed to shrink a little, not that she'd seemed very big to begin with.

"Her name is Starshine. My little Starshine." Nadine pushed Sydney away and took a step, with her arms out toward Daisy.

"Don't fucking touch me." Daisy yanked her arm away when Nadine tried to touch her, her legs shaking. "Go to hell." She was done with this. She wanted answers, not this drunken whore.

"I'm already there, baby. I need your help to get out."

The pleading hacked at her resolve. Daisy took a deep shaky breath. She couldn't let this woman suck her in.

"No. You had your chance. Obviously, you didn't love me enough to stay clean. Why would now be any different? You love your drugs and booze and whore-men more. I hope they take care of you when you're old, because you won't have me to do that for you." Her chest burned and she fought tears, but she walked away with her head held high. The last thing she heard was Sydney asking Tucker to escort Nadine from the property and Nadine swear she'd be back.

Daisy leaned against the side of the cabin and banged her head a few times. She wanted to scream, cry, and pound her fists like the tantrums her mother should have had to deal with when she was little, but didn't. She wanted to know why. Damn it. Why she hadn't been enough to keep her mother straight? Why hadn't her mother loved her enough to stay clean? Why hadn't she wanted her?

Instead of the sobs working their way to the surface, she let out one of Sydney's screams. Half-expecting Sydney to run to her, Daisy didn't know whether to take a walk or stay put. She needed her sister, but at the same time, needed time to make sense of Nadine's angry words and 'you owe me' attitude. What kind of mother blamed her child for ruining her life and wanted payment for stretch marks?

Never once had her mom said those things to Sydney. She'd never complained about the stretch marks. She'd always said they were her badge of honor for delivering such a beautiful child. The way she'd used her words hadn't made Daisy feel bad for not giving her any.

Really, Nadine *had* done her a huge favor by dumping her. She most likely would have turned out just like the woman. Though, she still wondered if she did have some of her mother's tainted ways. So many things she'd done might be because of the crappy DNA she'd inherited.

Granted, she tried not to sleep around, but still had her fair share of one-night stands and sex just for the sake of sex. She'd never done drugs. Never would. And she'd never found an obsessive streak about anything.

She was a bit odd, she knew that. Knew from the strange looks she sometimes received when talking about her interests. Maybe all photographers were just weird. She doubted that. She liked to take pictures others had told her they'd never thought of before.

At least, and it was a little comfort, she had talent and had managed to make a name for herself. Her work was requested and the few gallery showings she'd had sold out before the end of the first evening. Her repeat customer list grew all the time and she could now charge whatever she wanted.

Not that she would raise her prices to the level her agent wanted. Daisy consistently refused. Tripling prices over the span of two years seemed ridiculous to her. And vain. Somewhat calmer, she circled the pond. Wondering what her mother would try next stuck in her gut and she didn't know how she could continue to survive the confrontations.

Once had been enough.

She'd be stupid to believe Nadine wouldn't show up again. Not after some of the stuff she'd said. Obviously, Violet had painted Sydney as the evil step-sister. No big surprise there coming from The Vileness. They should have expected that. Jace hadn't said anything, but then again, depending on where he got his information there was no way he could have known.

Sydney called her name. Daisy ignored her and kept going. Hopefully, she could get her train wreck of emotions under control before talking to Sydney. She wished she knew if she was normal, or if she was some freak of nature like her mother.

She watched the fish shadows moving under the now clear surface. Sydney waited by the benches for Daisy to decide she was ready to talk.

Daisy truly was blessed. She needed to remember that. She was part of a team with Sydney. Both equals, with their own strengths and the same vision for this beloved ground. Gramps had never once treated her like anything but a true granddaughter. He'd often tell her she was God's gift to him because he had so much love to give his grandchildren and her parents hadn't been able to have another child after Sydney.

With a sigh, she approached her sister, knowing whatever she waited to tell her would not be welcome.

"She left you this." Sydney passed her an envelope.

Daisy opened it, removing the contents and dropping the envelope on the ground as she sat on the bench.

Baby pictures. The obligatory puffy newborn picture taken in the hospital when she was only hours old, and several snapshots over the next few days until Nadine walked out of her life. The last picture finally broke her and she sobbed in Sydney's arms. A mother-daughter portrait obviously taken shortly before her mother allowed her addictions to take over.

CHAPTER 14

Sydney wasn't sure what to do. Daisy's shoulders shook. Out of rage, sadness, or both? She'd never been as close to physical violence as she'd been when Nadine demanded Daisy pay her for all the damage she'd done to her life and body. Sydney didn't care about the nonsense Nadine spouted about her. Violet was good at rearranging the facts to suit her needs and obviously Nadine had willingly fallen into her trap.

Nadine cursed the whole way out of the campground. At least she'd left, crawling into the back of a filthy, dented van with the crappiest-looking guys Sydney had ever seen. She'd heard one of them ask Nadine if she'd gotten the money, but didn't wait around to hear the answer.

The horrid woman would be back. And soon, too.

The way Nadine's hands shook told the story. She was in need of a fix. Sydney seriously wondered if they should hire a security guard to make sure Nadine didn't come back during the quiet of the night. Would that help Daisy sleep any better? Or would it make things worse?

She didn't dare ask right now. Those pictures had sent her sister into an abyss she wasn't ready to come out of yet. Nadine was either good at manipulating people, or had followed Violet's sinister advice.

Drop off the baby pictures. Show the kid how great things had obviously once been. Give Daisy a link to a past she can't remember and make her wish for things that never were. Bitch.

Nadine would not do Violet's evil thing to Daisy. Sydney would make sure of it.

Daisy continued to squeeze her in a soul-crushing hug, the sobs wetting Sydney's shirt and breaking her heart. That Daisy had grown up with all the love in the world didn't matter right now. That her own mother had rejected her for a life of drugs, booze, and men hurt more than anything Sydney could imagine. She rested her head on Daisy's, her tears wetting Daisy's hair.

She was sure her sister knew how good her life was. That didn't mean she couldn't mourn how things should have been. How it would have felt to know your mother loved and cherished you no matter what. Not to have her dump you off, never come back, and then blame you for whatever destruction she imagined you performed on her body.

Sydney took a deep breath, wiping the tears away. "What would you think of going to meet your father? Maybe it would help?"

Daisy lifted her head. "How? To have one more person wanting something from me when they couldn't be bothered with me my whole life?"

"What if he doesn't know about you? What if Nadine never told him?" Sydney wasn't sure if her idea was a good one.

"Mom said he rejected Nadine when she told him. What if he's like her?"

"What if he's not? His business is successful. We saw that for ourselves. He was married for a long time according to Kay." They'd driven by, on purpose, Sydney was sure of it, on their way back from Kay's yesterday.

"I don't know. What help can it be?"

"At this point, what could it hurt?" Sydney wanted her sister to have some peace. Maybe her birth father would turn out to be the one to give that to her.

"Let me think about it. Okay?" Daisy rested her head on Sydney's shoulder with a sigh.

"Okay. Everything is up to you."

They sat in silence for a few minutes, until Sydney decided it was time to switch gears and get Daisy's mind off of her parents.

"So we passed inspection." Sydney jiggled her shoulder. "We've got the contracted work already paid for. The office is in good shape. What's next?"

Daisy took a deep, shaky breath. "We have to pay for the rest of the stone. Maybe hire someone to spread it? What about the pool? One more good inspection and we should be able to have it fixed. Or we could get the activity building ready?" Daisy sniffed, but the excitement in her voice gave Sydney hope.

"How many more inspections do we have? Four? Six? We may not pass all of them. We have the money we set aside for our first two months in business and for taxes and enough to do half the pool. Violet comes in two weeks. What's most important?" Sydney spouted off whatever thought came to mind, a normal brainstorming routine for them.

"With the money from today, we have enough to finish the pool. I think the pool is an important part of the campground. The estimate included some of the things we've already taken care of, like the electric and restoring the changing room. We might be able to knock a couple grand off the total. What if we wait until after the next inspection to start the work, then we'll have enough cash available?"

"What will we have to show them before next week? Yeah, the stones will be done and the campsites are nearly ready. The electric will be finished and the bathhouses underway. We need something big though, or we could fail." Sydney bounced her leg until Daisy dropped her hand onto her thigh and glared.

"Let's do the activity building and the playground first. I wanted to show you my ideas about adding a room so I could maybe give photography classes." Daisy grinned.

Sydney bounced with excitement. "That's a great idea. What about a place inside the activity building for kids to play when it rains? What do you think of offering a few hours of childcare per day? We'd have to find out the legalities and hire someone appropriate, but it may mean the difference of a few bookings. Maybe by next summer?"

"And a mini-golf course. I wonder how much that would cost."

"I have to meet with the plumber in ten minutes. Let's go over this at lunch. Kay's grandson is delivering. We need to interview him, too." Sydney stood and stretched before hugging Daisy.

"Okay. Thanks, Syd. I do feel better," Daisy said. At least Sydney succeeded in making her smile. That had to count for something.

After meeting with the plumber, Sydney found herself alone in the office. Alone with the weird box Marshal found in the hidden area. She'd searched the space and found nothing else. Why did the thought of opening the box make her want to do anything but?

Daisy would be here soon. She'd asked about the box twice this morning. Sydney had hated to admit she hadn't opened it yet. Sure, she was dying to know what was inside, but fearful at the same time. And why had the box only been addressed to her?

Time to find out. She picked at the edge of tape and finally yanked. The inside of the box smelled like Gramps, taking her by surprise and filling her with nostalgia. She let the tears fall as she peeled back the rest of the tape.

There was a newspaper on top dated five years earlier, which was shortly before Gramps died. The headlines revealed nothing spectacular. She'd read it once she finished with the inside of the box. An envelope was next. She opened it with shaky fingers and read:

My darling Sydney,

I know you are wondering why this box is addressed to only you and not Daisy as well. I have always felt her mother would come back to find her should she know of the inheritance I'm destined to leave you both. I know I can trust you to handle this with fairness and care. Ultimately, this will help you to overcome any obstacles in your path and reopen the campground.

My reasons for hiding this money are probably obvious by now. I cannot explain my actions to you. Suffice it to say I thought I was doing to right thing. Sometimes our path seems right and then we realize we've taken on more than we can handle. And sometimes we sacrifice much for the people we love. Right or wrong.

Leaving you this provides me much comfort. I can see your joy at realizing most of your financial problems are a thing of the past. If I could be there with you, I would. Maybe I am, but I don't know how the afterlife works yet.

Brookside is full of secrets and mysteries. I know you and Daisy love this place as I do and I trust the two of you will do whatever necessary to reopen.

I am so very proud of both of you and am blessed to have been your grandfather.

All my love,

G.

Sydney sniffed as she refolded the letter. Standing up, she peered into the box and found the money Gramps referred to in the letter. Lots of money. Enough to take care of the pool and any other job they could think of. She covered her mouth to keep the scream of joy inside as she did a little dance around the office. She couldn't wait to tell Daisy. They'd have no problems re-opening the campground now.

If they could just keep Violet and Nadine off their backs.

She didn't want to move the stacks, but had a feeling there was more to this box than the cryptic letter and a wad of money. She reached to the bottom, her hand closing around what felt like a book. Gramps' journal? Oh man. Sydney had expected to find this inside the house.

She rubbed her fingers over the embossed initials of her grandfather. A folded paper stuck out of the top and she sat down as she opened the note, her hands shaking.

We've never spoken of it, but I see the gift in you. Open your mind and heart and truly great things can happen.

Gramps had been big on the cryptic stuff. Sydney sighed, wishing she could ask him exactly what he meant. Seemed like everything was a huge puzzle and most of the pieces were lost or broken.

Opening the journal, she read the first entry dated fifty years earlier. Gramps' handwriting was strong and bold. He wrote of his experiences as the new owner of Brookside and his excitement shone through the aged words.

Wishing she had time to read the journal cover to cover, instead she paged to the middle and found a passage than made her sit up straighter.

The woman in the bathhouse hears me. I know she does. She just won't listen. I keep trying to help her find her way to where she needs to be, but part of me wonders if this is who she was in life. Someone who loved drama and pity. According to the records left to me by my father, she died in there shortly after Brookside opened. I wonder why she refuses to move on.

Creepy. And exactly what Sydney thought.

She flipped to the back of the book, noticing the weakness of the formerly bold handwriting mirrored the decline in Gramps' health. Choking back the tears, she read his last entry.

I want to say I'm sorry, but I am not. I can't be. I have loved two women in my life. Each has enriched my life in ways I cannot describe. I have been truly blessed. May I be further blessed with a quick death and not this illness that ticks years off my body with each breath I take.

Footsteps sounded on the porch and she wiped away the tears, then quickly scanned to make sure she hadn't left any of the money out. Tucking the journal into her briefcase, she stood and leaned over the top of the box, impatient to show Daisy their treasure.

Only it wasn't Daisy, but a harried-looking Tucker.

"Is Daisy in here?" Tucker's clipped tone unsettled her.

"No. She's supposed to meet me here. What's wrong?" Sydney straightened.

"We were supposed to meet. She didn't show. I thought she got tied up with the plumber, so I waited but she never came. She doesn't answer her phone and I can't find her." Tucker left the door open and glanced outside every few seconds.

"Daisy wasn't meeting the plumber, I was. She was getting her sketches together for the activity building and meeting me here for lunch."

"That's another thing. Lunch never came. The guys were waiting, but the order never came. Daisy called me and said she'd be late because the plumber had a few more questions."

"That doesn't make any sense. I watched him drive away and he didn't come back. Besides, he knew where to find me and I have the paperwork. He was told he was to only deal with me. That's how we split up the chores." Worry settled in her gut. "Call Kay and I'll find Marshal. Maybe she's with him going over footage or something." She tried not to worry.

Daisy's car was still parked beside Sydney's. Nothing to worry about. Except it was too quiet. Even the birds had stopped singing. Something wasn't right. Locking the box in her trunk for safety, Sydney rapped on Marshal's door. He opened it bare-chested and sleepy-eyed.

"Is Daisy here?" she fired off before he could even process who disturbed his sleep.

"No. I'm sleeping." Marshal stretched.

"We can't find her." She told him what Tucker said about the plumber.

"Some guy knocked on our door about an hour ago. Said he was the plumber and was late for a meeting with Daisy."

Sydney's stomach dropped. "What did he look like?"

Marshal's description didn't sound like the plumber or anyone she'd ever met. What the hell?

The entire cabin was up and searching the woods within a matter of minutes. Sydney found Tucker taking to Kay on his cell phone in the parking area. She watched him, wanting so badly to interrupt and ask every question roaming through her mind.

Finally, he hung up and turned to her. "Kay sent the lunch delivery with her grandson. He left an hour ago."

"Daisy doesn't answer her phone." She paced, trying to keep the fear away as she called Daisy's name out toward the pond.

The sheriff and his crew arrived. Several trucks and cars followed, the parking lot filling in a matter of minutes.

"We usually don't do this unless it's been over twenty-four hours, but with all the weird shit you two have dealt with here, I'm not taking any chances. Frank filled me in on everything. He's in Florida, but he checks in frequently. He's worried about you two." The sheriff had four search parties organized and sent them out with specific instructions leaving Sydney with the impression they'd done this type of work before.

"Can we make the office our command post?" The sheriff seemed more nervous than usual. "Tell me everything that happened today."

Sydney went through every detail. When she got to the part about the plumber the sheriff stopped writing.

"What's happened? What aren't you telling me?" Sydney stood in front of him, her hands on her hips.

"I received two calls today. One from some irate woman named Nadine accusing you of holding her daughter here against her will. I know enough of the family history to know who Nadine is." The sheriff rolled his eyes.

"I knew she'd try something." Sydney's fear grew. Was Nadine now holding Daisy for ransom? Was the woman really that crazy? "Who was the other call?"

"The other said he was a reporter. Started asking a bunch of questions about Brookside, Del and you two. They sounded weird, like they were reading the questions instead of asking. You know?"

"Maybe it was a new reporter?" This didn't sound good.

"I've dealt with lots of reporters, Sydney. My gut is telling me this person was not who he said."

"What did you tell him?"

"Nothing. They knew basic information. I refused to elaborate. The questions were really strange, too. He wanted to know about your pasts, where you lived before and if you were married. I guess that does make good human interest type stories. I'm not buying that. That kind of information is best asked of the person you want to know about."

"So now you believe us?" Sydney hated that the question came out so sarcastic. She hadn't meant it to.

"I'm sorry. It's not that I didn't believe you. I did, but I thought the trouble was caused by someone who really wanted the casino. Some of the debates in town about the casino are getting downright ugly. I broke up a fight at Kay's the other day. The young kids all think the change is exciting and see themselves making it big and leaving. The young families are appalled and the older folks are conflicted, because, maybe they want some excitement around here, too."

"Would those people go so far as to kidnap Daisy and sabotage everything we've worked for?"

"I don't know. Money's a powerful thing. The guy that hired the kid to scare you thought he was participating in a practical joke, too. We haven't been able to locate the person he says hired him."

"Do you really think Nadine would do this?" She told him her impression of her needing a fix.

"Possibly if she were desperate. Nadine's our biggest suspect. You know there's a chance Daisy went to clear her head and ended up in a hole or something." The sheriff didn't seem to believe that.

"Sure. That's why some guy saying he was the plumber asked where he could find Daisy."

Another shout sounded from the woods to their left and Sydney's hope grew as she ran toward the search party.

Sydney stood over the bones and shook her head. The skeleton was canine. She wondered if this could be the physical remnants of their ghostly visitor and decided once Daisy was safe, they'd properly bury what was left of the dog's body.

The sun was setting. Each minute Daisy stayed missing might bring her closer to death. No ransom note had appeared yet and her phone stayed mute.

Where was she? Sydney went back to the office, her steps as heavy as her heart. A vehicle stopped near the office. Sydney didn't bother to turn around. The next thing she knew, a hand grabbed her arm and spun her around.

Nadine.

"Where's my baby?" Her eyes were wild. Her hair stuck out in all directions and Sydney could swear there was a cigarette butt stuck in the crazy mess.

"For your information, she was a baby thirty years ago. She's a grown woman now and she does not belong to you. You're not welcome here." Sydney turned away.

"How dare you? You've poisoned her against me." Nadine's screech echoed through the trees.

"Where is she, Nadine?" Sydney spun and closed in, her fists clenched and the question quiet and menacing.

The shock on her face appeared genuine, but Sydney wasn't convinced. "You little bitch. Why would I kidnap my own flesh and blood?"

"Why would you show up and accuse her of wrecking your life? Why would you decide to come back now, after she's received half of an inheritance that holds enough potential to see us both into a comfortable old age? You leave your daughter to follow some band and you have the nerve to call me a bitch?" Sydney's volume increased. The next thing she knew the sheriff stood at her elbow.

"I'll take it from here, Miss Brooks. Ma'am, I'll need to ask you some questions." The sheriff had Nadine by the arm and steered her toward one of the benches.

"How did she know Daisy's missing?" Sydney let the door slam behind her. She felt like banging it again, or kicking the chair and screaming at the top of her lungs. She ended up doing all three.

Where was her sister?

CHAPTER 15

Daisy shivered against the metal floor. Her arms ached and her throat was raw. Where was she? The last thing she remembered was talking to the plumber.

Only now, she didn't think he really had been the plumber.

Why did the thought make her laugh? She was becoming delirious, no doubt. It was either sweltering or freezing. She'd had a sense of night, but couldn't see the sky.

Sydney would be insane by now. She'd have the National Guard searching for her and probably knock on every door. Why didn't that comfort her?

Probably because she was starving, freezing and had to go to the bathroom so bad she could barely move. Oh, whoever did this was going to get their ass kicked once she found a way out of here.

Just when she was considering using a corner of the metal box to relieve herself the door slid open and for a moment, the sun blinded her.

"Come on now. Let's go," a gruff voice commanded.

"Go to hell." She stepped back, wondering if baiting the person offering her freedom was really a good idea.

She moved before he could shut the doors on her, trying to adjust her eyes at the same time she contemplated which direction to run. Before she could take off, his hand gripped her arm, digging into her skin and causing her to yelp.

"Get your hands off me, you moron." When was she going to learn not to taunt the person who could end up killing her?

"Shut up." He dragged her with him, swinging her into an ancient outhouse. "Do your business quickly."

He slammed the door and dust rained down on her. Trying not to think about what kind of creepy crawlies probably inhabited the tiny stall with her, or about the possibilities termites had structurally damaged the wooden platform, her bladder demanded she follow his instructions.

She opened the door and checked the area. Her captor didn't seem around so she stepped out. Again, just as she prepared to run, he grabbed her.

"No way."

"Why did you do this?" She tried to wrench her arm away, not caring that his grip tightened.

"Why not?" His vague answer and obnoxious laugh made her want to kick him.

Weighing her chances, she pretended to fall, her shoulder popping with the impact. He didn't let go. Damn. And ouch.

"Where are you taking me?"

"You'll see. My boss is eager to speak with you."

"Your boss? What is he, like a gangster or something? What would he want with me?"

"Shut up. Just shut the fuck up." He yanked her arm and Daisy thought it might have come out of the socket this time.

"Why should I? This is stupid. Why didn't your boss just ask me to talk to him? Did you really need to lock me up to freeze my ass off all night? What kind of moron would treat someone so badly? This is insane. What the hell? Your boss has a lot of nerve. I want answers. This is fucking ridiculous," she railed, seemingly unable to stop herself.

"Why do you have to talk so much? Maybe I should put you back," he growled.

"Maybe you should take your hands off me. Maybe you should go fuck yourself. Maybe you should let me the hell go!" She wrenched her arm, kicking out with her foot at the same time.

Her kick connected with his kneecap and he released her as he bent over with a squeal of pain. A second kick caught him in the nose with a crack and a spurt of blood. Good. Without looking back, Daisy ran into the woods, hoping like hell she'd run into the guys she was certain Sydney had searching for her.

She ran with everything she had. Her lungs burned and tears streamed down her face. Where the hell was she? With her luck, she'd run right into a bear or get lost in this seemingly endless forest.

Finally, she found a trail and after a quick left and right, took off to the right on pure instinct. She had no idea how far she'd gone when the path widened to reveal a gravel road.

Could she really have made it back to the campground?

A man shouted, and she fell to her knees. The last thing she saw was Sydney's face, surrounded by Marshal, Graham, and Tucker.

Sydney paced the tiny front porch. Was Daisy ever going to wake up? They had no idea where she'd run from or how far she traveled, just that her face was scratched up, her arm was horribly bruised and her wrists were raw. Sydney's anger grew with each step.

Having Daisy back and not knowing who took her or why was almost as bad as when she was missing. Almost. Sydney hadn't spoken to anyone since Nadine's visit. She'd filled the sheriff in on what Nadine had said, but after that found she had nothing left to say.

Marshal had tried to talk to her. So did Jace. But she'd shaken her head and backed away. They seemed to understand. Each had hugged her, but hadn't asked for anymore from her.

She was grateful. They'd done so much for her and Daisy the past few days. Stuff they hadn't asked for nor expected.

Sydney wished she had even a smidgen of her former sense of humor. Right now, she felt nothing.

The door opened and the EMT taking care of Daisy stuck his head out. "She's awake."

Sydney moved to go inside, only to be stopped by a badge. "I need to ask her some questions."

"Then you can wait until after I make sure she's okay." Sydney moved around him. His hand closed around her wrist.

"Procedure, ma'am." He tried to seem sympathetic. Or at least she thought that was what it was supposed to be.

"I don't give a crap. Get out of my way." She gave him her best menacing glare, but he didn't move.

Thankfully, the EMT intervened. "She's asking for her sister. She doesn't believe she's safe."

Sydney quelled her urge to stick her tongue out at the sour faced officer and rushed to her sister's bed. "Hey, sleepyhead. You sure have a way of getting out of work."

She kissed her cheek, heartened when Daisy laughed in response. "They told me I was home, but I couldn't be sure. I guess it's the unfamiliar paint. Where am I?"

"In our soon-to-be conference room. The guys painted it for something to do while we waited. The cops kicked us off the search team." She went to her knees on the floor and hugged Daisy with a sob. "I was so freaking scared."

"Well, lucky for me I was out of it for most of the time. When I came to this morning I was pissed, so I didn't really get scared."

"Don't say any more, Miss. I'll take your statement in a moment," the guy who'd stopped Sydney at the door said.

"Not without my sister here you won't. I don't know you, so no, you don't get to talk to me without someone present I'm comfortable with." Daisy sat up, obviously in the same temper she'd escaped with. She winced when she moved her arm and despite not really wanting to know, Sydney moved the sleeve of her loose-fitting shirt, almost crying when she saw how awful the bruises there were.

"What the hell?"

"I swear the guy was trying to snap my fucking arm in half." Daisy tried to hide the pain.

"How'd you get away?"

The click of the door brought both of their heads around. Sydney's discomfort increased with the man's presence. She'd seen his badge, but that didn't mean he was really one of the good guys.

"I'd be more comfortable if you left the door open. It's kind of close in here. I'm a little claustrophobic," Sydney lied.

"Fine. I understand."

For the next hour, she sat in shock while Daisy told her story time after time. After the fourth round of questioning, Sydney couldn't take any more.

"Excuse me. I know you're just doing your job and all, but in case you've forgotten, my sister is the victim here. She didn't do anything to precipitate this. Why are you treating her like a criminal?"

"That's not my intention, ma'am. I just need to make sure I have all the facts."

Daisy yawned. "You had them all the first time. Why would I lie about being kidnapped?"

"Stranger things have happened."

"Not to me."

"I think you've drained her brain enough for right now. Let her rest. I'd like to talk to you outside though." Sydney stood, not caring how angry he looked.

"Good. I have some questions for you too." He preceded her out the door after a brief standoff.

On the porch, she spun on him. "Why would you question her like that? That's insane. She's innocent."

"Are you? Some folks think maybe you arranged this to take the inheritance for yourself?"

The idea was so ridiculous Sydney laughed. "What folks? What are their names? Like I'd really want to be burdened with the campground to run by myself." She didn't care that she'd shouted.

"No. So you can sell it and be a rich young woman."

"Oh. Now you're pissing me off. Why don't you find the real criminals instead of badgering innocent women?" She got in his face, knowing she needed to back off, but she was unable to stop herself.

"I am. I have to investigate the obvious first. I need to know everyone who's in residence here." His tone softened, but his face remained grim.

"I thought you gathered that information already?" She really didn't like this guy.

"I did. I need your opinions on them." He flipped his notepad open, his pen poised just above the page.

Sydney listed their names, even the guys from Tucker's crew. She really didn't think any of them were behind Daisy's kidnapping and told him so.

"That's quite a few men for only two women." A red haze blurred her vision at the undertones in his statement.

"You're a real funny man, you know that? Get your mind out of the gutter." She itched to slap his face for his innuendo.

"You mean to tell me you have the grandson of the woman trying to take this campground from you in residence and you don't think there's anything weird about that?" He raised a brow.

"No. Just because his grandmother embodies pure evil doesn't mean he does. I believe him. He's given me no reason to doubt him." Hopefully, her tone would end that line of questioning.

"I've seen the way he looks at you. Don't you think he'd tell you whatever you wanted to hear? He gets to sabotage your plans, maybe a sweet piece of ass, and his grandmother wins. I wonder what she's promised him for his role." Forget the slap, Sydney had to force herself not to punch him.

"A sweet piece of ass? Are you freaking serious? I'm going to pretend I didn't hear that. For now. If you ever say such a thing again I'll report you to your superiors."

"We'll see if my information matches yours." Why was he so snide and smug?

"Knock yourself out." She meant that literally.

"Here's my card. My cell number is on the bottom. If your sister remembers anything else, call me right away. I'll be back in the morning." He turned and stepped off of the porch.

Sydney kicked the wooden bench to her left, immediately regretting her show of temper. Damn that hurt.

What the hell? The guy was supposed to be on their side. Supposed to help find out who kidnapped Daisy and so far all he'd done was make assumptions and cast aspersion on their characters. She'd never call him, even if Daisy came up with the name of the people who'd taken her, but she would be having a discussion with his superiors. The way he'd treated them was ridiculous.

"You okay?" The EMT watched her limp back into the room.

"Yeah. I wish I could have kicked him in the head." She sank onto the couch.

"He's gruff and kind of an asshole, but he does good work. I've seen the results." He turned back to Daisy.

Sydney was losing her mind. "If you say so. He's not my favorite person right now. I don't want to have to talk to him again." She leaned back, fatigue making her sigh.

"Daisy's going to be fine. She's sleeping again. You should be able to hear her call from here."

"Thanks. You went above and beyond for us. I know she should have gone to the hospital, but she was adamant. When will the results of the blood tests be back?" She got comfortable on one of the new couches in the waiting area and wrapped the fleece blanket that had been hanging over the back around herself.

"Doc put a rush on them. He wanted to make sure whatever she was given will clear her system quickly. Expect headaches. If she has a headache that gets too bad, take her to the ER no matter what she says. I'll be back in the morning." He left, and panic climbed through Sydney.

They were alone in the cabin. What if this crazy asshole decided to come back for Daisy?

She stood and went to the door. Marshal stood with his back against the sign. Sydney almost screamed, but he silenced her with his lips. Melting into him, she allowed the physical needs of her body to override her common sense. His chest was solid against her and he tasted of coffee and sunshine. When he finally released her, guilt shattered her need and she rested her head on his chest.

Lifting her chin gently, he locked eyes with her. "Daisy's fine. There's nothing wrong with a little physical release in times of stress. Go to sleep. The campground is well-guarded. I called in a few of my part-timers. They're taping and patrolling at the same time. Rest easy. The bastard won't take her again. You have my word."

Sydney touched his face, realizing how easy it would be to give in to her hormones and let him take her away from this nightmare for a few blissful hours.

But then, Jace's face swam into her head and guilt was her new best friend. How had this happened? She'd gone from having no one in her life to dealing with the very real prospect of making a choice between Jace and Marshal.

How would she do that?

They were both wonderful men. Both spoke to her on a physical level and an intellectual one. Not to mention, they seemed to have the same morals and sense of humor.

She was screwed.

And judging by the way Graham and Tucker were acting, so was Daisy.

An owl called. Sydney sat up. Something was wrong. She just didn't know what. She stayed still, confused and concerned. Daisy. She threw the covers back and rushed to the room where her sister recovered. The bed was empty.

The windows were closed and locked. Whoever took her had to have come through the front door. *That's* what had awakened her, the sound of the door clicking into place.

She ripped the door open, startling Marshal.

"Where's Daisy?" She tried to control her breathing.

"Bathroom." Marshal motioned toward the outhouse they had to use until the new toilets were installed.

"Alone?"

"No, silly. Tucker and Graham are with her. Those two are going to beat the shit out of each other soon." He pointed, and she turned. Both men stood on either side of the bathhouse with their arms folded across their chests.

"Oh for crying out loud. What is going on in this place? Is there some kind of love curse or something?" She hadn't meant that last sentence to slip out.

"I believe so. I know how they feel." Marshal's words were quiet. So quiet she almost hadn't heard.

At least she wasn't alone in how she felt. It seemed to her that they were all confused.

"Try being me." She closed the door behind her as she went back to the couch to wait for Daisy's return. Standing on the front porch and discussing the decision she may have to make soon was not appealing.

The last thing she wanted was to hurt either man. Wasn't it supposed to be easy once you found your prince charming? Didn't all men pale in comparison, leaving no question as to who was your true destiny?

Except she felt like that with both Marshal and Jace. Could she be falling in love with both of them? She wasn't going to be able to choose. What would she do? Daisy's suggestion stuck in her head, but the whole thing seemed sleazy and slutty.

Sleep with both of them and whichever one made her quiver for hours afterward would be the man who was meant for her. How could she do that? Was she supposed to tell them? That certainly would put a lot of pressure on them to perform their best. She almost laughed at that thought.

What if neither did it for her? Or what if they both did? What would she do then?

She wondered if she could live with both of them. One of those alternate lifestyle type situations where they all lived together, sharing the chores, fun, and sex.

Shaking her head, she dispelled that idea. She'd be a wreck all the time and the whole thing didn't feel quite right to her. Much like sleeping with both of them to see which one suited her best. Her version was better than Daisy's though. Daisy suggested she sleep with both of them at the same time.

Besides the fact that the thought excited her more than she'd ever admit, she knew she'd never have the guts to suggest such a thing. Still, it was a wonderful fantasy.

She was better off forgetting the stupid idea and just getting a bunch of cats. Cats didn't care what you did as long as you kept their food dish filled, their litter boxes clean, and scratched them behind the ears every once in a while.

Yep. *That's* what she would do.

Become a cat lady who owned a campground.

Daisy waved on her way back to her makeshift sickroom. She appeared much better, and Sydney relaxed. Her mind wandered to candlelit rooms, oversized bathtubs, and two muscular handsome men waiting to take care of her every need and whim.

CHAPTER 16

Daisy rolled over, almost falling off the tiny cot. Her body ached and her head felt as if the hemispheres of her brain had permanently separated. She thought she smelled coffee and slowly stood to go in search of the magical brew. Her stomach growled.

Sydney smiled as she rounded the corner. "Good morning. How're you feeling?"

"Like shit. Why do you seem so happy?" Daisy didn't mean to growl.

"Because you're safe."

Guilt filled her, especially after that sweet reason. Maybe she should go back to bed until she could be nice. Sydney motioned to the chair beside her, a mug of steaming coffee and a plate of bagels and fruit in front of that.

"I figured you'd be hungry."

"Thanks. I am. I'm feeling a little disoriented. Sorry I snapped at you." She sank into the chair, feeling every ache in her body.

"No offense taken. It's probably because you haven't eaten in about forty-eight hours." Sydney pushed her plate away and stood.

"I wondered. I'm afraid I kind of lost track of time." She picked up a bagel, noticing Sydney had spread her favorite cream cheese on it already.

"Understandable after what you've been through." Sydney moved to the window. "Damn."

"What?" She turned her head, but the movement caused a crashing pain.

"That asshole investigator is back and as jerky as ever." Sydney filled her in on some of the comments the guy had made when he questioned her.

"He's a jackass." Daisy kept her head turned, concentrating on her bagel. "He was probably jealous. Thought we were running some kind of reverse harem and wants to join. Maybe you should interview him and see what hidden talents he has." Daisy watched Sydney's face turn red.

"Ha. Ha. I'm having enough trouble with your other suggestion on how to pick between Jace and Marshal." Sydney made a face and turned back to the window.

"Yeah. I'm having trouble with that one myself." The idea had seemed like a good one at the time.

Daisy finished off the bagel and the glass of orange juice beside her plate. "Think I could sneak out and shower before he wants to talk to me again?"

She stood and went to the window.

"There's no back way out of here. Hang on." Sydney dialed Jace.

Daisy could see Jace near the main house and she watched as he answered his phone. She could even see him nod in response to Sydney's explanation of their dilemma.

"Okay, Jace is going to divert him long enough for us to slip to our cabin. I need a shower, too." Sydney stood with her hand on the doorknob. "The EMT didn't want to move you last night."

She nodded, slowly so her head wouldn't explode. "Why'd you call Jace?"

"Detective Weiner-face has an issue with Jace. He seems to think his only reason for being here is to stop us and sleep with me."

"Sounds reasonable." Daisy couldn't help it. Watching Sydney's face turn red again brightened her mood.

"Very funny. Okay. We're clear. Let's go." Sydney opened the door and Daisy followed her out, not surprised when Graham and Marshal fell in step behind them.

"Captain's orders." Tucker grinned.

"You know he's going to see you and figure out where we are," Sydney pointed out.

"Not if we come in with you." Marshal winked at Sydney, and Daisy watched conflicting emotions travel over her face.

"I was kidding," Marshal said, only he didn't look like that had been the case.

"You know this isn't a covert op. When he finds out we're in the shower, he'll wait for us. It's not like he's going to cart us off to prison or anything. We didn't do anything wrong." Each step felt like her head would fall off her shoulders.

She'd hoped the ache would subside once the food and caffeine kicked in. So far, she hadn't been lucky like that. She didn't want to tell Sydney, didn't want to see the worried, guilt on her sister's face. She'd have to if the pain didn't stop growing in intensity.

By the time she'd rinsed her hair, she couldn't take it anymore. Wrapping a towel around her head and another around her body, she leaned against the side of the shower stall, certain she was going to be sick.

Daisy tried to call out for Sydney, but couldn't speak. She slid down the wall when her legs refused to support her. On her way down, she swung her arm out and knocked the shelf clear of every bottle and item stored there hoping Sydney would hear.

Bright overhead lights stung her brain and she squeezed her eyes shut tight. A voice she didn't recognize boomed near her ear. "She's waking. Get those lights turned down."

Thankfully, whoever they spoke to complied and she allowed her eyes to relax. She didn't know where she was, but from the antiseptic odors and barely audible footsteps, figured she was probably at the hospital.

The only reason Sydney hadn't brought her yesterday was because she'd thrown a fit and made her promise not to. She'd feared for her life so much at that point. In retrospect, she probably should have allowed it. Maybe she wouldn't be wishing for a decapitation now.

"How're you doing?" The same voice, only softer now.

Daisy tried to open her eyes, but even the dim light hurt.

"Don't. Not yet. Keep them shut. I can talk to you like this. I'm Dr. Keller. You're going to be fine."

He sounded nice. Daisy relaxed a little. "My head hurts so bad."

"I know. A combination of dehydration and the drugs your kidnapper pumped into your system. He used an odd combination of components that make no sense."

"Does that make him a stupid criminal?" Daisy tried for a joke but was pretty sure it failed.

"He was a stupid criminal for trying to kidnap you to begin with. Rest. You should feel better in a few hours. I'd like to keep you here at least until you can open your eyes without it hurting." He patted her shoulder.

She heaved a sigh and relaxed on the pillow. She should have let Sydney bring her here yesterday. Maybe she could have avoided this horrible pain and causing her sister any more worry.

Trying to clear her brain, she almost wished she would have allowed that jackass who drugged her to take her to see the boss. Almost. At least they'd know who they were dealing with.

The last thing she remembered was passing out in the shower. She was dying to know if any information had been discovered through her vague directional description of where she thought she'd been held. She'd been able to describe the outside area pretty well, including the falling down outhouse she'd been forced to use. The smell alone would probably make the place easy to find.

She drifted, wondering how she could be so tired.

Daisy opened one eye, then the other. The raging pain had eased to a dull ache and she pushed herself up. An IV stuck out of her left hand, attached to a bag of clear fluid. The room was dark. She looked around for a clock, but didn't find one. It had to be late though.

Great, what a way to screw up two, wait, three, days of work. They'd never pass next week's inspection. She must be recovering if she was thinking about work. The door opened a crack, the light coming through making her squint, but not cry out in pain.

"You're up." Sydney sat in the chair beside her, her face in shadow but the worry in her voice evident.

"I'm okay. Sorry I didn't let you bring me here sooner. Obviously it would have been the smart thing to do." She relaxed against the pillows, wanting to rip the IV out of her hand.

"That's beside the point. You're okay. That's all that matters now." Sydney patted her hand, fiddling with the tape holding the tube in place.

"Take that out, will ya?" She held her arm up.

"No way. They'll do it when they discharge you. Dr. Keller wants to wait until the rest of your bloodwork comes back. Should only be a few hours." Sydney sounded exhausted and Daisy knew it was her fault.

"I always seem to cause trouble, don't I?" Tears pricked her eyelids and she struggled to keep them inside.

"Don't you dare think any of this was your fault."

"It is. Except for the kidnapping stuff. I know I had nothing to do with that. But everything else. If I hadn't insisted on calling Marshal in, then you wouldn't be conflicted over which man is the one for you. Neither would I, for that matter.

If I hadn't initiated the search for my birth parents, Nadine wouldn't be raising hell for us." Daisy choked on the tears.

"How can you even try to blame yourself for any of that? I don't blame you at all. At worst, I'll end up with neither guy and never have to feel guilty or wonder if I made the right decision. Nadine can go to hell. You're not the one who brought her crashing through our door. That was Vile Violet, not you. If she hadn't told her about the inheritance then she would never have bothered. I know it hurts you to hear that, but it's true." Sydney grabbed her hand and squeezed.

"It doesn't hurt as much as it should. She's a sick woman. The only thing I feel for her is pity. And gratitude that she at least had enough sense not to screw up my life in the process of messing up hers." She took a shaky breath. The statement was like a bolt of lightning.

All the angst and anger she'd carried around with her faded. Her mother did love her in a twisted way. She'd done the right thing by leaving her with people who would love and care for her. Maybe, in time, she could have a vague friendship with the woman who gave her life. Maybe.

"What are we going to do about the guys?" Daisy rolled her head toward Sydney.

"Send them packing? All of them?" She'd said it as a joke, Daisy knew, but the thought of never finding out where her heart belonged stung.

"I'm still considering sleeping with them both." That had been intended to counteract Sydney's teasing.

"Me, too." Sydney's eyes were serious.

Silence hung in the air between them. She knew her sister's morals and how shocked she'd been at Daisy's half-joking suggestion of a one-night stand. Now her prim and proper sister was actually considering sleeping with two men just so she could make a choice?

"I don't think that's a good idea anymore."

"Good. I don't either. But then again, what if it is? What if they both suck in bed?" Sydney's laugh brightened the room and lifted some of Daisy's melancholy.

"You could only hope that they do." She wiggled her eyebrows, but doubted Sydney could see that in the dark.

"What if they're both excellent, both make me see fireworks and witness God? I've considered that. How do you choose then? And what if I don't and always wonder if I made the wrong decision?" The worry was back in Sydney's voice.

"And how do you tell the one you chose that's how you made your decision?" Daisy picked at a piece of tape.

"Why would you?"

"I don't know. Honesty maybe? Would you lie if they straight out asked you?" Daisy hoped Sydney really wasn't considering forgetting her morals just to try to make this decision easier. As if it would.

"Oh. I never thought of that. Not that I'd ever be able to go through with something like that anyway. This whole situation is stupid. It's very rare that I even have one guy interested in me."

"It shouldn't be. You always do that. Sell yourself short. And it sucks. You have a lot to offer, Syd, you just need to figure that out for yourself." Sydney didn't look at her. She only shook her head and faced the window. Daisy figured that conversation was now over. "What are we going to do about the next inspection?"

Sydney sniffed. "No worry. We're in good shape, not that I would care if we weren't. I hired Kay's grandson and some high school kids to spread the stones and paint the activity building. The bathhouses are under construction and the pool contractor starts in the morning."

"How'd you get all that done?"

"Well, when Dr. Keller told me you were going to be fine, I had to do something or go crazy worrying about you.

I've been working from the waiting room all afternoon, the guys have been calling in with updates every few hours."

"How are we affording the pool renovations now? I thought we had a plan for that?" Daisy couldn't quite remember what their last conversation entailed.

"I'll explain that on the way back." Sydney acted like she thought someone was spying on them.

"Secretive, are you? Fine. I'm ready to go." She sat up, amazed at the difference in her head.

"Okay. Let me find the doc and see what he says." Sydney stood as the door swung open.

The dim light kept Daisy from seeing who came in. Her heart pounded, her head echoing the beats with the remnants of the pain. The terror of being held captive filled her and she struggled to remember she was safe.

"Good. You're up. I'm turning the lights on." The doctor's voice.

Daisy relaxed and covered her eyes with her hands, waiting a few moments until the initial sting passed. The ache was still there, but in the background.

"How're you doing now?" Dr. Keller opened her chart.

"Better. Much better. Can I go?" Daisy watched him study her treatments over the past few hours.

"You're good to go. The drug you were given has mostly cleared your system. The headache will linger for a little while yet, but if it becomes severe again or doesn't completely go away by this time tomorrow, call me immediately. You should be nice and hydrated. Continue to drinks lots of fluids and don't forget to eat properly. I'd like to check you in a week, just to make sure you're not suffering any long term effects from your ordeal and to check that bruise." He handed her a list of instructions.

"Thanks, doc." She held up her arm with the IV tubes.

"The nurse will do that. Don't forget, fluids. Be well." He shut the door behind him.

Sydney stood and rummaged around in a bag beside her, producing a pair of jeans and her favorite T-shirt.

"Ah. Clothes. I guess I arrived without any." She wondered who'd carried her out of the bathroom.

"Yep. Naked as the day you were born. Here." She tossed panties at her next. "You should have seen the guys. Graham was beside himself. Tucker was ready to punch Graham. Marshal was yelling at both of them to quit acting like babies."

"Why?" She almost hated to know the answer.

"Because they both wanted to carry you out. Marshal did it and they were both ticked. Marshal was like 'Well, if you want to stand around discussing this like kindergartners go ahead but she needs to get to the hospital.'" Sydney's impression of Marshal made Daisy laugh.

"I have a feeling they're going to drive you crazy when we get back. They were convinced you were knocking on death's door. Marshal had to make Graham stay behind and I had to remind Tucker his crew needed his guidance. They call every half hour or so. I had to turn my phone off when I came in to see you."

Daisy groaned. She was honored and flustered by their attention. And not looking forward to dealing with their questions when she got back.

Finally, after dealing with shocked disapproval from the nurses for taking the IV out herself and listening to another lecture on hydration and proper diet, Daisy buckled into the passenger seat of Sydney's car.

"Are you hungry?" Sydney asked.

"Starved. Can we just grab take out? I don't feel like sitting in a restaurant." The thought of dealing with the unnecessary noise and odors didn't sit well.

"Sure. Any preference?" Sydney signaled at the hospital's entrance as she listed the choices.

They finally settled on one of the two fast food places in town. Daisy wanted to ask Sydney to spill her secrets, but waited until they'd gotten their food and merged onto the main road toward the campground.

"Okay. What aren't you telling me?"

"This has to stay between us . . ." Daisy listened as Sydney told her what was inside the mysterious box found behind the secret compartment.

"Holy shit. Gramps is a freaking genius." Daisy rested against the seat, relief mixing with excitement.

"I just can't help but wonder what kind of hold Violet had over him. He had to have agreed to the stipulations she wanted on the campground or they would have never held up in court. I don't understand why he did it, or why she wants this property so badly." Sydney sounded frustrated and Daisy's guilt load resurfaced.

"It's not like we can come right out and ask either of them. Violet would only lie. What did the journal say?" She was with Sydney. How could Gramps have allowed this?

"I don't know. It's locked in my briefcase. I only glanced at it. What I did read was confusing, as if we would expect anything else. Gramps knew he was dying and almost pleaded for death." Sydney sighed and shook the ice in her cup.

"Where is the box?" She trusted all the guys at the campground, but Gramps had hidden it for a reason.

"Relax. I locked it in the trunk, too. No one knows anything. They know I have the box, but not what's inside, let's tell them the box was filled with old photographs." Sydney cast her a sideways glance.

"Okay, so we take the money out and put pictures in. I have a ton we can use. We'll put the old ones of the campground we're going to frame on top, leave the box on the table in the cabin and see what happens. I hate to say this, but I really think one of our trusted guests is working for the other side." Daisy rubbed her arm, the bruise throbbing in time with her heartbeat.

"I do, too. Who else would know that the plumber was due for a meeting? You still think it's Jace, don't you?" Sydney's voice cracked, but her face showed no signs of distress.

"Not really. He does have the most to gain from us losing the campground, but I don't think he's interested in anything but you. I hate to say this, but what about Kay?"

"What? You can't be serious."

"What if she's working with Violet? She already said she'll always have a soft spot for her. Kay knows a lot of what's going on at the campground, probably way more than we realize. What if Kay sees this as closure between her and Gramps? I can't help but wonder if she is bitter because she didn't end up with him?" Guilt turned Daisy's stomach. Kay had done nothing but support them.

"No. I'd never believe that. She stayed with me until the doctor left. No."

"Good. I don't believe it either. I'm sorry. I just had to put it out there. Who else could it be? Someone from Tucker's crew?"

"Or Marshal's?"

Daisy's stomach burned. "I trust Marshal with my life. He's been my friend for a long time."

"I know. I didn't say Marshal himself. But how well do you know the guys with him?"

"They've been with Marshal since I met him. Except for Graham." Daisy hated how that sounded. How could she be suspicious of Graham?

"I really don't believe the guys are involved. Why would that kid be hired to scare us? If Marshal, or anyone with him, was involved the technique would be more realistic. Jace really seems like he was unaware of Violet's business practices. He's not defending her since he learned what she's done."

Daisy could tell how much suspecting Marshal or Jace hurt Sydney. Was this what Violet wanted? To divide them and watch their progress fall apart from the inside? She organized her thoughts enough to tell Sydney what was going through her head.

"You're too smart. That's probably true. She's planting seeds of distrust. Evil woman." Sydney slapped her hand on the steering wheel.

"Okay. So we present a united front. We'll discuss this with our little crew and tell them what we think." Daisy wondered if the tactic would send Violet off the deep end, but decided she didn't care.

"Tell them everything except for the money." Sydney slowed to make the turn into the campground, glancing her way with a nod.

"Right." Daisy took a deep breath, amazed that just arriving at the campground relaxed her. The stress of her pain and visit to the hospital melted away as Sydney drove the short distance to their cabin.

Coming here had always been this way for her, except for a few times lately. Daisy suspected Sydney had a similar experience because she breathed deeply, a sound of contentment escaping as she relaxed against the seat for a moment before shutting off the ignition.

"Home sweet home." The words were quiet. "I'd thought whatever I felt protected me here had crossed over, but I don't believe that now."

"I would never let that happen unless I had no choice," Sydney said.

Before she could climb out of the passenger seat, the area around the car filled with their guests. Daisy groaned and forced a smile as she accepted Graham's hand.

Figuring questions would give the headache root to return, she tried to prepare herself for the destined barrage. Except it didn't come.

She closed the door and leaned against the car, surveying Graham and Tucker in front of her. Dread settled in her stomach when she realized Graham had a bruise on his cheek and Tucker a swollen lip.

Had they fought? Over her?

They were going to demand she make a decision.

And she still didn't know which one of them was her true destiny.

CHAPTER 17

Sydney watched as Graham and Tucker circled Daisy like a couple of bruised buzzards. Irritation at their childishness made her hurry to Daisy's side.

"You two are ridiculous." She gently took Daisy's arm, careful of the bruise.

"We want to make sure she's okay." Graham stepped forward as Tucker shot him a death glare and matched him step for step.

"She's fine. You see her standing in front of you, don't you? She's tired and has been through a lot. Don't act like jerks. You might be surprised at the outcome. If I were her, I'd tell you both to fuck off. Really, you jerks? Fighting like a couple of twelve-year-olds?" Sydney shook her head as she guided a dazed Daisy between the two men. Or was that little boys?

"We just want to make sure she's okay," Tucker repeated.

Sydney stopped and turned back to face them. "I told you she's fine. If her headache comes back, she'll have to spend a few days in the hospital for testing. I'd hate to be responsible for that happening, wouldn't you?"

She didn't know if her threat was believable. They were giving her a headache though and she didn't have to choose between them. Daisy turned on her with wide eyes and she winked, hoping Daisy understood she lied.

Apparently, she did, because she pressed the fingers of her free hand to her temple. Both guys backed away, glaring at each other.

Once inside, Daisy laughed. "I should be mad. I mean, I am mad. How dare they do that when I'm just coming back from being at the hospital? Jerks."

Daisy didn't sound as angry as Sydney thought she should. "Assholes."

"Sweet assholes though. They fought over me." Daisy sank into a chair with a sigh.

Great. Sydney wanted to scream. Daisy had always had a fairy tale view of life. Most likely, she believed one of the two men would be her knight in shining armor. Sydney's stomach turned. That kind of thinking really made her want to vomit. She hated the idea of a helpless princess just waiting for her sturdy prince to make life better.

From the time she was a child, she'd wanted to scream at the poor, unprepared heroines from those stories. Tell them to get off their butts and make changes on their own. To stand on their own two feet and not to rely on their fashionable prince to make their lives happy and complete.

So, maybe she was a cynic, but Sydney didn't think happily ever after came without both sides of the equation doing their best. Sure, there was room for one to take the slack when the other struggled, but the effort should be a joint one, not a dependent one. Weak women drove her crazy.

Daisy wasn't weak. Not by any means. Was she wrong because she held on to a romantic view of the world?

Maybe Sydney was the one who was wrong. Maybe there was a layer to those fairy tales she'd missed. She'd always wanted to know what happened next. Did the princess ever learn to make her own decisions or did she turn into a shadow, standing behind the prince and losing her identity in the process?

Did the prince think that just because he'd rescued her that he owned the princess? Did the romance lose its luster once life settled into a routine? Did Prince Charming only marry Cinderella because she knew how to run a household?

God. She *was* a pessimist.

Daisy cleared her throat, her expression confused. "What are you thinking about?"

"Believe me. You don't want to know." Sydney smiled, shaking her head at the ridiculous thoughts. No wonder everyone thought she was overly sarcastic. They only thought that because she was.

Of course, she'd never admit that the idea of being rescued by a handsome prince appealed to her on some level. Except she wouldn't be the helpless flower like those other chicks. She'd be capable, working hard to get out of the situation by herself, and wouldn't let him help her unless he could admit she was his equal in all areas.

Maybe she was just plain crazy. Maybe she should call the humane society and take all the stray cats off their hands now, instead of waiting to collect them in increments as was her obvious destiny.

"It's clear out there now." Daisy stood at the window. "Go get the box."

Sydney nodded, grateful for something to take her mind off her bizarre thoughts. She opened the trunk and grabbed the nearly empty bag she'd taken with Daisy's clothes, their jackets, and the box nestled between the garments in an effort to slightly conceal it.

Except maybe they should let anyone watching see that the box would be inside the cabin. She purposefully allowed their jackets to slide off the top and made a big production of putting the box on the hood of the car to retrieve the windbreakers from the ground.

Daisy shook her head from the window and moved to open the door for her. "You're such an actress."

Sydney smiled. "Clever, huh?"

She put the box on the chair, waiting until Daisy closed the curtains to open the top. "We need to put the money in something."

"I have a shoebox," Daisy offered.

"Too obvious. So is a suitcase or under the mattress." Sydney looked around the room for something they could use. The problem was that the cash took up over half the box. They'd have to divide it.

"How much will the pool cost?" Daisy fingered one of the stacks of cash.

Sydney named the estimate and watched as she counted out the amount, plus a third more and placed it in an envelope. She wrote 'pool' on the front and stuck the package in her briefcase. They did the same with the other projects they needed to fund.

"Gee, I thought taking that out would make a great impact on the pile." Daisy seemed concerned. "That's a lot of cash to hide. Should we take it to the bank?"

"I'm not sure. What if Violet has someone there working for her? What if she's alerted to our good fortune?" Sydney chewed her lip.

"We could use a different bank. In a different town. Your name would have to be the only one on the account though. To keep my mother away from the money. Legally, that money is yours. You have a signed, dated, and notarized letter from Gramps to prove it. I say copy all the documents and put the money in the bank and the proof in a safety deposit box. Just not in this town." Daisy paced, her eyes going back to the stacks of cash each time she passed.

"Technically, our privacy should be protected in this town, but I'm not taking the chance that The Vileness doesn't have her ways. Let's save some out for the renovations on the house. We'll put the money in the bank after we do some shopping." Sydney watched Daisy's eyes light up.

"We'll need a list." Daisy grabbed a legal pad from her briefcase.

"What are we going to hide the money in?" Sydney didn't want to think about shopping until they had the money safely out of view. She scanned the room, stopping on the basket of laundry.

"Tomorrow is laundry day," she announced, picking up the basket and taking out the top layer of clothes.

Sydney made two trips to the trunk with her two baskets of dirty clothes and glorious cash, hopefully she was as convincing as her act bringing the box inside. By the time she yawned, they'd placed a bunch of old pictures in the box and left it in the chair and she'd put her locked briefcase in her room.

"What if . . .?" Daisy tried to act brave, but Sydney could see her fear.

"No worries. You're safe. Marshal's filming tonight and we even have an off duty deputy who volunteered to stand guard. He'll be here soon. They won't get close to you."

"Thank you." Daisy rubbed her temples.

"Is the headache back?" Sydney searched her pockets for the instructions the doctor gave her.

"No. It's like an after ache. If that makes sense. It's a little tenderness where the pain was the most severe." Daisy stood, her balance fine, and Sydney relaxed a fraction.

"Wake me up if it comes back. We're not messing around. Don't feel guilty and decide to ride it out. Got me?" Sydney knew she sounded stern and motherly, but her worry for Daisy did that.

Daisy nodded with a smile. "Yes, Mother." She blew her a kiss and disappeared into her bedroom.

Sydney sat at the table, scribbling in the margins of the extensive list they'd made. Now that they had the funds, they could do what they'd talked about when they first found out they would inherit the campground. Each of them would have a private suite, with a bathroom, sitting area and kitchenette. That was so they could work without tripping over each other. Two guest bedrooms would round out the second floor and the kitchen and open living area would make up the first floor. Each would have a private balcony on the second floor as well as a grand deck off the first floor, away from the prying eyes of guests.

Sydney wondered if Gramps would approve of the free way they planned to spend his hard-earned money. A twinge of guilt almost made her wake Daisy so they could scale down their big plans. Except, her gut really told her Gramps wanted them to renovate the house. There was plenty of money to run the campground. More than enough, especially after this legal mess was finished and they received the cash that was tied up with the red tape. Sydney sighed, leaned back in her chair and reached for Gramps' journal.

She read page after page of ghostly encounters and strange happenings. The experiences of guests and Gramps were all different, except for the Native American travelers. It was like some kind of portal was located somewhere on the property.

As she flipped the page, she realized Gramps had thought that, too. He'd even considering finding out how to close it, but changed his mind because he felt that would be messing with destiny. At least that's what she thought he meant. Why was it that the ghost tales were clear and concise, but all of Gramps' personal thoughts were in some kind of obscure language? Sydney could think of several different meanings for each private entry and didn't know what to believe.

A chill touched her ankle. She looked down, seeing nothing. She shifted her legs. The cold followed, moving up one leg and then back down.

Sydney closed her eyes, too tired for spiritual interaction tonight. When she opened them again, she almost fell off the chair. Why she didn't know. She'd seen some pretty freaky things lately. Why would a ghost cat startle her?

Maybe it was the earlier thoughts about becoming a cat lady. Maybe that was truly her destiny.

Figured.

She went to bed. Disgusted with herself and the world.

When Sydney woke, the smell of coffee reminded her of today's plans and she rushed to get ready. Getting that money safely tucked away was priority one. Daisy sat at the table and drummed her fingers.

"What is it? What happened? Is your head okay?"

"I'm fine. My head is fine. Where did that damned cat come from?" Daisy pointed to last night's visitor perched on the windowsill.

The cat cleaned itself as if it could actually be dirty.

"He's mine. I've decided to become a cat lady." Sydney moved to the dead animal, expecting her hand to go right through. Instead, she met with soft fur.

Confused, she picked the cat up, surprised to feel the purr the animal produced. The orange tiger cat nuzzled her hand.

"Umm, he showed up last night, but as a ghost." Maybe she should have left that part out.

"Seriously?" Daisy didn't seem convinced.

"I swear. Of course, I couldn't tell what color he was. He about froze my leg off with his rubbing." Sydney shook her head. The cat on her lap was very real and very warm.

"Is that even possible?" Daisy reached over to stroke the cat's head.

"Beats me." Sydney figured it all had something to do with her negative, cynical view on happily ever after and fairy tales.

This was a warning, like Scrooge's three ghosts.

"Are we keeping him?" Daisy scratched the cat's ears.

"I don't know if he's ours to keep, but we should let him hang out if that's what he wants." The cat seemed to nod in agreement and Sydney wondered what the next ghost to show her how terribly she handled her life would be like.

"He'll need a name." Daisy patted her lap and the cat complied, settling in and purring.

"And then what? We'll get all attached to him and he'll decide to leave. We don't need that kind of pain. If we don't name him, we won't get too used to him." Sydney caught the glare the cat shot her and wondered what she'd said that was so offensive.

"When are you going to learn that life isn't about protecting yourself from pain? It's about going with the flow and living each moment to the fullest. What happens next isn't important. You aren't doing yourself any favors by hiding from life." The cat moved and nuzzled Daisy's cheek as if telling her she was right.

Sydney sighed. "Thomas."

The cat looked bored.

"Fred."

It opened one eye.

"Prince."

That got them a satisfied sounding meow.

Figured. Maybe Sydney should drop this money off and then check herself into some kind of treatment center. She certainly felt like she was cracking up.

Daisy placed Prince on the chair by the window and patted his head. "We'll be back, okay? We'll bring kitty food."

"He's a ghost."

"Is not. He's real and needs to eat." Daisy glared at her.

"The contractor's here. Let's go."

Daisy waved at the cat, and Sydney thought she might be sick.

As they left the circle of cabins, Daisy stopped in front of the only other cabin they might be able to rent when they opened. The windows were clean and the weeds trimmed.

"Graham took it over. He cleaned for an entire day according to Marshal. Said he was sick of the noise and constant activity in the cabin with the rest of the guys." Sydney watched Daisy's reaction.

"Oh. Graham cleaned? I didn't think he knew how." Daisy shook her head.

"He did a good job. I don't think he's as prissy as you believe. Of course, he's the only guy here who looks perfect no matter what he's been doing."

"I was thinking he pretty much fits the 'metrosexual' description. Don't you think? So not my type." Daisy turned her head so Sydney couldn't see her face.

Sydney wasn't sure if she'd done that on purpose. "I think that when the love bug bites, types and what you thought you wanted doesn't matter anymore." Ha. Had she really said that?

Daisy only grunted.

The contractor turned out to be a big, muscled man with long hair tied in a ponytail at the base of his neck. Tattoos lined both arms and a braided goatee completed the picture. Sydney was a little skeptical, but Daisy warmed right up to him.

After listening to him talk about his twin sons and beautiful wife, Sydney couldn't shake the guilt. Had she really been so shallow that she'd judged the man on his appearance?

Allowing Daisy to show the contractor through the house and explain their plans was fine with her. Sydney didn't know if she wanted to cry or throw up. She waited in the living area, lost in her self-pity when they finally came back from the tour.

"Pick out your fixtures, but don't purchase them yet. I'll have an estimate by tomorrow. I love your ideas. This place is going to be great, trust me." He smiled, revealing perfect white teeth and dimples on both cheeks.

Why hadn't Sydney seen how attractive the man was? Had her twisted vision only allowed her to see the tattoos and earrings? She already knew the answer to that. She was as shallow as they came. Daisy tugged her arm and she followed outside. After saying the appropriate goodbyes, Daisy turned on her.

"What the hell is your problem? You turned into a moron in there." The anger didn't quite reach Daisy's eyes but still, Sydney knew her sister wasn't happy. "What? You're going to say we can't hire him because he has a tattoo of a snake?"

Sydney burst into tears.

Daisy dragged her into the house. "What is wrong with you?" Daisy demanded, though her voice was soft and comforting.

"I'm going to turn into a cat lady." Sydney sobbed. When her tears finally subsided, Daisy just stared at her.

"Why do you think you're going to turn into a cat lady?" Daisy asked with patience, as if Sydney was a distraught child.

Sydney sniffed and explained her thoughts from last night. How she'd decided that romance was stupid and not for her, and how she should probably start collecting cats. And then how Prince had shown up and insisted his name be Prince. By the time she finished, Daisy laughed hysterically.

"You're not right. Coincidence. That's all." Daisy hugged her though she continued to laugh.

"What if it's not?" Sydney couldn't help but lose some of her distress.

"Then I'd say that's up for you to decide. Are we going to hire Lloyd?" She stepped back.

"Tattoos and all. I really am a shallow, judgmental person, aren't I?" Sydney asked, the laughter leaving her system.

"Not really. Only sometimes. Lloyd's a great guy. I loved the way he described his wife. It was so sweet. Why can't all men be like him?"

The description had been sweet. Romantic and almost sickening, but Sydney kept that to herself. "You have two gorgeous hunks fist fighting over you. Some would call that sweet."

"They're jackasses and you know it. Let's get out of here." Daisy hooked her arm with Sydney's and closed the door behind them.

Tucker approached the car and asked where they were going. Graham was nowhere in sight.

"We have some errands in town and we need to take care of our laundry." Daisy gave him a bright smile and Sydney watched how he responded.

"Be careful." Tucker stepped back, but didn't seem to want to leave yet.

Marshal approached from Sydney's side and she really didn't want him to see her tear-streaked face. "Let's go. I don't want him to see me like this. You don't even understand. I'd never expect him to."

Daisy hit the gas, spinning the new stones behind them as they left the guys in a cloud of dust. "They're going to be upset with us."

"Why? They're not our guardians." Sydney couldn't help the belligerent tone.

"Actually. They are. They've done more for us than anyone else has, without expectations or demands. We owe them a lot." Daisy's expression dared her to disagree.

Sydney stared out the window for a few minutes before turning back to Daisy. "You're right. Let's do something to show them how much we appreciate them."

Daisy smiled and hit the gas. "Now you're talking. What do we do?"

They discussed different ideas, finally settling on the barbeque they'd talked about when Tucker's crew first came on. Sydney took notes as Daisy spouted off ideas and what they'd need.

"We'd better call and let them know not to make plans for dinner." Sydney reviewed the list.

"I got it." Daisy dialed after parking in front of the bank.

Sydney watched her face as she told Marshal to spread the word about the evening and asked what brand of beer would be the best to bring home. This little party just might do them all some good.

CHAPTER 18

By the time they stopped for lunch, Daisy's concerns about Sydney had eased. What happened to her this morning, Daisy wasn't quite sure. As the plans for their appreciation party solidified, Sydney managed to get herself together and act almost normal.

Getting the money into the bank and the documentation tucked away in a safe deposit box had eased both of their minds. They'd breathed a huge sigh of relief upon leaving the bank.

"Let's forget shopping for anything but the party stuff," Sydney said as she settled into the booth across from her.

"Okay but why?" Daisy didn't want to admit that the shopping trip had lost some of its appeal.

Sydney shook her head. "I don't know. It just doesn't feel right."

"Okay. Good enough." Daisy would be worried if she didn't have the same feelings.

Marshal and Graham looked at them as they drove by, but made no move to approach the car. She'd had enough of being worried over. Sydney constantly questioned her about the status of her head and other aches.

"Where should we set this shindig up?" Sydney asked as they got out of the car. "The barbeque people will be here soon."

Even though they'd decided to cancel their all-out shopping trip, what they did purchase and arrange took far longer than either of them had wanted. Daisy stopped and stared, amazed at the transformation the campground had taken on since her ordeal. The stones were spread, the trees around the campsites trimmed to accommodate larger vehicles and there wasn't a trace of poison ivy. At least in this area, the campground was ready for business.

"Let's set up right here." Daisy motioned to the grass between the cabins. "We can move the vehicles to the empty sites and use the whole area."

Sydney nodded, grabbing an armful of bags from the trunk. "Sounds good to me."

Daisy joined her, picking up a can of cat food that had fallen out of one of the bags. "We'd better feed Prince first. I'll bet he's starving."

"I'll bet he's gone. I told you, he's a ghost." Sydney had that spooked sound again.

Daisy followed her inside. Prince circled Sydney's legs with a loud meow. Sydney stood by the box where the money had been. Nothing seemed touched.

"Okay, but how did he get inside?" Sydney seemed wary of the orange cat, but still pulled the lid off a can of cat food and dumped it onto a paper plate.

Without waiting for her to place the food on the floor, Prince jumped onto the counter and went to work on what must seem like gourmet fare.

"Ghost cats wouldn't be starving. I don't know how he got in. Maybe there's a hole some place. Maybe he followed us in and we didn't see him." She dropped the litter box onto the table, figuring she'd best get the kitty potty set up before they started finding cat presents all over the cabin.

Daisy sniffed. Checking the cabin and couldn't believe they'd stupidly left the animal locked inside all day. When she found nothing, she sat the pan in the bathroom and brought Prince to show him his new throne.

The cat scratched for a moment, then turned to look at her as if to say *Leave me alone now.*

He arrived back in the main room with a meow before plopping down on the chair where she'd left him this morning. Daisy shook her head. She'd never admit it to Sydney, but there was definitely something weird about that cat.

Two hours later, delicious aromas chased Daisy during her inspection of the bathhouses with her constant guards, this time Ron and Eric, who probably wouldn't notice if anyone tried to sneak in and grab her again. The caterers, friends of Kay's, arrived shortly after they'd unloaded the car and went to work.

As she approached the designated party area, the transformation amazed her. The scene was like something out of a magazine and the exact vision of the party she'd always wanted, but had never been able to achieve. Twinkling lights and beautiful potted flowers hung from the trees, torches had been placed at the edges of the space, and there were candles on the tables. She clapped her hands and gave Sydney a thumbs-up. The tension of the past few days eased away and she felt free and alive again. With a smile, she went to get dressed.

Closing the cabin door, she called for Sydney, hearing the water turn off in response. Prince meowed from his upholstered throne, an answering meow catching Daisy off guard.

Two cats?

Sydney emerged from the bathroom, a towel around her head. She had the same expression she'd had this morning when Prince helped choose his name, kind of like she'd seen a ghost.

"Where did this one come from?" Daisy asked, reached out to pet the mostly white calico.

"She was here when I came in to get ready. It's a sign." Sydney stepped back with a wary sigh.

"A sign of what?" Daisy had to admit, the growing cat population concerned her as well.

The calico was clean and appeared in good health. Not once since they moved in had they even seen a stray cat. Now they had two healthy-looking felines magically appearing in their home.

"A sign I'm going to be a cat lady." Sydney eyed the cats with a wary shake of her head. "I should probably buy cat food in bulk. Maybe litter, too."

"You're nuts. So, okay, we seem to be attracting cats. Maybe Violet thinks we're allergic and is sending them to make us sick." Too bad neither of them had ever had an allergy to anything.

"That's good. I hadn't thought about Violet doing this. Kind of lame, don't you think?" Sydney appeared to relax.

"Yeah, but who knows? She might be grasping at straws." Daisy doubted that, but her suggestion had helped Sydney out of whatever freak-out mode she'd been about to embark on.

Sydney tried to accept Daisy's theory, but couldn't. Violet hadn't sent the cats to make them allergic and sick. She supposed Daisy would never make such an outrageous statement if Sydney had hidden her reaction better.

To her, the new cat was a sign.

The only problem was, she didn't know exactly what to do. Did this sign relate to Marshal and Jace, or something else entirely? Was it her attitude toward romance and true love or the way she treated all people?

Sydney didn't think she routinely treated others badly. She always tried to be nice even if she didn't feel like it. So why the cats? And where had they come from? She opened another can of food, placed it on the floor next to the self-watering dish Daisy insisted they buy, and went to get dressed, her emotions as tangled as her wet hair.

When the guys emerged from their cabin, showered, clean-shaven, and handsome, their expressions made the day of planning and shopping worthwhile. Daisy stood on a chair and asked them all to gather around, pulling Sydney up on the chair beside her.

"We just wanted to thank you all for everything. Your kindness touches us more than we can ever say." A tear slipped out of Daisy's eye.

"And we want you to know that you're not obligated to stay on here. We know you each have your own lives and though we appreciate everything, we understand if you have to move on. Just know that we'll never forget what you've done." Sydney meant every word and struggled not to cry.

"Do you really want us to go?" Graham asked, looking up at them in confusion. "Is this what this party is about?"

"No. We didn't want you to think that. We wanted to give you a night off after everything you've done for us. Marshal, Graham and the crew only came to find evidence of ghosts and ended up helping with heavy labor. Tucker and his crew came for training and have helped with stuff not even in their realm. Jace, though Jace is really only here to piss off his Grandmother, Jace has done more in a few days than Sydney and I have managed in two weeks. We wanted to say thank you. That's all." Daisy stepped down, surrounded by laughter and hugs.

Jace offered his hand as Sydney went to step down. "I guess she figured out I'm not here to sabotage the campground?"

His smile melted some of the ice that had taken hold since the cat arrived. "She's pessimistically optimistic."

"Fair enough. Thanks. This is a really great setup. You should have seen how excited everyone was all day." Jace carried the chairs to the fire ring.

"I'm glad. We've all been under a lot of stress. Daisy's

ready to call the funny farm on me." She tried for a laugh, but knew the statement was more true than not.

"I won't ask. Okay. I will. Why?" Jace moved in. Too close.

His scent filled her senses and she swayed toward him, wondering again why it was a bad idea to sleep with him before she decided if she even needed a man in her life. Catching herself and her errant thoughts, she bent to pick up a stick and tossed it in the already burning fire before answering.

"Have you seen any cats around here?"

He appeared confused and she didn't blame him.

"Not a one. Why?"

"Look in our window." She pointed at the two sets of cat eyes watching the party from the front window.

"Where'd they come from?" Jace studied the cats and Sydney felt a surge of relief.

If he had said he didn't see them, she'd be on her way to check herself into that mental health facility.

"We don't know. The orange one arrived this morning. The calico when we came back today. They're clean, healthy, and friendly and seem already acquainted with each other." She watched as Prince licked the calico's back.

They'd have to name her, but the idea sort of freaked her out. What if she wanted to be called "Princess?"

"Weird. They have to be someone's pets. Maybe they were displaced in the storms?" Jace turned back to her.

"Oh. I never thought of that. We should call the humane society and see if anyone is missing them." She stood on her tiptoes and kissed his cheek. "Thanks."

"For what?" His eyes softened. He reached up and placed his hand over where she'd touched her lips to his skin.

"For your logic." She held his hand for a brief moment.

The idea the cats were storm victims made her feel a little better. Not because they were lost from homes that had obviously loved and cared well for them. It meant that no one was trying to send her a sign from above. Maybe she wasn't in danger of being a crazy cat lady after all.

"Who's that?" Sydney asked Daisy as a dark-blue van drove into the area they'd designated for vehicles.

"A surprise." Daisy grinned.

Daisy had hired a local band to come and perform for them. Kay and Ed arrived next, smiling and glad to be invited. Kay had recommended the band and most of the guys in residence had gone into town to hear them play more than once. Sydney was out of the loop, but that was okay. She was about to join the fun.

By the time the caterers cleaned up, packing the food into coolers for them and some for Kay and Ed, Sydney had danced with every guy in camp, except for Marshal and Jace.

She felt guilty. If she danced with one, what would the other think? She was better off steering clear of both.

But then, Kay called Jace over for some legal advice. The next thing she knew she was in Marshal's arms. And she was melting.

"You've been ignoring me," Marshal whispered in her ear, sending awareness through her whole body.

"Not on purpose. There's been a lot going on." Did he know she was conflicted between him and Jace? How could he not?

"I know. I'm glad you and Daisy planned this party. I think we all needed it. And I'm here for as long as you want me." The low timbre of his voice rumbled against her chest, comforting and arousing.

Sydney was pretty sure that last sentence had more to do with her personally than the campground. She couldn't respond. Instead, she looked into his eyes and realized he meant the statement. And she felt like crap.

She wanted him. And she wanted Jace. How could that be?

Weren't you supposed to know when the man of your dreams arrived? More fairy tale bullshit. How she'd held onto that notion after rejecting the happily ever after was beyond her. This wasn't about romance. It was about practicality. Who was best suited for her based on personality, hobbies, and habits, not anything else.

There was no magic chemistry or knowing. Relationships happened and thrived because both people wanted them to. Marshal was her opposite. At least what she used to consider her opposite when she denied her place in the paranormal world. Now that she'd re-opened herself to her gifts, they were well suited for each other.

And so were she and Jace. Both men had all of the qualities she admired and wanted in a man, but which one?

Jace was pretty much how she'd dreamed of her ideal man. Professional, handsome and kind. Everything else was a bonus. And Marshal had each of those qualities as well. They were equals, evenly matched in a confusing playing field.

What the hell was she going to do?

For now she was going to enjoy this dance, the closeness that felt right. The feel of Marshal against her. She kept the melancholy away. She could cry over how to make her decision later. For now, she was going to live in this moment and love every minute.

Daisy watched Sydney dance with Marshal and had to admit she was a little jealous of how easy her sister seemed to be taking the situation. She smiled, talked, and laughed with both men throughout the evening, without looking guilty.

Daisy couldn't seem to find that balance. Of course, Marshal and Jace weren't circling each other like pro wrestlers either. That just pissed her off. She sat in a chair by the fire, putting her back to the lone couple on the makeshift dance floor. Most of Tucker's crew had left, leaving the full-time residents the only guests. And Kay and Ed. Jace spoke with them by their car, goodbyes already said.

Ron and Eric had snuck off shortly after dinner, as was their routine. They'd become more open about their relationship over the past few days, but still couldn't seem to allow anyone else to view the depth of their emotions for each other. Daisy could see and hear Ron's true feelings when he talked about Eric. Despite that she told him how truly happy she was for him, he didn't seem to believe her.

She figured both of their families resisting their relationship had something to do with that. Maybe time would make them see this group didn't judge them and only wanted them to be happy and secure.

Daisy sighed, her thoughts heavy and morose. A hand tapped her shoulder and she looked up to find Tucker's smiling face. His smile faded and she figured her irritation with his behavior must have shown a little too much. What was she supposed to think when he acted all sweet one minute and then did the 'I'm so confused' stuff the next?

He sat down in the chair beside her and put his hand on the arm of her seat. "I'm sorry for acting like a caveman."

She turned to him. "While it's flattering that you're willing to fight for me, I'm not impressed. You and Graham are acting like children and I will not be the meaty bone between you. If you two can't play nice, I'm not talking to either one of you. I can't change who I am, or what I want, because you want me to."

Graham sat on her other side and she stood to leave, not wanting her description about being the meaty bone between them to come true.

"Don't leave. I wanted to apologize, too. Tucker and I talked about how awful we've been acting. And we're really sorry. I'm sorry. We're going to try our best to be nice, to each other and to you." Graham placed his hand exactly as Tucker had done on his side of her chair.

She felt trapped.

"The thing is, I don't know where I want to be. Who I want to be with or where my life is going right now. I like you both, but you know what? Neither of you has given me the chance to really get to know you. Tucker and I have a past, but it's one colored with lies, hurt, and now expectation. Graham, you and I don't see eye to eye on a lot of things. There are issues to be resolved and I simply cannot talk to either of you if you both act like I'm your personal property. I don't want to have to choose and I'm not sure either of you even care what I think." She leaned back in her seat, not sure if her words had come out the way she intended.

"Fair enough." Tucker grabbed her hand. "Then, let's just be friends. If something develops again, we'll take it a day at a time."

Graham grabbed her other hand, as she figured he would. "Sounds like a plan to me."

They both seemed sincere. The way their colognes merged to create a seductive smell didn't help her frame of mind. They were both very attractive and for a minute she closed her eyes and imagined them as one perfect man.

That thinking was dangerous. Soon her one perfect man daydream turned into a full-blown fantasy of two perfect men and one her. Soon she had to move or end up suggesting something she wasn't sure she was comfortable with. Or maybe she was too comfortable with the idea and figured that would be a quick way to lose them both.

With a sigh, she stood. The band started an upbeat chord and she grabbed both of their hands. "Let's dance."

She headed down a path that either lead to despair or the best night she'd ever had. Tucker smiled, gripping her hand tightly. Graham hesitated, and then shrugged, joining them with a broad smile.

Soon, Daisy lost herself in the beat of the music. She'd forgotten how good it felt to dance her troubles away. She grew bolder as her body hummed with exertion and the fantasy that took on a life of its own. When they sandwiched her between them, she thought she might have an orgasm right there on the dance floor, fully clothed and in full view of anyone who happened to be paying attention.

The sensation was amazing and she loved the feel of their hands on her. At first, Graham was timid, barely touching her, but soon grew brave, each pass of his hands more bold. Graham and Tucker seemed to find some kind of common ground, each satisfied to share what she offered. She turned, staying within the circle they'd created around her.

After a while, she forgot who was who, giving them both equal attention with her dancing body. Sweat mixed with their clean-shaven odors and turned into the most sensual scent she'd ever smelled. Graham lost all of his apparent reservations about group dancing and his hands brushed her breasts and stomach while Tucker copied his movements on her back.

The music slowed and both men moved in, her body gloriously crushed, Graham's arousal pressed into her stomach while Tucker's pressed against her back. The whole scene was surreal.

Each seemed to have their side, either by agreement or default, their heads moved to her neck and she almost forgot to breathe as each kissed her flushed skin.

"We could take this somewhere private." Graham licked the sensitive spot under her ear.

"We could. We definitely could." Tucker kissed her neck and moved his hips against her back.

Daisy melted, unable to speak, she could only nod. She briefly glanced around for Sydney, wondering what her sister would say if she realized what was about to happen. Daisy decided she didn't care. Sydney might be offended, but she'd be better off if she encouraged the same type of treatment from the two sniffing around her.

At least they'd be without secrets. Daisy made no promises to either man, and they'd made to promises to her either. Could this be one of those situations where she could have the best of both worlds?

Of course, she might hate herself in the morning.

Somehow she highly doubted that as a shudder worked its way through her overheated and highly aroused body. A hand slipped under the hem of her shirt and unhooked her bra. Excitement and energy surged through her as she went with Graham and Tucker to Graham's cabin.

CHAPTER 19

Sydney blinked, not sure she'd just seen that. Had Daisy actually left the dance floor with *both* Tucker and Graham feeling her up? How much had her sister had to drink anyway?

She noticed the beer bottles floating in the barrel by the fire. By her quick count, Daisy had no more than the few beers Sydney had so she definitely wasn't as trashed as Sydney feared.

Unsure if she should break up the little ménage or create one of her own, she struggled with conflicting emotions. Sure, the fantasy was one of great erotic possibilities. Two guys, one girl. The whole thing would revolve around her pleasure.

Only she didn't think things would be that easy in the real world. As much as the idea of having two men at her sexual beck and call made her hot, she didn't believe she'd ever be able to go that far.

Would Daisy?

Sydney shook her head. Daisy would if she wanted to and that's all there was to it. That was Daisy's decision to make, and Sydney would stay out of it, even though she knew she'd have to pick up the pieces when the whole affair came crashing around her. Eventually, the great sex would end and Daisy's self-respect might go with it.

The dancing part looked like fun. Too bad she didn't have the guts to suggest even that. Didn't matter anyway since the band was loading the gear into their van. She hadn't even danced with Jace and that upset her. For Sydney, the night was over. She might as well go back to her cabin, feed her cats, and get used to the idea that all her nights would end this way.

Marshal was busy setting up equipment near the pond. He hadn't asked her to join him tonight and that bugged her a little. From the looks of things, he'd end up solo since Ron and Eric hadn't reappeared and Dave had a family emergency half way through the evening.

Jace hadn't come back after seeing Kay and Ed off. She'd heard a cell phone ring and watched as he disappeared into his camper. The lights still burned, but no movement shadowed through the windows. With a sigh, she climbed the steps to the cabin, tired, disappointed and worried for Daisy's mental well-being. Sure, and a little jealous, too.

Trying not to think about it, she opened the door to the meows of her future.

After feeding the cats, she sat at the table, going through the mail that had arrived during their trip into town. Some personal banking information, a postcard from their parents' cruise. Too bad they'd arrived home yesterday and had already relayed the information written on the back of the card. Since nothing seemed important, she tossed the envelopes in the basket with the rest of the unread mail. Eventually, she and Daisy would have to go through the stack, mostly advertisements and stuff related to the campground.

She tried to concentrate on tomorrow's plans, but that didn't take her mind off worrying about Daisy and wondering what kind of mental backlash came from sleeping with two men at once. Not that they'd do much sleeping. Sydney snorted, covering her mouth even though the cats didn't seem to mind her outburst.

The same cold sensation wrapped around her legs. She moved her sore feet to the chair closest to her. Still the chill seemed to continue over the backs of her legs. She looked down, knowing she'd see nothing and was correct.

What was the deal? Did they have ghost cats as well as an infestation of real cats? She'd been glad to see their numbers hadn't further multiplied while they'd been at the party. Two cats were more than enough.

A soft knock sounded at the door. Sydney paused, not sure who would be visiting this late. She peered through the window and saw Jace.

She opened the door, trying to act unsurprised and casual and knowing she came off as a bundle of nerves. Jace stepped inside, his attention on the new houseguests.

"So these are your new friends?" He reached out and scratched each cat in turn.

"Lazy beggars." She tried to sound stern, but her tone definitely wasn't.

"Names?" The calico seemed especially interested and Sydney couldn't help the sting of jealousy. Jealous of a cat?

She was going mental.

"Prince and we haven't gotten around to naming the female yet. She only just arrived."

"And she seems completely at home. I think you should call her Princess." The cat meowed and Sydney refused to think it was for any other reason than his vigorous scratching.

"Sure. That was my thought, too."

He stopped scratching and faced her at her sarcastic tone. "You don't like cats?"

"I do. I'm just . . ." Was she really going to tell him that she was afraid she'd end up as a pathetic cat collector?

"Just what?" He stood only inches from her now. His heat and scent filling her senses.

"Nothing. I like cats. Okay?" She swayed toward him.

He caught a section of her hair in his fingers. The next thing she knew she was closer to him than she'd ever been and didn't want to move away.

"I'm sorry I didn't get to dance with you. There was a

problem at the office I had to diffuse." His words were soft, his breath caressing her cheek.

"You're on vacation." She tried to remember what he'd said.

"Yeah. That's the problem with being the boss. You get to take care of everything and everyone." His lips were now inches from hers, and she swallowed.

"Doesn't it make you crazy?"

"Doesn't it make *you* crazy?" He barely brushed her mouth and she swayed closer. "You make me crazy. I've been watching you all evening. Wanting you."

Sydney lost her train of thought. She lost her ability to think. The only thing she wanted was to feel him, as close to her as possible.

He groaned. Or was that her? She had a brief moment of relief that she'd turned the main lights off before he knocked on her door. After that, she doubted she even knew her own name.

His kiss was tender, hot, and perfect, and she melted against him, loving the feel of his hands on her. He moved against her and it took several seconds until she realized they danced.

Moving his hands down her sides, Jace cupped her bottom, bringing her even closer. They moved in a circle, meshing as if they'd done this dance a thousand times.

Her back now against the wall, the seductive movement of the dance slowed as their hands took up the rhythm. Jace seemed to touch her everywhere, not lingering too long in the places she wanted him the most.

Sydney was drowning and didn't care. Her reservations vanished as soon as Jace took her into his arms. If they could move like this, dance like this, without music she could only imagine what making love would be like.

Was she about to find out?

She stopped. As much as she wanted to, her heart was torn. Being in Jace's arms felt right, but then she'd felt the same way when Marshal held her. Jace rested his forehead against hers. She reached up and touched his face, feeling the slight stubble on his cheek.

"It's not you." That hadn't come out right.

"I see." Jace released her waist.

Before he stepped away, she grabbed the front of his shirt. "That didn't come out right. I'm not ready for this. There's so much going on right now. I don't even know what I'm doing anymore."

He stayed, his expression unreadable and guilt filled her.

"It's okay. I'm sorry. I didn't come here with the intention of seducing you. I just wanted to talk since I ended up missing most of the party."

"Don't be sorry. I'm the one who's sorry. I had this whole thought . . . Never mind. Believe me when I say this isn't about you. It's about me and my stupid morals. I just can't, not like this, not without more. I'm not a one-night stand kind of girl." She rested her head on his chest.

"Don't tell me you're still a virgin?" There was no humor or shock in his voice.

"I'm not, but I don't have a lot of experience either." She met his eyes, wishing he understood what she tried to say.

"What makes you think we would be just having sex? You don't see a future between us?" He backed away and that stung.

"I don't know what I see in the future, except a lot of work and stress with this campground. I don't know what I want and I don't want to have to decide." She watched him rub Prince's chin. How bad had she screwed this up?

"You're talking about Marshal?" He didn't turn away from the cat.

"Not necessarily." She laughed, a hoarse, sarcastic sound. "I don't know what to do, how to feel, what to think."

He turned, understanding and compassion softening his words. "You're saying is you feel pressure from both of us."

"I've never had so much attention before. But, yeah. I am. My main focus has to be the campground and making the grand opening without letting your grandmother win."

"Where does that leave us?" She hated the sad finality of his words.

"The same place we've been. If you're still willing to help us then working toward the same goal. If you're not, then I don't know." She tried to smile but was sure the action failed.

"Hey, I'm not going anywhere. I promised you I'd help make up for what Grandmother is trying to do. Besides, I haven't had this much fun in ages. And before you ask, that ghost thing you do doesn't scare me one bit. Gramps could do it, too. I don't think he knew I saw him." This time his smile was genuine.

Sydney nodded, relieved. And sad. "I really am sorry, Jace. You had me. My inner voice just wouldn't be quiet." She touched his arm expecting him to shake her off.

He surprised her by leaning over and kissing her tenderly. "No apologies. If it's meant to be, those voices will let you know. Now isn't the time. Doesn't mean I'm going to stop trying to convince you of what a great guy I am."

He kissed her again, patted both cats and went to the door. "Thanks for the party. The food was great, everything was."

"You're welcome. Our pleasure." Worry over Daisy popped in and must have shown on her face.

"What?" He leaned against the doorframe and she had to remind herself that she'd made the right decision.

"Daisy. She went off with Graham and Tucker." She looked out the window, wondering again if she should intervene.

"What do you mean?"

She figured he must not have witnessed their little sexy dance party. "Well, they were dancing . . ." She explained the scenario, letting him fill in the blanks on his own.

"Oh. She's an adult, Sydney. Capable of making her own decisions. You said yourself she wasn't drunk, so she went with them of her own free will." He didn't sound appalled by the concept and Sydney didn't know what to think of that.

"I know. I just worry that she's going to beat herself up in the morning. Or get hurt, or too far into something she doesn't want to be in." And she was the slightest bit jealous of the freedom Daisy seemed to have. And because, after tonight, Daisy's decision would probably be an easy one.

Jace raised his eyebrows but, thankfully, didn't twist her words into sexual innuendo. "All you can do is be here for her if it all comes crashing down on her. Maybe she is making a mistake, but it's her mistake to make."

"You're right. I know you are, but that doesn't stop me from worrying."

"I know. It's your job to worry. Just remember you don't have to take on everyone's problems. I see you doing that and it's not healthy." He reached over and grabbed her hand.

"I can't seem to help it." She had to admit, talking to him like this seemed to put things into perspective. It was nice to kind of share her load.

"That's what makes you so darned cute." He kissed her nose. "It's useless, I know, but don't worry about her. She's a smart gal and knows what she's doing. I'll see you in the morning."

She leaned in, giving him a hug that hopefully conveyed some of the things she hadn't been able to explain. Being with him like this had only confused her more. He actually listened to her and respected her opinion.

The problem was, so did Marshal. Both were equal, and Sydney had no idea how to make a decision. Her head hurt and so did her heart. How could she have managed to put herself in this position? Trapped between two attractive, nice, romantic, and perfect men?

As tired as she felt, she knew she wouldn't be able to settle in any time soon. For one, there was Daisy to worry about. She might not even come back tonight. Sydney had no idea how long something like Daisy's little ménage would take. She would hope at least hours.

Shaking her head, she stepped over a cat, wondering again where they came from. Tomorrow she'd call the local shelter to see if anyone had reported missing pets.

She'd never had a cat. But she wasn't sure she wanted to give them up now. The pair made the cabin feel like a home. With every chore she could think of done. She went to bed. Maybe she'd wake up with a brand new perspective.

As if.

She locked the door and went to her room. If Daisy wasn't back by now she wouldn't return tonight. The guys would keep her safe, no matter what happened.

CHAPTER 20

Sydney rolled over, feeling a warm body protest her movement. Make that two warm bodies. Both cats were curled around her, one at her side and the other at the top of her head. She stretched, further displacing them and was subjected to threatening meows.

She was still tired. Now that she'd opened her eyes and thought about Daisy, she wouldn't sleep any more. Besides, she had a long list of things to take care of today. If she was lucky, she'd get them all done. The cats followed as she made her way to the kitchen, meowing and trying to rub against her legs. An echoing meow sounded from the main room and Sydney stopped in her tracks.

A third cat. This one white, sat in the middle of the table. The beast seemed a little haughty and impatient, maybe because she'd taken so long to become aware of its presence.

"Well, hello." She reached out, letting the cat come the remaining distance to her hand. Scratching the soft head, she picked up the cat and sat her on the chair. "Another girl. What are you two, his harem?"

The white cat meowed and jumped back onto the table.

"I don't know if that's going to work. See, people eat there. I'm not real sure I want your cat butt where I put my food." She shooed her off the table. A waste of time.

Soon she'd have cats everywhere. Her home would belong to the four-legged purr boxes. Everything she owned would be subjected to claws, fur, and hairballs. She might as well get used to it.

She filled the dish with a sigh, and then grabbed the coffee can. "You already have me trained. I'm feeding you before my caffeine needs."

"You're already turning into that cat lady. I didn't think I'd ever hear you actually talk to cats." Daisy's voice startled her and she jumped, sending coffee grounds all over the counter.

"I didn't think you were home." That came out a little more accusing than she'd meant.

"I know. You locked me out. I had to crawl through the window. I felt like I was back at home, sneaking out because Mom grounded me." Daisy laughed and Sydney compulsively hugged her.

"You okay?"

"Just peachy." Daisy sighed and sat down. "Hey. Where did this one come from?"

The white cat had jumped onto Daisy's lap and almost glared at Sydney.

"She was here when I woke up. I wonder if she came in with you when you crawled in the window." That made sense.

"Doubt it, but maybe. Now we have to name two more cats." The white cat rubbed its head against her chin.

"I believe our first girl is to be called Princess." Sydney pointed and the cat meowed.

"How'd you come up with that? I think she likes it."

"Actually Jace. She meowed exactly the same way when he said the name."

"Jace was here? When?" Daisy stared at her.

"Last night when you were out. What are we going to call the white one?" Hopefully that changed the subject, at least for now. She was dying to ask Daisy for details, but couldn't bring herself to just yet.

"Snow White." Daisy grinned and the cat meowed.

"Fine then. Next we'll have Cinderella." Sydney shook her head.

"I think we'll have the dwarves next. Miss Snow White has been fooling around. She's got kittens in there." Daisy had her hand on the cat's belly. "They're moving."

"Great. Dwarfs. Perfect. I'm a cat lady already."

"So. What happened with Jace?" Daisy pointed at the chair across from her and Sydney sat.

"Nothing to tell. Except he's a great dancer and kisses like a dream." She smiled and Daisy narrowed her eyes.

"And? Did you?"

"No. And it really makes me mad. He was so understanding. He didn't get mad or try to convince me. Jace being a jerk would make this whole decision much easier."

"Ah. Sorry to hear that. You really didn't think he'd get all mad did you? I didn't think he was that kind of guy. Of course, you never do know. Sometimes the ones that seem really great are the biggest assholes and think no means yes." Daisy rambled a minute before she caught herself.

"What happened?" Sydney leaned forward, her worry tripled. Why else would she have said that?

Daisy shook her head. "Nothing."

"What do you mean nothing? I saw the way the three of you left. Things were happening right then." She tried to keep her voice neutral.

"That's true. That was the hottest dancing. I knew Tucker had those kinds of moves, but had my doubts about Graham. He didn't even want to dance. He warmed up pretty quick." She fanned herself and leaned back in the chair.

"I saw that. You had them right where you wanted them. Or where they wanted you. The whole thing seemed mutual." And yeah, she was still jealous, just a little.

"Definitely. And then Graham suggested we take our dance party somewhere private. Seemed like a good idea. I knew what I was doing and didn't care. I mean, both of them? At the same time? Isn't that a fantasy? Well, at least a lot of women's anyway. Whether they admit it or not, the idea of having two hot guys attend your every need is pretty damn hot. Right?" Daisy talked a little too fast.

"Okay. I'll agree with you on that. So did it live up to your expectations?" Sydney wasn't sure she wanted to know.

Daisy shrugged. "I don't know the answer to that one. We went to Graham's cabin. It was incredible. The things they said, the feel of their hands . . . well, you get the picture. Someone took off my shirt and things were progressing. I didn't have time to think about what was going on."

"You said 'were'. What happened?" Sydney relaxed a bit. Right now it didn't seem like she'd have to help Daisy pick up any emotional baggage.

"I don't know. I just couldn't. It was like I suddenly heard this voice in my head that said I was about to make a huge mistake. That if we went through with it, I'd lose them both. I didn't want to do that because what if one of them is truly meant for me? That's weird I know." Daisy shook her head.

"Not as weird as you think. That's pretty much the same reason I put the brakes on Jace last night. Almost like so much hinged on that decision and even if he was the one for me, going any farther would totally impact the outcome of whatever is happening." Sydney sighed as Daisy nodded vigorously.

"Exactly. And they were both totally cool about the whole thing. We played cards for a while. Graham and Tucker actually managed to speak civilly to each other and we had a great time." Daisy jumped up and grabbed two cups as the coffee maker finally stopped gurgling.

"Weird night. I have to admit, I was a little jealous. I doubt I'd ever be bold enough, but hell, it's nice to think about." Sydney accepted the steaming cup with a smile.

"I think it's better as a fantasy. I've had one other experience with two guys. Things went a little farther. I realized a threesome wasn't for me when the guys seemed more into each other. Kind of killed the passion, you know?"

"I would imagine. That's what most guys want, though. Two girls who are just as into each other so they can watch. At least that's what I hear."

"I guess that's the difference. I have no desire to watch two guys get it on and I really have no interest in two girls and a guy. Not that there's anything wrong with that. I just want it to be all about me."

"I'm jealous. I don't have nearly as much experience." Sydney didn't realize how much she'd needed to tell her sister that.

"I don't have as much as you think I do. Tucker and I didn't make love until we'd been dating for about six weeks. So, regardless of what you might think, I'm not a slutty girl."

"I have never thought that. Really. You're more open. I don't know half of the stuff you know. I didn't mean I thought you'd actually done them." Sydney hoped she believed her.

"I know. It's my own fault if you did with the way I talk and the suggestions I make. I should probably try to tone that down a little."

"No. I don't want you to. The way you talk makes me laugh, makes me think, and breaks up the monotony. Like when you suggested what our bald electrician could do with his head. That's something I would have never thought of. It's a pretty hot scenario." Sydney still thought so.

Daisy jumped up and came around the table to hug her. "Thanks. I was feeling like a jerk."

"I'm really getting tired of thinking about this, you know?" Sydney patted her arm.

"I do. Just when I think I have it all figured out those two surprise and confuse me even more." Daisy moved back to her seat and dropped down with a sigh.

"Exactly. Both Marshal and Jace suit me perfectly. I can see myself with either of them. I'm going crazy." Sydney set her cup down a little harder than necessary.

"You and me both. Let's forget about them and try to open early. I've been thinking about what we still need to do and we could be ready for the weekend before Memorial Day if we hustle." Daisy leaned back and grabbed a notepad from her briefcase.

"Our stipulations say nothing about opening early, just that we have to open by June first. Let's check with Al to be sure." Sydney leaned forward.

"What about the ghosts? Are we going to advertise them or wait?" Daisy numbered the page, putting advertising at the top and website reservations second.

"Let's talk to Marshal. He's been doing a lot of recording and we haven't heard much of what he's caught on tape. If he's not going to say the place is haunted I don't want to advertise it. I'm not sure I do anyway. What if it scares families away?"

"What if we don't tell people and they end up having an experience that makes them never want to come back? If they know there's a possibility, they'll know what they're getting into."

"True. Okay, write it down. Maybe we'll know which areas have a higher level of activity and we can designate campsites accordingly." Sydney watched Daisy write as she laughed and shook her head.

"What's so funny?"

"You are. When we first moved in here you said didn't believe in ghosts. Now you're talking about them like an expert. It's just amazing."

"Yeah, well. Nothing like having dead people show up in your bedroom to change your mind. God, our lives have turned out weird. Seriously, we have a box of money, ghosts, kidnappings, and sexy, hot men at our beck and call, more men than we need. My old life was very dull compared to this."

"I heard that one. I think the kidnapping stuff, and my birth mother, is a little too much to deal with though." Daisy's demeanor changed when she mentioned Nadine.

"I know. I agree. Maybe she's gone." Sydney doubted that.

"Yeah. Okay. She left without a dime from me." Daisy didn't appear to be as angry as she sounded.

"You're not planning to give her money, are you? She'll never quit coming back." Sydney couldn't stop her from giving her mother money, but she hoped she'd at least listen to reason.

"I don't want to, but I don't want her hanging out here either. If I give her a couple of bucks, she'll go away." Daisy didn't seem like she believed that would solve the problem anymore than Sydney did.

"Yeah, until she needs a fix. She'll drain you in no time and you know it."

"I know. I'm going to have to tell her straight out I don't want her in my life unless she's clean. After she dries out, we'll take it from there. I did realize that she did me a huge favor by dumping me with you. Otherwise, who knows how I would have turned out?" Daisy smiled, tears shimmering in her eyes.

"You're right. I understand. At least I think I do." Sydney reached out and patted her hand.

A knock sounded on the door and Sydney got up to answer, not expecting the sheriff this early.

"Ladies." He didn't smile as took off his hat and stepped into the cabin. "I have some news."

"From the look on your face, I don't think it's good." Sydney tried for a laugh, but failed miserably.

"Kay and Ed were in a car accident on their way home last night."

Daisy shrieked, and Sydney dropped to a chair. "Are they okay?"

"In County General. Kay is in stable condition. She has a few fractures and a goodly amount of stitches. Ed is in critical care. They don't expect him to make it through another night."

"Oh my God. What happened?" Daisy wiped at the tears streaming down her face. "Neither one of them even had a drink while they were here."

"Run off the overpass by a van and flipped onto the highway below." The sheriff shifted his stance, and Sydney had a feeling there was more bad news on the way.

"And?" She wished he'd just get on with it. Dishing out bad news in increments was never a good idea.

"We're fairly certain Nadine was involved. Kay said the driver was male. The female passenger fit Nadine's description."

"Shit. I won't post bail. When you pick her up tell her I said to leave me alone. She can sit in jail and rot for all I care." Daisy stood, shoving the chair back with a force that made it topple. She had her hand on the doorknob when the sheriff told her to stay put.

"I'm not asking you to bail her out, but you should know she's going to be behind bars for a long time. Not only is she wanted for questioning for the accident, but she'll be charged with your kidnapping." The sheriff held his hand up when Daisy swore loud enough to disturb the cats. "She's already been arrested. She arranged the kidnapping. One of her boy toys squealed when we picked him up for attempting to purchase illegal drugs from an undercover officer. He said if you wouldn't give her the money willingly, then she'd take you. She planned to hook you on the same stuff she's on. Said she figured it would be easier to get money from you if you needed a fix, too." The sheriff moved quickly, catching Daisy before Sydney had a chance to move from her seat.

"Come on, girl. You're going to be just fine." He sat her in the cushioned chair, patted her hand and stepped back.

"What kind of a monster is she?" Daisy spoke quietly.

"The worst kind. We've arrested all her cohorts. They're singing now. She planned to use you as a source of income when your inheritance ran out. Prostitution, drug running, anything to keep you all in supply. Not pretty, but you're safe."

Daisy collapsed into Sydney's arms, her sobs deep and soul rendering. Sydney couldn't help but cry with her. To think Daisy had come to some kind of peace with the way Nadine dumped and forgot her.

Anger surged as Sydney released Daisy, handed her a wad of tissues and faced the sheriff. "Daisy's been through enough because of Nadine. I don't want that woman even attempting to contact her. Ever."

"I understand. You may want to retain legal services to counsel you through this. You'll most likely have to appear in court when she faces the kidnapping charges." The sheriff turned to leave, his expression revealing his compassion.

"What about the other threats? We know they didn't all come from Nadine." Sydney's brain reeled with a million questions. "Is there a chance Violet put this kidnapping idea into her head, or paid her to do it?"

"I don't know yet. Time will tell. Call me if you have any questions. I'll be in touch." He put his hat back on and let himself out.

Daisy stared straight ahead, her expression as blank as her eyes.

"Come on, honey. Everything is going to be okay. You'll see." Sydney hugged her, but Daisy didn't respond. "Get mad. Cry. Do something. Don't sit here and let her do this to you."

Still, Daisy didn't move. Sydney wasn't sure what to do. The reaction was the last thing she'd expect from Daisy, but clearly, her sister had taken all she could handle from the woman who was supposed to love her and protect her.

The door opened and Tucker, Graham, and Marshal rushed in, each with a concerned expression that grew after seeing Daisy's passive face.

"We're going to see Kay. Do you want to come?" Marshal stood in front of Sydney, blocking her view of Daisy.

"I don't know what to do to help her." She told him what the sheriff said and didn't realize she was crying until Marshal wiped the tears from her cheek. At that tender gesture, the floodgates opened. She sobbed, resting her head against his shirt and allowing him to comfort her.

"She's going to be okay. She needs to process everything. Even though Nadine betrayed her from birth, this is a little much to take in." Marshal rocked her and she tried to relax.

"I'm okay." Daisy's voice cut through the tension hanging in the room. "I am. Let's go see Kay."

She stood, swayed a little and ended up in Graham's arms. He held her for a minute before she moved away. "I need to get dressed."

Her voice sounded wooden and her movements were jerky. Sydney couldn't help the sobs, her sister was hurting and there was nothing she could do for her right now. Sydney had always been the one with the answers, the cure and a way to make things better. This time she didn't know what to do.

Or did she?

She stepped out of Marshal's arms and grabbed her cell phone off the table. Stepping onto the porch, she dialed her parents' number and prayed her mom was home. When she answered, it took Sydney a few seconds to compose herself enough to explain what happened. When she finished, she realized her mom and dad were both on the line.

"We'll be there this afternoon. Don't worry," her dad soothed.

"But your allergies, how are you going to manage here?"

"I don't care. I need to be there for you girls. Don't worry about me. Just hang on to Daisy until we get there. I promise everything is going to be okay." She believed him and hung up, hoping she'd done the right thing.

CHAPTER 21

Daisy felt nothing.

She heard the worry and pain in Sydney's voice. The emotion or words to let her know she was okay wouldn't come. Daisy didn't even know if she was okay.

All hope for a relationship once Nadine got clean was gone. Nadine threatening Sydney and demanding money from Daisy had hurt enough. But to be behind a kidnapping scheme that had her enslaved and drugged? And to decide if Daisy wouldn't give her the money she'd find a way to make her produce income, well, that was unforgivable. And to hurt Ed and Kay?

Hell, everything about Nadine was unforgivable.

What if she turned out like her?

Her actions of last night made her wonder if she really wasn't any better than her disgusting birth mother. She'd almost slept with two guys at once, just for the hell of it, and not for the first time. What did that say about her character?

Anger surfaced through the nothingness, bubbling up and then erupting as she smashed her fist into the wall. Daisy dressed, eager to make sure Kay was okay and to apologize for bringing this mess to the sweet couple. Kay had already been more like a mother to her than Nadine ever had been. Nadine had tried to take that away, just like she'd denied Daisy her love as a child.

Damn her.

She slammed her door, realizing she'd shocked everyone in the room with the noise.

"Good. You're mad. Now stay that way." Graham didn't come to her. He probably figured she'd slug him. Smart man.

"You're damn right I'm mad. How dare she?" She picked up a coffee cup, but set it down. Daisy wanted to throw something. She wanted to scream and cry.

But she didn't.

Instead, she tried to shake off the emotions and go back to feeling numb. She didn't want to care about anything right now. Maybe she should grab the bottle of whiskey from the cupboard and finish it off. Maybe that would help. She went to the cupboard and stopped before reaching for the handle. That had probably been the stupidest thought she'd ever had. She was stronger than Nadine.

She was stronger and she'd prove it.

"Let's go see Kay." She slammed the door behind her for good measure.

No one spoke on the way to the hospital. Sydney glanced into the backseat every once in a while, but never asked how she was doing. Probably a good thing. Daisy didn't know that her answer would be very nice.

Tucker and Jace had already left. They planned to stop by the sheriff's office before the hospital. Daisy wasn't sure she wanted to hear what they had to say when they arrived. She didn't want to know anything her mother said.

Kay smiled as they entered her room, the action not reaching her eyes. "I'm okay. Don't fret."

Sydney went over to hug her, but Daisy leaned against the wall. This was her fault. She'd brought this on these wonderful people. Now Kay would likely face the rest of her years alone because of Nadine's selfishness.

"They won't tell me anything about Ed. Do you think

you could find out?" Kay pleaded with Graham, who nodded and left the room.

Daisy didn't think any news he found out would be good. She didn't know what they'd told Kay, so kept her mouth shut and tried to contain the tears that threatened.

"Come here, girl." Kay pointed at her and patted the bed.

Daisy hesitated. Kay gave Marshal and Sydney a look that brooked no arguments. Without a word, they closed the door behind them, leaving Daisy alone with Kay.

"Listen. You had nothing to do with this. I can see you're feeling responsible. Nadine is trash. She always was. Always will be. You're the best thing she ever did. And like it or not, she loved you. The drugs and lifestyle made her forget. All she sees is her next fix and you as a means to achieve that. None of this is your fault."

Daisy sat on the bed and burst into tears. "It *is* my fault. If I would have just given her some money, maybe she would have left and none of this would have happened."

"You did the right thing. That would have only made her more determined to drain your bank accounts and the end result would have probably been the same. The loss in all of this is Nadine's. She doesn't know what a great daughter she gave birth to. I can only pray one day she dries up enough to realize what she's done to you." Kay hugged her with her un-bandaged arm.

Daisy couldn't speak. She couldn't fathom how this woman could be so understanding after all that had happened. What if Ed died? Would Kay change her mind about Daisy's involvement in this whole mess?

Graham stuck his head in the door, his expression cautious. Daisy was certain the news was not good. She stayed at the edge of Kay's bed, determined to comfort her even if Kay changed her mind about how she felt.

"Well?" Kay sounded impatient.

"He's resting." Graham stayed at the foot of the bed.

"Listen to me. They won't tell me anything and they won't let me see him. I know he had to be resuscitated at the scene. Now, damn it, tell me." Kay gripped Daisy's hand with a force Daisy didn't think possible.

"He's in critical condition. His prognosis isn't good. I couldn't get them to tell me anything. I had to charm one of the nurses into telling me that much." Graham didn't look at either one of them.

Daisy knew she should feel jealous, but she wasn't.

"Thank you. Now help me get up so I can see him." Kay sat up and moved her legs to the opposite side of the bed.

There was no way they would talk her out of seeing Ed. Not that Daisy would dream of doing so. She deserved to spend what little time he had left at his side. Grabbing a second hospital gown from the bedside table, she urged Kay to put her arms in it backward and tied the front.

"You should probably use this." Graham pushed a wheelchair into the room.

"No way." Kay took a step and faltered.

"Yes way. Sit." Daisy threw the pillow from the bed on the seat and pointed.

After Kay positioned herself, Daisy covered her legs with the blanket and moved the IV bag to the pole attached to the chair.

"You two better go. I don't want you getting in trouble for my stubbornness." Kay moved the wheelchair forward but Daisy didn't let go of the handles.

"Nope. Lead the way Graham." For the first time since finding out what happened, Daisy actually felt more than anger and guilt. If Kay wanted to see her husband, Daisy would do whatever she could to make it happen.

A stern-faced nurse stopped them outside of Ed's door. "No visitors."

"Like hell. That man is my husband and I will see him."

"You're not supposed to be here. Go back to your room."

The nurse blocked the door as Kay stood, the blanket falling to the floor.

"I will see him. You can't stop me." Kay took a shaky step forward.

"I can and I will."

Daisy stepped from behind the chair. "Excuse me. Can I speak with you for a moment?"

She moved to the other side of the hall and waited for the nurse, hoping Graham would take Kay inside while she had her occupied.

"I can't let her in. You have to understand that. Please talk to her and explain." The nurse at least had some compassion in her voice.

"Do you know they kept his condition from her? She was in the accident with him. She knew he had to be resuscitated. You'd deny her spending his last moments with him? That's cruel." Daisy used a polite, but firm tone.

"I have to follow the rules." The woman straightened and Daisy figured security now stood behind her.

"Who's her doctor?"

"I am."

Daisy turned to see the same doctor who'd cared for her after the kidnapping. He didn't appear very pleasant right now, even if he did seem surprised to see her.

"She has every right to see her husband." Daisy ignored the nurse as she turned to face him fully.

"I don't care that she listed you and your sister as her next of kin and decision makers, Kay is a heart attack waiting to happen. I'm afraid the shock of seeing him will be too much." At least he sounded like he cared.

"So letting her sit alone in her room, worrying and being denied information about the man she loves is any better for her? Give me a break."

"It's my choice to make. Ed's in rough shape. Seeing him like that might kill her."

Daisy looked over his shoulder. Kay sat on the bed beside Ed, his hand in hers. "It hasn't yet."

He turned, started to move toward the room, and stopped with a sigh. "Not a good idea."

"Are you married?" Daisy asked, hoping he didn't take her question as a come on.

"No. Why?"

"Because when you love someone as much as those two do, you have to realize that they heal better when together. They're connected by more than just years and a wedding band. Ed might not improve and he might not live, but at least they'll both have some peace and comfort. She'll let him know if it's time for him to go and he won't leave her unless she tells him to." Daisy swallowed to keep the tears away.

"Okay," he said with a sigh. "She can stay. I'll have her transferred here until she's released. If my boss has anything to say about this, I'm sending her to you so you can give her the same speech you just gave me." He motioned to the nurse.

Daisy opened the door, the smell of impending death heavy.

Kay smiled. "Thank you."

The sadness on her face broke Daisy's heart. It seemed she'd been right in Ed needing Kay to give him permission to go and Daisy hated that.

Tubes of varying sizes were attached to him everywhere. Monitors, IVs, and breathing equipment filled the room and the enormity of the damage her mother caused hit her hard. She breathed deep, not wanting to lose her composure here when Kay needed every ounce of strength for Ed.

"He's okay." Kay wiped the tears from her eyes. "He's going to be fine."

Daisy watched as Ed squeezed his wife's hand. A sense of peace filled her. Maybe he would live.

The door opened and the same argumentative nurse stepped in. "I apologize for my rudeness. His doctor gave permission for you to stay. I'll get your bed set up in a minute."

"Thank you. He's going to be okay. I think." Kay moved back to let the woman check the papers shooting from the machines.

The nurse shook her head and held up a strip of paper. "I think you might be right. His blood pressure has stabilized."

"You two do need to go. I've broken enough rules for one day."

Kay beamed and moved to hug her before she left. "Thank you. If it wasn't for you and whatever you said to the doctor, Ed would be gone by now."

Daisy didn't know if she'd go so far as to believe that, but Kay certainly seemed to. She kissed Kay's cheek and went into the hall with Graham. Sydney and Marshal waited just outside the door.

"What did you do?" Sydney grinned.

Daisy shook her head. "She had to be with Ed. I just helped. She'd have done it with or without me."

"You did a good thing. If we were at any other hospital they would have arrested you." Sydney laughed. Stopping when she must have realized what she said. "I didn't mean it like that."

"I know you didn't. It's okay. I'd gladly go to jail if it meant making sure Kay and Ed were okay. As long as they don't put me in a cell with Nadine, that is. Otherwise, I'd probably spend the rest of my days in prison." She didn't elaborate. Sydney knew what she meant.

"Let's go home." Sydney hooked her arm with Daisy's.

Back at the campground, the amount of work they'd neglected seemed like a lead weight around her neck. Every time they decided to try to open early, tragedy happened.

Maybe someone was trying to tell them something. What, Daisy couldn't say.

She needed to work on the advertising and website. And then she realized they didn't have phone service yet. She had no contact number to put down on any of the ads. A phone company truck pulled in.

"Who called them?" Daisy looked out the office window. Sydney shrugged. "I haven't had time."

"I did," a familiar voice said, and she spun around to find her dad. And her mom.

Daisy burst into tears.

The next thing she knew, they had her wrapped into a three-way hug. "Sydney called us. We just wanted you to know that no matter what, we're always here for you. You're our daughter by choice and you always will be."

Daisy cried even harder. They had chosen her when they could have easily insisted Nadine take her back. They'd protected her when Nadine tried to reclaim her.

"Thank you," she somehow managed through the sobs.

Sydney nudged her way into the family circle. "I called them. I didn't know what else to do. You wouldn't respond."

"I'm glad you did." Daisy hugged each of them.

When she got to her dad, she stopped. "You're going to die here. What about your allergies?"

He smiled and shook his head. "Nah. I saw the doctor before we left. He gave me a shot and a prescription. And one of those allergy pen things in case I get stung or something."

"I can't believe you're here. And you called the phone company."

"Sydney told us the highlights. When we got here and realized how close you were to opening, we wanted to help. You girls have done an incredible job. It looks better than the last year Gramps was open." Her mom let out a sad sigh.

"Your contractor left this." Her dad held an envelope.

"Which one?" Sydney took what probably was an invoice. Which job had completed while they were busy being kidnapped and partying?

"Oh. The bathhouses are done. And the plumbing in the main house." Sydney held the bill up and did a little dance.

"Sweet. Let's go see." Daisy needed to do something to break up the emotional fest or split apart at the seams. She'd had enough drastic changes lately.

The bathhouses were exactly as she'd envisioned. Even the most squeamish camper would feel comfortable. The warm colors gave the bathrooms a homey feel. The ladies' side had a station for hair dryers and curling irons, the result of how they'd felt during their teenaged years.

It didn't matter they were camping. She and Sydney had to go all out, just in case there were any cute boys around, and that meant hair and makeup. The area attractions would make any woman want to look their best before leaving. Now they could do that easily. Daisy was pleased with the results. Now all they had to do was wait for the coin-operated washers and dryers to be delivered, which was supposed to be the day after tomorrow.

"I can help with the website, if you want." Her dad bumped against her as they made their way back to the office.

"Excellent. I have the basic layout done." She told him her ideas.

The pool contractor stopped them on their way by. The transformation of the weed- and sludge-filled pool was amazing.

He grinned when they said so, his dark mustache twitching at the corners of his mouth. "A Santa suit, eleven bullfrogs, a bunch of eggs, a dead squirrel, couple of dead birds, and a six-foot-long snake."

"A Santa suit?" Scenarios filled her head and Daisy laughed.

"That's nothing. I've found weirder things. At least you didn't have a dead body."

Daisy shuddered. She ignored the prospect of a dead body and kept the humor of the Santa suit. The good feeling lasted until afternoon. By dinnertime, the website had launched and most of the advertising had been prepared. Having their parents in house had helped Daisy overcome most of her black mood. Though she still didn't want to talk about what Nadine had done.

Everything had turned out well for them today, despite Ed's injuries and the death she'd smelled in the hospital this morning. The last report from the hospital had been good. If everything went well, Ed would be out of critical care by morning. Despite all the good news, foreboding crept in as Daisy waited for the rest of the family by her parents' minivan.

Something bad was about to happen.

CHAPTER 22

Sydney couldn't shake the irritation that had grown all afternoon. Daisy pretended all was well, probably for their parents' sake. The act was getting on Sydney's nerves.

To go from nearly comatose to bubbly and carefree wasn't setting well with Sydney. If her guess was correct, her sister was due for a major breakdown.

Jace and Marshal stayed away most of the day. Jace had called to update them on Ed's condition, but didn't say when he would arrive back at the campground. Marshal said he had work to do and disappeared shortly after their parents arrived.

She couldn't help but feel relieved. The last thing she needed was her mother asking a million questions about the guys and hearing her lecture on the appropriateness of her and Daisy allowing so many men to live at the campground.

If her mother only knew.

Now she wondered if calling the folks had been a wise decision. Some of her freedom had been swept away with the arrival of the parents. Decisions were talked through four different ways instead of the two usually required. At least they'd made some much needed progress today. If nothing else happened, they'd be ready to take reservations next week, and open the following week. Two weeks early.

Sydney couldn't help but wonder what Violet would do when she saw the ads they'd placed. They'd covered every newspaper and advertising magazine and linked to camping searches all over the Internet. They'd even started a blog where they would post pictures and progress related to opening, and then campground events and activities once they opened. They even planned a billboard and radio spots.

She only hoped guests would come. Marshal advised leaving the ghosts out of this round of advertising. They'd agreed that unless the spirits interacted with the paying customers that they'd continue as Gramps had. Sydney still wasn't sure how she felt, but since nothing bad had happened she supposed it was the best course of action. Once they re-established Brookside, they'd consider a different approach. Even though her nerves were stretched thin and her irritation was at an all-time high, the prospect of opening had her excited.

Graham had hung out for a few minutes this morning. Until her mother had made some sort of comment about inappropriate behavior and the Dawson's twenty-two-year-old daughter having sex with every guy she met. She figured he was pretty smart for leaving. The next questions would be aimed at him and his opinions on the matter.

Tucker waved as he passed on his way back to town with some of his crew. Sadly, their job was nearly done. Sydney was going to miss him. He'd become a brother figure. She could definitely see what Daisy found attractive about him. Admitting he was handsome was as far as that went though. She figured how she felt was what Daisy had meant when she talked about Marshal.

She wasn't sure how Daisy would react when everyone left. Marshal and his crew, including Graham, couldn't hang out much longer. The two weeks they'd been in residence was far longer than they'd planned. They all had their own lives.

Hell, she wasn't sure how she was going to feel either. By Sunday, everyone would be gone. Hopefully, that figure included their parents. Days remained and she was no closer to deciding which man belonged in her life.

Maybe things were better this way. Maybe she shouldn't choose. That thought hurt and she tried to brush it off as Daisy bounced down the stairs toward her.

"I'm so hungry." Daisy checked her hair in the reflection of the car window.

"You are such a liar. How can you act like nothing is wrong?" Sydney faced her, certain they shouldn't have this conversation right now, but not intelligent enough to stop the accusing words.

"Nothing is wrong. Everything is great." Daisy turned on a bright smile.

"Everything is not great. Ed's not going to die, but that's about it. I'm sorry I called Mom and Dad. I shouldn't have. But get off whatever cloud you're on and come back to earth with me," Sydney said quietly.

"You did the right thing. Look at how much we got done today. We're in great shape. Nadine is behind bars and we're going to beat Violet. How much better can it get?"

"Oh, please. Spare me. Cut the 'happy girl' act. Tucker is leaving tomorrow. Graham by the weekend and you can pretend everything is fine?"

Daisy spun, her words were hard and quiet. "Mom and Dad are leaving in the morning. So yes, until then I can pretend. Once they go, I'll fall apart. You might want to do the same. Otherwise they'll be our first reservation and it might be permanent."

Sydney leaned against the car and sighed. Daisy was right, but that didn't mean she had to like it. "Fine. I'll play your game, but don't lay the act on so thick. Mom will see right through what you're trying to do."

"10-4, Chief." Daisy mock-saluted her, and Sydney smiled even though she felt like throwing up.

Somehow, Sydney lived through dinner. And the car ride back to the campground. By the time they reached the parking lot, her dad sneezed constantly and his eyes were red and watery.

He cursed as he turned off the car. "I'm sorry to do this. I can't stay. Your mom and I are going to head home. My system can't take anymore."

Sydney hid her sigh of relief. "Oh, Daddy. We don't want you to leave, but I don't want you to be sick either."

She hugged him from her seat behind him, her brain spinning with the evening's conversation. Twice their mother had asked if they were sleeping with the guys she saw milling around the campground.

The first time, she'd answered her truthfully. The second time she told her they'd had a huge orgy just the other night and how wonderful it'd been. Her mom's eyes had gotten huge and Daisy gave her a thumbs-up. She'd never said anything so drastic to her mother before and it felt good. After that, they'd gone back to talking about Violet and the different ways she tried to get them off the property.

Finally, their parents drove away. Sydney stood beside Daisy and waved. It had been good to see them. But now she could breathe again. They had helped, but she did worry for her dad's health. His allergies couldn't even be called allergies, more like a ticket to the funeral home if the amount of toxins in his system became too much. The shot the doctor had given him wore off far sooner than it should have.

When the headlights finally faded, Sydney turned to Daisy. "So, do you think Mom believed me?"

"That was freaking perfect. I taught you well." Daisy one-arm hugged her. "An orgy. I couldn't have done better."

They walked in silence for a minute, the darkness settling around them like a comfortable blanket.

"You know you've always been so serious, just not about sex. I think Mom is shocked to her toes."

Daisy unlocked the cabin and as they stepped inside, they realized they had more guests.

The white cat was curled up in the upholstered chair with tiny furry bodies surrounding her.

"She had her babies. Look." Daisy stood over the cat, awe on her face.

"How many? Wait. Don't tell me. Seven." The kittens were cute. Too cute.

Daisy counted, shaking her head. "Seven. We have our dwarfs."

"I can't believe this. Ten cats. This is so wrong." Sydney peered at the tiny furry bundles and smiled, despite the sinking in her stomach.

"What did the shelter say?" Daisy patted Prince, Princess, and Snow White, scratching under their chins and complimenting them on the new kittens even though it was absurd.

"No missing cats. The sheriff didn't know of anyone who's lost a cat. I even called the vet. No luck." She sighed.

"Too weird. I guess we should make this crew check-up appointments soon. We have ourselves a cat family. I definitely don't want to add to these numbers."

"No doubt. It's a sign."

Prince meowed and Sydney glared at him.

"I don't know. You could be right. None of the guys came around after Mom and Dad arrived. Marshal and Graham holed up in the cabin. Tucker did physical labor for the first time since last week and Jace stayed away all day. What does that tell us?" Daisy put her briefcase on the table.

"That we're doomed. I'm going to call and check on Ed. Kay told the nurses station to update us. Hopefully they'll actually do it this time. They keep forgetting we're next of kin." Sydney punched in the number and waited. She explained who she was and why she called. The nurse sounded pleasant and put her on hold while she checked on Ed.

The time dragged. Sydney was about to hang up and call back when the woman's voice came back on the line. Sydney had the impression the news was going to be bad.

"Sorry it took me so long to come back. His wife said to tell you there's healing power in love. Ed is off the respirator and breathing on his own. There is no apparent permanent damage from the heart attack and besides a few bruises and a broken arm, he's going to be fine. He'll definitely be under the doctor's care to monitor his health from now on. They're moving them to a regular room in the morning. Kay's ready to be released but she won't go without her husband."

"Excellent. Tell Ed and Kay we send our love and we'll be in to see them tomorrow," Sydney said goodbye and hung up, wondering over Kay's remark about the healing power in love.

Was that meant specifically for her? Or had she just said it as a general statement?

Jace came back. Sydney called into Daisy that Ed was fine and gave her the outline of what the nurse said. "Jace is here. I'm going to find out what he knows and why he stayed away all day."

"Keep your clothes on." Daisy laughed, and Sydney closed the door with a bang.

Jace smiled when she approached. "How'd your day go?"

"With our parents here?" She laughed. "I'm glad I called them even if mom grilled us about why all you guys were staying here and if we're having sex with you."

"She's just worried about her little girls." Jace kissed her forehead.

"Where have you been all day? Too chicken to meet the folks?" She tried to keep her tone light.

"Well, kind of. I didn't know how they'd treat me seeing as how I'm Violet's grandson."

"I hadn't thought of that." And she hadn't. She'd been too busy being mad at him for staying away.

"I talked to the sheriff. Nadine is probably not going to see freedom for a long time. I saw her. She looks even worse than the other day, if that's possible. She's coming down off whatever she's been on. It's not a pretty sight."

"Do you think she'll remember what she tried to do?" Sydney hoped so. Maybe that would make Nadine see what a terrible person she'd become.

"Hard to say. Her man friends are talking. The only thing she said when I was there, was that you two were sluts and she wished you would have been in the van they ran off the road."

"So she's admitted having something to do with Ed and Kay's accident?" She leaned into him, enjoying the comfort and not realizing how much she'd missed him.

What did that mean?

"That's the only thing she's admitted. There are enough charges against her to keep her behind bars even if she doesn't remember the kidnapping. And there's evidence to convict her even if she never remembers."

"I guess that's good for Daisy's sake. She doesn't deserve what that woman's done to her."

"I agree. So what did you guys get done today?"

Sydney filled him in, trying not to think about the ease of their conversation. Trying not to think about how right it felt to share her day with him.

They ended up at her cabin. "Come in. I want to show you something."

Jace followed her inside and to the cats. He peered at the furry little beasts, his smile melting her heart.

"Aren't they cute? I love kittens. Seven? What are they the seven dwarfs?"

Daisy and Sydney burst out laughing. Sydney still swore there was some kind of message being sent to her. She just couldn't figure out what the heck she was supposed to understand.

A knock on the door sent Daisy to answer. Sydney heard her greet someone and the next thing she knew, the room filled with all the missing men.

She had to slap Tucker's hand away when he tried to pick the new kittens up, and stop Graham from doing the same thing. Marshal was the only one who seemed unaffected by the babies.

He grunted and seemed distracted. Sydney didn't know what to do. Should she ask him what was wrong or wait until they were alone? Was he upset with her or just tired from a long day of processing video and audio?

"Did you guys find anything interesting today?" She tried to sound casual.

"A few good clips and sounds. Not much different than what we've already found. We'll show you once we get everything organized. Probably tomorrow. I'd like to tape one more night before we head back home Sunday or Monday." Marshal talked to her, but didn't really look at her.

What did that mean?

Sydney didn't want to lose him by default. She didn't want him to give up because he thought she'd already made her choice. She hadn't. At least she didn't think she had. Truth be told, she was more than half in love with both of them.

She'd already been more than half in love with Marshal when Jace appeared and she finally stopped hating him. Her feelings for Marshal hadn't changed. At least she didn't think they had.

With a sigh, she realized how different things were going to be around here in just a few days. This support system that had assembled itself would be gone and it'd be down to her and Daisy.

And the cats.

And the ghosts.

At least Violet should leave them alone once they opened and her hopes of getting her hands on Brookside were canceled. Sydney wasn't stupid enough to believe she'd ever completely give up, but at least she wouldn't have a legal leg to stand on.

She'd never have to deal with the woman again.

Unless she and Jace had a future. Then the woman would be a part of her extended family. The thought made her sick to her stomach and was almost enough to change any thoughts she had of being with him.

The next morning, Sydney woke with a heavy heart. Tucker and his crew were officially finished today. Sure, they'd see them often for maintenance. A contract Sydney had insisted upon even though Tucker said he'd take care of the property for free.

The campground looked official. The grounds were spotless and well-groomed, the finishing touches far more than Sydney could have hoped for or dreamed up herself.

Daisy was already gone by the time Sydney came out of the shower. She'd planned to visit Kay and Ed, drop off the advertising paperwork at the various locations, and pick up lunch for Tucker and his crew.

Marshal waved as he opened the door to his cabin. A distracted hand movement that seemed more an obligation than desire. Sadness filled her. He'd avoided her at every turn and even though she knew what his lack of interest probably meant, she didn't want to admit it.

Jace's car was gone. She tried to remember if he'd said anything about errands and couldn't. She walked the property, pleased, excited and sad. Life was about to change and she didn't know if she was ready. She and Daisy would move from their cramped little cabin to the house where they'd have their own space in a few weeks. She would miss the little wooden house at the edge of the woods. As weird as that was.

Jace pulled in, too fast, but since there were no children around she decided not to mention his speed was unacceptable. He stayed in the car and appeared to yell into his cell phone. She wasn't sure if he'd seen her and decided not to wait.

A bundle of wildflowers sat in the center of the desk she'd claimed in the office in an old soda bottle. There was no note. A tiny spider crawled over a white petal, disappearing into the center of the bundle and Sydney decided smelling the flowers was out of the question.

She moved them beside her computer and turned on the machine, staring out the window until the system became operational. Jace continued to sit in his car, only he didn't appear busy anymore. He had his head against the seat and his eyes closed, his posture reminding her of defeat.

Sydney wanted to go and talk to him, but wasn't sure how he'd react. Forcing her attention back to the computer, she clicked on the email icon, hoping for a reservation request or at least an email requesting more information.

Nothing. She shouldn't be disappointed. The web page had only been operational for a few hours. They'd have guests their grand opening weekend. They had to.

She stared out the window again. Jace wasn't in his car and she had a ping of disappointment that he hadn't come to see her. Not that she really had time to chat. The pile of paperwork she needed to take care of seemed to have grown in a few hours. Grabbing a file from the top of the stack, she opened it and did her best to put both men out of her mind.

Someone decidedly male cleared his throat.

Sydney looked up from the spreadsheet to find Jace standing in the doorway.

"You busy?" He seemed nervous.

"Yeah, but I could use a break. Come in." She saved her document, stood and stretched. "I have coffee, but it's probably burnt by now."

Jace wrinkled his nose and shook his head as he offered her a take-out cup with steam drifting from the top. Apparently, he'd been out when she was wrapped up with her stack of work.

"Thanks. You've been busy." She figured that was better than coming right out and asking him what he'd been up to.

"You could say that. We need to talk." He sat down, his smile gone.

"Okay." She resumed her seat, her stomach turning. Violet had to have done something. "What is it?"

"I've been working on research. Trying to figure out why Gramps would marry my grandmother. I think I have the answers."

"Good. I can't wait to hear what you found out. This is going to change everything." Answers meant that she now had a weapon to fight Violet.

"Yeah, it's definitely going to change everything. It changes more than you realize." Jace shook his head, his face full of sadness and something she couldn't name.

"What? How bad could it be?" She reached out and placed her hand on his arm. He brushed her touch away.

"I'm your blood uncle." He dropped a thick file on her desk. "Your grandfather is my father."

CHAPTER 23

Sydney stared, trying to absorb what he'd said. How could that be? "That doesn't make any sense."

"I know. Grandmother came to visit and she and Gramps kind of painted the town red. You already knew there was something between them in high school. Your Gram was away for the weekend and apparently Violet took advantage of the situation. She stayed for the weekend and then went back home."

"What? That doesn't make sense. He would have never cheated on Gram."

"She never called to tell him about me. She was still married, not to my grandfather, or my father. Hell, I don't know. I'm so confused. Del was Violet's third husband. After her first husband left her, she married the ex-husband of one of her ex-best friends. They'd only been together a few months when she got bored and decided to visit Gramps. So she came here and went back home to discover she was pregnant. Her husband believed the baby was his. Except he died a few weeks before the birth."

"You mean a few weeks before you were born?" Sydney couldn't seem to wrap her brain around this twisted deception. How could any of this be true?

"Yeah. It's easier if I speak in general terms. Anyway, Violet didn't know what to do. She felt a woman her age having a child was preposterous. She hid her pregnancy, spending the last few months out of state and having the baby where no one knew her. At the same time, her daughter, who I thought was my mother, died due to complications from a difficult pregnancy. When Violet went home, she told everyone I was her grandson."

"What about her daughter's husband?" None of this made sense. How on earth did Violet manage such an elaborate scheme? And at her age?

"There wasn't a husband. Violet always told me my parents were killed in a skiing accident when I was very young. What really happened was that her daughter got pregnant and refused to name the father. Violet sent her away because she wanted to maintain the appearance that she had a perfect family. She made up this elaborate story about how her daughter had married a wealthy businessman and now traveled the world with him."

"All of this is very twisted. Her daughter had to be at least twenty. Right?"

"Eighteen. Violet was forty when I was born and it gets worse. Apparently, Violet had two children to your grandfather. Me and another daughter, not the one I thought was my mother. What doesn't make sense is why she waited so long to tell him about either of us. The daughter was long dead and I was in college. There had to be a reason she waited."

"No wonder she's so adamant on you having the campground. She feels it's more yours than mine."

"I guess that's her odd thinking. Gramps and I talked about his legacy before he died. He told me how much he wanted you to have this place to continue the family legacy. Remember I wasn't a little kid. I didn't know he was my father either. That wouldn't have changed anything. Don't get me wrong, I loved the man and fully supported his decision to leave Brookside to you. I did wonder why he left me what he did. Now it makes sense."

"Why didn't they tell you?" Her eyes burned.

"I don't know. I guess the lie had been told so many

times Violet believed it, or was too afraid to admit what happened."

"No. This can't be true. Gramps would have had to cheat on my grandmother and he would never, ever do that. He loved her more than anything. When she died, we thought he would die with her. No. He didn't do that." Sydney knew she was probably wrong. After what Kay had told her, she knew Gramps had been in love with Violet. The stark truth made her angry and threatened the foundation she'd always depended on.

"They both cheated. That file is all the documentation my private investigator found. The only thing I haven't done is confront Violet." Jace rubbed his fingers at his temples.

Sydney almost asked if she could be with him when he talked to his mother/grandmother. The matter was private, though, and she had no right to be involved. Her heart broke for Jace. To find out your entire childhood had been a lie had to be the most earth shattering event. To learn the cold woman who raised you was actually your mother and that she'd chosen to hide behind rules and etiquette instead of giving you the love you needed and deserved had to hurt more than anything she could think of.

She wrapped her arms around him, hoping to give comfort.

"We can't do this, Sydney." He pulled her arms from his neck and stared into her eyes. "I'd hoped we could have a future together. I've discovered so much about myself since I met you. I'm happy to be with you, in your company, hearing you laugh or holding you when you cry. I love the way your face lights up when you try to deny that you're in love with those little kittens. I love the way you defend your sister even when you know she's wrong. I love the way you love this place and I love your vision of what you want to do with this cursed campground. Damn it." He stood, knocking the chair to the floor.

Sydney stepped back, unsure of what she should say.

"Damn it, Sydney. I love you. And I'm your uncle. We can't even ever be friends because of how I feel about you." He slammed the door, rattling the pictures hanging on the wall.

Sydney didn't move.

Jace loved her.

Jace was her uncle.

Sydney ran a hand over her tear-stained cheeks. She wasn't sure how much time had passed since Jace left. The emptiness inside her prevented her from caring. Her heart broke, for Jace and for herself.

"What's wrong?" Daisy dropped the mail on her desk and rushed over and wrapped her arm around her shoulder, leading her to the couch where she'd slept when Daisy was missing.

"What's happened? Sydney. Talk to me." She shook her arm.

Sydney raised her head.

And burst into tears.

Somehow, she managed to tell her everything. Repeating much of it because of the sobs she wasn't able to control. Daisy passed her tissues, but didn't interrupt.

"And he loves me." Sydney blew her nose, tears dripping onto her hands.

"Shit. That's messed up. Oh, honey." Daisy hugged her, and Sydney gave in to another round of tears.

"How could Gramps do such a thing?" Sydney sniffed and tried to find self-control.

"It happens. Gramps was a great man and this doesn't change anything. Sure, he screwed up, but I think he paid plenty for his mistakes," Daisy said.

"And now I'm paying for them." She hated to feel that

way. Hated the anger and bitterness threatening to swallow her whole.

"So you finally decided Jace was your man and then this happens?" Daisy sighed.

"The thing is, I hadn't consciously decided. The whole story is like some stinking soap opera. A bad one at that."

"Obviously, you decided. Now what?" Daisy pushed and Sydney fought the urge to snap at her.

"I don't know. We open the campground and try to sift through this mess." Sydney picked up the pile of tissues. She was worn to the bone and didn't have a clue what she should really do.

"Come on." Daisy stood.

Sydney followed her to their cabin like a robot. Daisy ushered her inside and closed the door.

"You need to rest." Daisy pointed to her bedroom.

"I don't think I can. There's too much in my brain." Sydney sat at the table and dropped her head to the surface with a bang, ignoring the cat that jumped on her lap.

"Drink this." Daisy pressed a glass of amber-colored liquid into her hands. "Don't smell, just gulp."

Stupidly, she did, regretting the action as the liquor burned her throat and made her eyes water. "What the hell is this?"

"Don't worry about it. Drink." Daisy filled the glass again, setting a bottle with a black label on the counter behind her.

"I really don't think this is going to help." She drank anyway and numbly watched as Daisy filled the glass a third time. At least her throat didn't burn any more.

"It'll help you sleep."

She did, and the next thing she knew the cup was full again. She held the glass like a lifeline, ignoring Daisy's insistence to swallow again.

"No wonder Violet insisted the campground go to Jace. She felt Gramps owed her for the daughter that died and the son she had with him." The last few words came out slurred. Sydney wondered what else her sister slipped into the glass. Until she remembered she hadn't eaten yet today and her tolerance for whiskey was low.

"Drink and don't think." Daisy pointed and Sydney followed instructions. "Now. Go to bed. I'm going to call Al and see what he has to say."

Sydney stood, swaying a little. "Okay. But don't be stupid and call Mom and Dad. At least yet."

"Yes, ma'am. God, you're a mess. Remind me to try a different tactic next time." Daisy shook her head, and Sydney stuck her tongue out.

Daisy tugged her shoes off and for a minute, Sydney couldn't stop laughing. It felt wonderful to lie down. She tried to remember why she was so tired, but gave up when her eyes closed by themselves.

Sydney sat up in confusion after shutting off her alarm. She didn't know why it had been set. She hadn't needed to use it since coming to Brookside. Her heart pounded as she tried to remember how she got into bed. Getting up, she went to the bathroom, her head fuzzy and her mouth dry.

Daisy forcing her to drink whiskey surfaced, along with the reason Sydney had been so upset. Jace was her uncle. Gramps had fathered two children with Violet, one while married to Gram.

She caught the edge of the sink to steady herself and tried to put everything into perspective. Even though she was angry and betrayed by Gramps' infidelity, she had no right to judge his actions.

But why did Jace have to be her uncle? She hadn't been aware that her heart had chosen Jace. Knowing that now, no matter what, she could never be with him shattered her soul. She loved him.

She showered, hoping to bring at least her body back to life. Thinking about Jace's kiss and the way he touched her brought tears that shook her body and made her fall to her knees in the tub.

Sydney put on enough makeup to cover the traces of the crying. The last thing she wanted to do was answer a million questions from everyone she was bound to run into. Violet had some things to answer for. Sydney would get those answers and try to find a legal way to keep her from interfering in her life from now on.

She dialed Al's office, leaving a message and wondering what Daisy already said to him. That she'd slept a full eighteen hours bothered her. The whiskey was probably mostly to blame, but she didn't like how much she'd missed.

There was a note on the table. *Meeting in office. Now.*

Daisy would have been on a rampage, demanding justice for Sydney. Usually Sydney would stop her, but this time she didn't really care. She opened the office door, almost leaving when she saw Jace sitting behind her desk. Maybe he'd decided that since the truth was out, he'd just go ahead and claim what his grandmother saw as his birthright.

He smiled tenderly as she banged the door behind her. She'd been so caught up in seeing him that she'd failed to notice the room was full. Al, Daisy, and Violet stood in the reception area. Daisy had a mean look on her face and Violet wore the same haughty indignation she always had. The woman's bra had to be too tight.

Sydney laughed, despite the serious tone in the room. She was done. Finished with all of this nonsense and trying to follow the rules and make peace with everyone.

Daisy rushed over, her eyes showing her concern. "You

weren't nipping at that bottle this morning, were you?" Her voice was a whisper.

Sydney shook her head.

"I should have." She took a step, planting herself in the middle of the room. "Good morning, everyone. I'm glad you're all here. I find I'm in need of some answers."

"Wait, Syd. We need to talk first." Daisy put her hand on her arm, but Sydney brushed it off.

Violet turned, her face red and Sydney wondered if she'd start shooting lasers out of her eyes. "So am I. Where did you get the money for all of this?"

"That's none of your damn business and I plan to see this campground stays that way. You have no right to be here and you are not welcome here. However, I do have some questions for you before you go." Sydney squared her shoulders and moved toward her vile step-grandmother.

"I don't have to tell you anything." Violet seemed to shrink and Sydney wondered how long it would take before Jace bailed her out of Sydney's angry communication.

Daisy grabbed her arm again, this time squeezing hard enough to get her attention. "I mean it. We need to talk before you go any farther."

Sydney shook her head, not taking her eyes from Violet.

"Wrong. How dare you? How dare you come in here and demand the things you have? How dare you use my grandfather?" Sydney wasn't exactly sure which issue she should address first, but since the words were out there she went with them.

"Now it's my turn to say none of your business. What was between Del and me is my business. Not yours." Violet sniffed and Sydney wondered how long it would be until she pretended to faint.

"Wrong. When you come in here and try to override his wishes with your silly demands and tricks it became my business. You've done everything to try to stop us from fulfilling Gramps' final wish. It's my business. I think you have a few confessions to make." Sydney stepped toward her, not willing to let Violet's now pale face make her back down.

"I don't know what you're talking about." Violet sat and reached for a tissue.

"Sydney, wait. You don't know what you're talking about right now either. I need to talk to you." Daisy pinched her hard enough that her words finally soaked through her anger.

"What?"

"Outside. Now. Just shut up and don't say another word." Daisy tugged her arm and Sydney glared at Violet as she followed her sister.

"What?" She nearly yelled.

"It's a lie. Everything is a lie." Daisy paced in front of her, her arms crossed over her chest.

"What's a lie?" Daisy sat on one of the benches and Sydney followed. "Tell me what's going on here."

"All that stuff Jace told you yesterday is a lie."

Sydney's heart lightened.

"Most of it anyway. Some is true."

The feeling vanished, her heart settling farther into her chest.

"Would you quit beating around the bush and just tell me what the hell you're talking about?"

"Gramps never cheated on Gram. He did father Violet's daughter. The daughter that died delivering Jace. He's not our uncle, but our cousin."

"What difference does it make?" She leaned back on the bench and rested her head against the side of the building with a sigh. "Violet still has no right to make demands for him. He may technically be a true heir, but it was Gramps decision not to leave him the campground. From what Jace told me, Gramps talked to him about his plans and he did take care of Jace in the will."

"I know. That is the issue though. Al's not sure what's going on. He wants us to stick to the issue of the will and not bring up their daughter right now. He's sending DNA samples so we know what we're talking about. You're the last one he needs." Daisy tapped on the window and pointed inside.

Al came out, gently taking her arm and moving to an area where they couldn't be seen from inside. "Something doesn't make sense to me. I want to try this. The results will tell us how to proceed. Keep your tongue and I'll take care of Violet."

He swabbed the inside of her cheek before giving her a hug. "It's probably best if you don't come back inside. Violet is up in arms about how you paid for the improvements. She feels like the agreement has been breached and wants to take immediate possession of the campground. She even called her contractor to set up a start date."

Sydney tried to move past him, her fury returning.

"No. Jace has already informed her she has no legal right to demand anything. She's listening to him for now." Al held her arm and she didn't struggle.

"What about the contractor?" She so badly wanted to confront the evil woman and had a hard time listening to Al's reason.

"Won't come without proof of ownership and the proper permits. Since the town is so divided about what Violet wants to do here, he won't take the chance of ruining his business. We're fine here. Go and let me handle Violet."

"Fine, but I need to know everything as soon as you do." She tried not to sound like a bitch, but she felt like this whole thing was set up without her.

"I promise. She's coming. Get out of her sight." He

pointed and though she didn't want to, she followed his instructions.

Sydney followed one of the new hiking paths, one she hadn't had time to check out before. The trail led from the office to the activity building, then to the pond. Jace's idea. The pain in her heart hadn't changed. Jace was still off limits. The sadness inside of her threatened to make her not care anymore. What was the point anymore? They'd worked so hard to get the campground ready and beat Violet.

Even though they'd met every stipulation and challenge, there was still a chance Violet could win. Sydney kicked a rock in the center of the path, hearing the resulting thud as it smashed into a tree.

She passed the activity building, the smell of fresh paint following her. She should have stopped and checked out the finished product, but didn't feel like it. She'd return once she'd worked off most of her anger and continued down the path and into the woods.

This section of trees was thicker than the rest. The temperature difference did nothing to cool her hostility and bitterness. She reached the halfway mark before she started to calm. A bench sat on each side of the path, the area widened to give people a chance to rest if they needed to. Wildflowers had been planted immediately surrounding the area and even though most of the trees still held fresh buds, the scene was perfect.

She sat on a bench. If she wasn't careful she'd let bitterness consume her. The sheer irony of the situation should tell her how screwed up she was. The sense she wasn't alone filled her as the scent of Gramps' aftershave eased through her confusion. Sydney wished he was really here so she could hug him and ask for the truth. She almost asked her questions anyway, but before she could, the familiar smell vanished.

"Read the journals." Sydney wasn't sure if the whispered words were something she made up in her own mind, or if Gramps said it to her before he vanished.

God, she was cracking up big time.

Someone came toward her. A moment of panic filled her but she fought the urge to run away. There was no one here that would hurt her. At least not more than she'd already been hurt.

Marshal finally appeared at the curve in the path. Sydney considered getting up and going by him. She didn't know what to say to him, didn't know how much he knew or what he felt. She didn't want to hurt him. Even though Jace was off limits she couldn't be with Marshal either.

"Having a rough day?" Marshal sat on the bench on the opposite side of the path.

"You could say that." She sighed and tried not to make eye contact.

"Want to tell me about it? Everyone is acting really weird around here lately. What's going on?" Marshal kicked at the ground like the last kid picked for the dodgeball team.

"I can't tell you yet. My legal counsel has advised against speaking of the situation." She sounded snotty. Hopefully he realized she didn't direct that at him.

He gave a half-laugh. "That good, huh? Listen, if you need some money I can probably help. I'll try to help regardless of what you need."

The innuendo in his words made her want to cry. She shook her head. "Thanks. I think things will be okay. And I'll tell you what's going on when I can."

Yeah, things would be okay. Maybe for everything but her heart.

Marshal shuffled his feet before getting up. "Listen, I can't be the guy you need and that's my fault. I guess I have some issues to work out before I can actually have a relationship. I realized that over the course of the last few days. It has nothing to do with you and Jace, though I know you will be really happy together."

His honesty brought tears to her eyes. "I'm not sure things will work out, but thank you. You're a good guy, Marshal. One day you're going to be some girl's perfect man."

"Only because you gave me what I needed to figure myself out." He grabbed her hand and squeezed.

"How? I didn't do anything but flirt with you."

"Just because of who you are, how you handle yourself, and how you stand up for the people you love. You treated Jace and me fairly. You didn't play us off each other and use us. You're a true lady, Sydney."

She squeezed his hand. "Thanks. You gave me a chance to be free for the first time in my life."

"Yeah, I think you still owe me. I never got to collect from our pool game." He wiggled his eyebrows, but laughed.

"You cheated. No dice." She didn't feel threatened. Marshal had many chances to collect on their bet and hadn't. Probably because he sensed she didn't know how she felt anymore.

"If Jace breaks your heart, you come and see me. I'll kick his ass. I'm not sure I want to be a consolation prize, but if things don't work out, I'm here. I can at least help you find yourself again." Marshal's sincerity brought tears to her eyes again. She couldn't tell him things with Jace were already in the toilet.

"Thanks." She reached up and hugged him tight, kissing his cheek before touching his face.

"Nice." A sarcastic voice sounded behind her. "You move fast. I know I don't have a thing to say about it and maybe I'm glad of that now."

Jace walked by them, his posture angry.

Sydney watched him, guilt, hurt, and humiliation making the tears fall.

Marshal guided her to a bench. "I'm going to go kick his ass."

"No. Let him go. There's a lot going on right now. The simple truth is we might not be able to work out what's between us. It might be impossible." She stared down the path but Jace was long gone.

"Nothing is impossible." Marshal patted her shoulder.

"This might be. It is already. I'm sorry I can't tell you what's going on." She stood.

"You know where to find me. I meant what I said. If you need me, I'm yours." God, the man exuded sexuality. Too bad that even though he was the second most attractive man she'd ever met, she wouldn't act on what was now the memory of her fascination with him.

She'd been so unfair to him.

He left her alone on the bench.

Sydney was sick of crying, sick of feeling sorry for herself and sick of the pity everyone seemed to send her way. Even the ones who supposedly didn't know what was going on seemed to know something.

Locking herself in her bedroom, she opened the battered journal where Gramps had recorded parts of his life. Sydney still wasn't sure she wanted to read his personal feelings, but maybe some of the questions would be answered inside.

She sifted through page after page of mundane campground experiences—angry customers, animal and insect infestations, and fishing stories. Just as she was ready to give up, she found a section of ghostly experiences. Page after page of interactions with some of the same spirits Sydney had encountered, now and when she was younger.

Why hadn't Gramps told her she'd inherited this ability to see and talk to spirits from him?

The ghost stuff was interesting, but not what she needed to know right now. Skipping past that, she flipped to the back of the journal, landing on an entry written close to her grandmother's death. Sydney swiped at the tears as she read, feeling Gramps' pain as he faced a future of loneliness. By the time she got to the section where Violet came to town the last time, Sydney didn't know what to think.

She almost felt bad for being angry with Gramps for possibly cheating on Gram. Obviously, he loved Violet, too, and had for most of his life. Still, she hadn't found anything that referenced the children he supposedly fathered with her or why he married her.

Then she did.

And it was as cryptic and confusing as any of Gramps important words.

She's in there. I know she is. The girl I loved way back then. The girl I still love. I see her sometimes, but not often enough. I know I can help. I know I can bring her back. I have given up much to try, lost much. If they could only see her like I do, they would understand.

What?

Sydney grabbed her car keys and purse and got behind the wheel. Jace appeared at the edge of the clearing. She looked over, wanting nothing more than to go to him.

No. No matter what, they couldn't be together. She started the car and drove away.

CHAPTER 24

Daisy tapped her pen on the desk. Damn this situation. Damn Violet and damn Gramps for bringing this on them all. Her heart broke for Sydney. To finally figure out who your future belonged to only to have the entire dream pulled out from under you like some slippery rug.

That sucked. Almost as much as your own mother trying to kidnap you for financial profit. Daisy picked up the phone to call their parents, dropping it before even dialing. There was nothing they could do. There was nothing anyone could do.

Thinking about Sydney kept her own sorry love life out of her mind. Tucker was gone and Graham was acting like the biggest jerk on the face of the earth. Really, her mind was already made up. Apparently there was nothing she could do about it though.

Tucker didn't bother to say goodbye.

He hadn't even looked at her when he'd left.

It didn't matter how much she loved him. She wasn't willing to have the babies he so obviously wanted. And that was the deal breaker.

She threw the pen and pushed back from the desk as Sydney tore out of the parking area, taking several layers of stone with her in the process. Jace stepped onto the porch when she opened the door. From his expression, he was in the same mood she was in.

"Where the hell is she going?" Her words were accusing and she knew it.

"How would I know? I'm not in charge of her."

"What did you say to her?" She should leave and not even try to talk to him.

"Something I shouldn't have. Not that it matters." His voice was sad. "Call me if anything weird happens. If Violet comes back. You shouldn't have to worry about Nadine, or her cronies."

Daisy placed her hand on his shoulder. "I'm sorry, Jace. I really am."

"Yeah. Me, too." He gave her a quick hug.

Marshal stomped up the porch, his gaze fixed on Jace. "I ought to kick your ass."

"Go ahead." Jace turned, obviously ready for a confrontation.

Daisy stepped between them, placing a hand on each solid chest. "You two are idiots. Knock it off." They pushed against her hands until she finally stepped away. "Fine. Freaking idiots. Go ahead and kill each other. That's just perfect and will solve so many problems." She slapped them both and walked away with a frustrated scream.

Sydney knocked on Kay and Ed's hospital room door before peeking around the corner. Ed appeared to sleep while Kay fiddled with a floral arrangement. She smiled as Sydney stepped into the room. Kay patted the bed beside her.

"So you know."

"Why didn't you tell me?" Sydney reached for a tissue, pissed at the tears that kept falling despite the fact she no longer wanted to cry.

"It wasn't my story to tell. Del and Violet, as mismatched as they were, had this connection. Different from your grandma, but still deep and abiding. Time changed Violet and she shifted into someone Del didn't know anymore. I think he wanted to save her. But he ended up killing himself in the process." Kay grabbed a tissue from the box and dabbed her eyes.

"Why didn't Gramps tell us about their daughter?"

"Probably figured that it didn't matter because she died before he and your gram married."

Sydney sniffed, stopping and replaying Kay's words. "What?"

"The little girl died before she was two. I think she got the whooping cough, but I don't know for sure." Kay offered her the tissue box.

"Wait. I don't understand." She told her both versions of the story she'd heard, watching shock and horror cross Kay's face.

"Oh my. No wonder you were mad at me for not telling you. Honey, I had no idea you and Jace were related. None at all or you can be sure I would have said so." Kay shook her head, her eyes narrowed as if going over her memories.

"Well, what Jace found out is different than what Al says." She told her about the DNA samples and how strange Al acted. "He didn't even want me near Violet, though I think he was afraid I'd take her apart with my bare hands."

Kay laughed, her smile turning into a frown. "I think you ought to listen to Al. When Ed wakes up, I'll ask him what he remembers. I know there was a chance that little girl wasn't Del's. Del was furious Violet hadn't told him before the baby died, that she hadn't allowed him to be a part of her too short life. But even then, he wasn't convinced the child was his. He would have treated her like his own regardless."

A spring of hope started in her chest. "Really?"

"Now that was a long time ago. I don't know. No one talked about those kinds of things. Del wouldn't have thought that for no reason. Don't get your hopes up, sweetie. As for Jace being Del's, I just don't know. It's possible. Violet did come back here once when your Gram went home to bury her mother. She stayed the weekend in a cabin at the campground and left before your Gram returned."

Sydney waited around for Ed to wake, visiting with Kay and hoping to keep Jace from her mind. She'd already ignored the request for visitors to leave for the afternoon so when the nurse came in, she figured she'd better go or end up in big trouble. She and Daisy already had reputations in this hospital. Sydney didn't doubt they'd toss her in jail if they could find a good reason. She stood, kissed Kay and Ed goodbye and headed out. Wishing for things that would never be.

Jace's camper was gone.

Sadness filled her, but Sydney fought the tears. She couldn't feel this way, couldn't mourn what could have been if it wasn't for that stupid DNA they shared. Her broken heart was wrong.

Marshal met her at the car and hugged her as soon as she got out. "Remember what I said. I'll always be here for you. No matter what."

"You deserve better. You deserve a woman who will love you with her heart and soul." She sniffed. She would never be that woman and they both knew it.

"Doesn't seem to be in the cards for me. I'm okay." Marshal took her packages. "I know I'm not ready for a relationship right now, but I'd try for you."

"It's just not fair. Why couldn't I have fallen in love with you? Things would be so much simpler." She regretted the words as soon as they left her mouth. Marshal was hurting, too and she'd done that to him. "I'm sorry. That was unfair."

"No. It's okay. I wish things had worked out that way, too. But we can't fight fate."

"Yeah, fate leaves me hopelessly in love with a man who's most likely my uncle, at the very least a cousin. How fair is that?"

"You know in the old days that would be considered a perfect match." Marshal smiled and though he was gorgeous, she didn't get that hitch in her heart she felt when Jace smiled at her. Why hadn't she noticed that before?

Sydney shook her head. "Ick. And all our kids would be genetically challenged. Sounds like a great life."

"See that? At least I got a smile out of you." Marshal waited for her to open the door, then he set the bags on the table. "I hope you brought cat food. Daisy said this crew is going through it."

"I did. I guess I'm destined to be a cat lady. I'd better get used to buying cat food and litter by the truck load." She sighed and moved to feed the meowing herd.

"I hope not. That would be a damn shame." Marshal helped by filling the water dish. "I have footage ready for you to view. When you're ready."

"Great. Any idea where Daisy is?" She might know if she listened to the message Daisy left on her phone. She should have by now, but had forgotten.

"No. She said she was going to call you."

"She did. I forgot to listen to her message." She activated the mailbox on her phone.

Daisy's fake cheerful voice erupted in her ear. "Hey, Syd. Just to let you know, I have to go into town and sign some papers regarding Nadine. I'm putting it off as long as possible because I'm hoping you'll come with me."

Sydney looked at the clock. She exited out of the message center without hearing everything Daisy said and hit the button for Daisy's cell phone.

Daisy answered on the first ring.

"Where are you?" Sydney hated herself for being so wrapped up in the tragedies of her personal life that she'd neglected to take care of her sister.

"Just got to the sheriff's office." Daisy sounded nervous.

"Wait for me. I'll be there in a minute." Sydney finished feeding the cats and turned to Marshal. "I have to go. Daisy needs me."

"Anything I can help with?" Did he have to be so completely wrong for her?

"Thanks, but I don't think so. I don't want her to be alone. Nadine has put her through enough." Sydney grabbed her keys.

"Call if you need anything. If Daisy's up to it when you get back we can go over the evidence. We'll probably head out tomorrow. As much fun as I've had here, I have to get back to the real world." Marshal's expression was unreadable and Sydney couldn't spend too much time thinking about it or she'd cry again.

"Okay. Thanks, Marshal." She gave him a quick hug and rushed to her car.

Daisy sat on a bench in front of the sheriff's office when Sydney arrived fifteen minutes later. Daisy gave her a grateful smile.

"What exactly do you have to do here?" Sydney hugged her as she stood.

"Give another statement about what she did. I don't know why. Sign some papers. I'll probably have to testify at her trial too."

"We'll get through it. I'll most likely have to testify, too. The important thing is making sure she doesn't bother you anymore. I know you had high hopes for the future, but I think it's just too late for Nadine. Her way of life has finally caught up to her." Sydney didn't know if she was helping or making Daisy feel worse.

"I know. I keep trying to remember that she did me a favor by abandoning me. It's hard, though. All my life I just wanted her to want me, to love me like Mom always does. She doesn't have it in her though. It's all about what I can do for her and how I can help support her habits. It's not fair." Daisy's eyes filled with tears, but she didn't cry.

"I know, honey. It isn't fair. You deserve better than that." She hugged her. As she squeezed, Daisy let go of the control she'd managed, her body shaking as she sobbed.

"I can't find someone who loves me no matter where I go. I mean, besides you and Mom and Dad. What is wrong with me?" Daisy sobbed into her shirt.

"You will. You will. I think you're trying too hard. Trust me, there's someone out there perfect for you. Someone who will treat you the way you deserve to be treated and who will love you so deeply it humbles you." The words caused Sydney to fight her own tears. She might have had that, if Jace hadn't turned out to be a relative.

"I'm sorry. I know comforting me when your world has fallen apart isn't easy. You know exactly what to say to make things better." Daisy straightened, wiping her nose with a tissue pulled from her pocket. Seemed like they both needed a never-ending supply of tissues these days. "Let's get this over with. We have a campground to open."

Sydney followed Daisy inside, hoping they wouldn't have to face Nadine. Somehow, she didn't think that was going to come true.

Sure enough, Nadine sat in the room where Daisy was ushered. At first they told Sydney she had to wait in the tiny, dank waiting room, but she'd insisted and they finally relented and allowed her to stay with her sister.

Nadine dabbed her eyes as they entered, her face showing a regret that Sydney couldn't help believe was fake. "Oh, my baby. I'm so sorry."

Daisy ignored her, facing the officer with irritation. "You didn't tell me she would be here."

"She's not supposed to be. We're waiting for transport to the county jail. I apologize. You were to be shown to the other room." He stood, giving Nadine a warning glance and moved to open the door behind Sydney. "If you'll go across the hall, I'll be with you shortly."

Sydney stepped backward, not taking her eyes from Nadine. Daisy held her head high as she turned to leave the room.

"I've always loved you. I didn't mean to hurt you. I'm so sorry," Nadine wailed.

Daisy spun, and Sydney caught her arm. "The only loving thing you've ever done was dump me off. Trying to use me to support your habit is not love, hurting people I care about is not love. I'm sorry, too, sorry that you're my mother and that every day I have to fight the idea that I'm going to end up just like you. I'm even afraid to have children because I don't want to share your genes with innocent children. I don't want to know you. I have always been nothing to you and now you are nothing to me."

Daisy left and Sydney shot Nadine a glare as she followed her to the identical room across the hall. She banged the door shut behind her and gathered Daisy into her arms and held her as she cried.

Sydney could hear Nadine screeching from the little room. She demanded to be able to talk to Daisy and try to explain why she did the things she did. She screamed to be released, saying she didn't have any idea why they were treating her like a criminal and that she didn't do anything wrong. That she'd made sure her daughter was provided for and hadn't broken any laws. From what Sydney could tell, the officer with her either didn't say anything or spoke very quietly.

Obviously, Nadine had gone over the edge. She didn't seem to remember that she'd kidnapped her own daughter for profit and future income or how she'd purposefully hurt people her daughter loved. Sydney hugged Daisy tighter, not saying anything as she cried out years of pain and frustration.

Finally, Daisy stepped away and dried her tears. "I don't hate her as much as I should."

"No one said you had to hate her. She's messed up. Had she not fallen off the wagon she would probably be a different person. None of this is your fault, you know." Sydney wasn't sure she was saying any of the right things. She couldn't seem to find her usual comforting words right now.

"I know that. She infuriates me and yet, I feel sorry for her. For how she chose to live her life."

"Chose is the right word. She made these decisions on her own and they had nothing to do with you. What did you mean when you said you have to fight to not end up like her?" Sydney worried over that last question. Never had she seen any signs that Daisy would end up like her erratic mother.

"Just an idea I've had since I was little. If the apple doesn't fall far from the tree, will there be a point in my life where I'll be faced with the same decisions Nadine made? I wonder if I'll make the right choices." Daisy didn't seem like she wanted to share more than that.

"You make the choice to not be like her every day. Besides you grew up on a different tree, so I think it doesn't apply to you. If you had grown up under Nadine's influence it might be a different story. You've already faced and dealt with more than Nadine ever will. She hides from her problems with booze, drugs, and men. You face them head on. I don't think you have anything to ever worry about."

Daisy nodded. "Logically. I know that. It's just one of those fears that will probably color every decision I ever make. It has so far, ever since I heard that phrase for the first time. The last thing I ever want to do is turn out like my birth mother."

"Then you won't. It's that simple. You're aware. I don't think Nadine ever was. I'm not trying to change your mind about having children, but I think you'd be a great mother. You know exactly what not to do." Sydney watched Daisy's control slip back into place.

Just in time. The door swung open and a different officer entered the room. "Sorry. That should have never happened. She was supposed to be long gone. The transport van got a flat tire. She'll be on her way before we're done with this paperwork."

He dropped a stack of forms in front of Daisy.

"Nadine claims you will take full financial responsibility for her." He pointed to the top page. "If you sign that, she'll make bail."

Daisy shoved the paper back at him. "Not a chance."

"Good. I'm required to make sure." He marked a big X over the page and stuck it in the back of the folder.

"Am I responsible for her, financially?" Daisy fiddled with the pen.

"Not if you don't want to be."

"Good. That's what started this whole thing."

The officer's eyes widened as if he hadn't been aware of the situation. He shook his head. "I hadn't made the connection. We have another family dispute going on here. I'm sorry. I would have never given you that page had I understood the situation." He reached for the stack of papers, returning only one to Daisy.

"Protection from abuse order. Just in case. One for each of you."

Daisy quickly scribbled her name on the page and handed it back to him as Sydney did the same. "What about the legal stuff?"

"You'll be contacted. You don't need to be there for the preliminary." He rustled through the papers. "There's quite a bit to sift through before her trial can be set. She needs to be clean and she's not. A psych consult to see if she's even fit to stand trial. There's a lot to do before we get to that stage. Don't worry. You're the victim. So far we have enough on her, without what she did to you, to keep her behind bars for a very long time."

"Like?" Daisy leaned forward. Sydney did, too, trying to see what was written on the top page.

"Illegal drugs, sale, and manufacturing. Prostitution. Attempted murder. That's the biggies, without the kidnapping. She admitted to trying to kill Kay and Ed. She said they were trying to steal you away." He shook his head, and Sydney hoped he wasn't feeling sorry for Daisy. Or Nadine.

"Ha. She dumps me off at my aunt's house when I'm tiny and now worries that someone is trying to steal me away. And she signed the adoption papers." Daisy stood. "I assume I'll be contacted. My uncle Al will serve as my legal counsel. Thank you for making me come in here. And thank you for screwing up so I had to see her."

The officer seemed upset until Daisy smiled.

"Listen, if the mix up hadn't happened, I wouldn't know that I've made the right decisions. Nadine abandoning me was the best thing she's done in her life. I'll never forgive her for not being stronger than the drugs she loved more than me, but at least she didn't try to take care of me. Thanks for your help. Let me know if I need to do anything else." Daisy held her head high as she left the room.

Sydney followed. Peace settled inside of her. Her sister was going to be just fine.

Would Sydney?

Marshal waited for them in the campground office. His van was the only vehicle Sydney could see. She figured Graham had already gone. Daisy didn't seem to notice and she couldn't help but wonder how things had been left between them. Sydney didn't believe there was more than slight attraction between Daisy and Graham, but she couldn't say for sure. She'd been so wrapped up in her own tragic love life she hadn't seriously thought about what was going on with her sister's heart.

"Guess we're on our own now." Daisy commented as they got out of the car.

"Yep. We're going to be just fine." Sydney hoped so. The words felt like a lie.

Marshal hugged them before moving to the conference room at the back of the office. The only equipment present was a laptop computer. She and Daisy settled themselves around the screen as Marshal dimmed the lights.

"Graham sends his apologies. His mom was rushed to the hospital this morning. Things don't look good. He left as soon as his sister called." Marshal shook his head. "He's supposed to update me as soon as there's news."

"Crap. I'm so sorry to hear that," Daisy said, her heart breaking for Graham.

"Keep us posted, okay? Let us know if there's anything we can do for him." Sydney sat at the table.

There was a few seconds of awkward silence. Marshal checked his phone one more time and moved to the table.

"You know how much I hate to say there's no scientific evidence to dispute odd phenomena." He glanced at Daisy, who nodded.

"I have to say it here. This place definitely has a lot of paranormal activity. From what we found, there is nothing to be afraid of, mostly memory spirits who don't interact with the living. There are a few others that seem to want to interact, though. You both have seen evidence of that, I believe." He hit a few keys and brought up a screen, pressing play as he settled back in his chair.

"What are we seeing here?" Daisy leaned in and Sydney had to reposition herself so she could see.

"The woods outside the first bathhouse. The spirits can see and even touch people. There's no malice. Listen to this." Marshal opened a smaller screen and paused the first, preparing to start them at the same time. "This is a voice recording done at the same time we taped the figures in the trees."

He pressed 'play'. Sydney stared at the screen as the tape played a scratchy, nighttime recording. Two figures came into view, moving slowly and toward each other. At first she thought they were Marshal's crew, but soon she realized she could see right through them.

Whoever manned the recording device asked if there was anyone who would like to speak to them. One of the figures turned toward where the question had been asked.

She could see the figure nod. Goosebumps rose on her arms but she wasn't scared.

"Why are you still here?" the voice on the recording asked.

"I cannot leave him. He is my one true love. He cannot go yet," a faint female voice said, sounding like she was speaking directly into the recorder.

The other stayed put, reaching arms out toward the female figure.

"Why can't he go yet?" Marshal's voice asked.

"He won't. He won't forgive himself so he can go. I must stay with him until he sees that his sins have been forgiven." The voice sounded sad and resigned. The woman appeared to know Marshal could understand her.

"Why does he torture himself?"

"It was such a terrible accident. He had no way to know that I would come through these woods. He knew the traps were here, but didn't warn me. He blames himself for not making sure. My father was watching me. I had to find another way."

Intrigued, Sydney scooted forward on her chair.

"I must go to him."

"Do you see me or just hear me?" Marshal asked.

"I see you. I see much. I try to help when I can but sometimes I only scare." The woman leaned close to the camera, her soft features further blurred by the wispy whiteness of her face. "Don't ever give up on love. The one you desire is not the one for you. She belongs to someone else and always will. Your heart's love is out there. You will find true happiness."

Tears sprang to Sydney's eyes and she couldn't believe Marshal had shown them this clip. Especially since the woman obviously spoke about her and Marshal. The video continued to run, showing the woman returning to the male figure and holding him in her arms. Finally the video ended and Sydney couldn't find a single thing to say.

"Whoa. That was interesting. What happened?" Daisy leaned forward, looking at the screen where the video stopped showing the lovers entwined in each other's arms.

"We didn't find much. Local lore tells of a young couple from rival families. Kind of a version of *Romeo and Juliet*. The older brother set a trap. The boy found out, but felt confident the girl wouldn't come that way. She ended up with a metal spike through her heart. He found her the next morning after being angry all night that she hadn't shown. They were supposed to elope. She forgave him on her dying breath and he shot himself right there. Sad story. Don't know how much of it is true." Marshal clicked out of the video.

"Interesting. What else?" Daisy bounced with excitement but Sydney could only feel sad.

"Your Native American travelers. It's highly possible this was part of the Trail of Tears. They're just memory spirits. I think the whole journey is done over and over again. Look at this." He clicked 'play' and Sydney watched as several blanket-wrapped figures passed in front of the camera. "Back there." He pointed to where three figures stood around a child-sized mound of dirt. "Many died on the journey. We have hours of this type of footage. It's different every time. I'll leave this with you to go over at your leisure."

Daisy practically bounced in her seat. "There's more, isn't there? I told you, Syd. We have to use this on our marketing. People will pay to stay here just to see a ghost."

Sydney couldn't find her voice. She nodded in a noncommittal kind of way.

"This video is of the pond. I think they were ice skating. You've both seen this and it seems to happen every week. This was part of an estate at one time. The main house burned down with the entire family inside. And then there's your bathhouse death." Marshal pushed a button. "She's gone now. Thought you'd want the tape. There's also this." He pushed another button and Sydney watched as several cats appeared on screen.

"Ghost cats?"

"That's how it appears. I don't know. I'm leaving you with about thirty hours of clean footage besides the pond and the trail. All of it shows something different and we've noticed the activity seems to go in cycles. Nothing appears threatening. If either of you feel like that's changed, call me right away and we'll reassess the situation." Marshal popped out the disc and placed it into a case before handing it to Daisy.

"Thanks, Marshal." Daisy hugged him.

"I'm thanking *you*. This was the best vacation I ever had. For many reasons." He shot Sydney a sideways glance and what was left of her heart shriveled up and turned to dust. "We really learned a lot by being here and I think you've helped make us an even better investigative team. I wonder if you'll let us come back in the off-season for training and stuff."

"Absolutely. You're always welcome here. Even if you just want to get away from it all." Daisy hugged him again, and Sydney wanted to cry.

"I might take you up on that. That is, unless Sydney minds me hanging around." Marshal's need for reassurance poked at the ashes in her chest.

She nodded. "Anytime."

Sadly, Marshal would always be just a very good friend and nothing more. What felt like a cold hand on her shoulder comforted her. Sydney didn't know if that was Gramps or some other spirit, but it didn't matter. She whispered a thank you.

CHAPTER 25

The next few days passed in a whirlwind of preparations, shopping, and phone calls. As soon as the ads hit the papers, the phone lines had gone crazy. They'd booked nearly the whole campground for the next month within a few hours. And that was without the added benefit of being able to advertise that Brookside was actively haunted.

Sydney still didn't know if she wanted that to be a well-known fact. She was all about having ghost tours, but didn't know if capitalizing on the spirits in residence was a good idea. It felt wrong and she told Daisy so.

"I agree. I'm fine with just doing the ghost tours. And not yet, either. We need to re-establish Brookside." Daisy leaned back in her chair and grinned. "We're doing it, aren't we? Making Gramps' wish come true."

Sydney nodded. She hadn't been able to say much lately and let Daisy be excited for both of them. Nothing felt right in her life right now. Except re-opening the campground. Even the spirits that had come to her for help avoided her now. Maybe she sent out too much negative energy or something. Or maybe they were acting on the compassion they had in life and knew she was hurting.

Guests were due to arrive by noon tomorrow. Everything was ready. They'd gone all out for their grand opening. The weekend would be filled with music, food, and fun activities. Daisy practically vibrated with excitement. Sydney was having trouble finding even a smile.

So far, Al hadn't given them any more information, even though they called him every day. Jace had left without a goodbye and Sydney refused to torture herself by calling him.

Violet had stayed out of the picture, too. Since they were reopening the campground ahead of schedule, her plans were finished. Even though Sydney was pretty sure Jace stopped her legal action against the property, she wouldn't put anything past the woman.

The lack of information was draining.

She stood and stretched as the phone rang. "Your turn. I'm going for a walk."

Daisy answered, a smile on her face and in her voice and Sydney heard her say what they'd both been repeating constantly since they started taking reservations.

There were maybe six sites left for this coming weekend. And the calendar was similar until well into August. At least she'd be too busy to moan over her broken heart and terrible luck. Now if she could only apply that and actually be happy they had achieved what had seemed impossible only a few weeks ago. Of course, Gramps' hidden money had helped immensely. She couldn't help but wonder if they would have been able to ever open without the extra cash.

She wanted to think they could have. They'd had a great plan, one that required many sacrifices of their own comfort and a slightly higher rate than they were now charging. Gramps' money only made things easier.

A car stopped but she kept going. Daisy had arranged for one of the local papers to come out and do an article about the re-opening. Sydney knew they wanted to talk to both of them, but figured she'd catch up with them in a few minutes. Once she had a chance to clear her head and stretch her legs.

She passed the circle of cabins where they'd spent so much time and couldn't help the pang of loss and loneliness that settled over her. The guys might have been a huge pain in the butt but having them here had been fun.

As far as she knew, Daisy hadn't spoken to Tucker since the morning he came to see the kittens. Then again, Daisy kept her cell phone off most of the time. Sydney wanted to ask her but could never find the courage. Bringing up Daisy's love life hurt as much as thinking about her own. She had to get over Jace.

She had no choice. They could never be together.

Her brain knew that. Her dreams were a different story. Every night she dreamt of him and what their future could have been if it wasn't for the shared DNA. Every morning she woke in tears, her heart breaking all over again for what she'd never had the right to want despite him being perfect for her in every way possible.

Lately, sleeping had been a chore. She didn't want the dreams so she stayed up as long as possible in the hopes that she would be so tired they wouldn't come.

But they always did.

Her cell phone rang but she ignored it. Daisy was probably reminding her that they were scheduled for this interview and photo shoot. She forced her feet to move past the little cabin where she'd learned so much about love and life. Her phone rang again and she pressed the silent button on the top, not looking at the number and not caring who tried so hard to get a hold of her.

Reaching the edge of the property, she sat on one of the benches that closed off the rest of the land Gramps left them. They had a few years until they could expand the campground, if they even would. Sydney kind of liked that the land was free and the animals that sometimes ventured from the woods into the campground. Except for the bears. At least they'd moved on for the season, with the help of some park rangers with tranquilizer guns.

Still, the sites that bordered the woods often brought deer into the campsites. She worried about that. Worried that the campers would make the animals depend on humans for food. They'd adopted a strict no feeding policy to deter that and to keep the peskier types of critters from over taking the campground. The last thing they needed was a band of raccoons or squirrels ravaging through their guest's belongings. Hopefully it worked, or else they'd at least have to put up a fence to keep at least some of the animals out.

Peace filled her. She couldn't help the feeling that Gramps approved of what they'd done and the sense grew stronger with the smell of his aftershave. Since his journals had turned out to be mostly cryptic messages and odd references, she figured she'd never know the dynamics between him and Violet. The sense that he felt he could save her stuck though, and for the first time since Violet started issuing orders and acting strange, Sydney found some compassion for the woman.

Her phone vibrated this time and she finally checked the caller ID. She still didn't pick it up, knowing that was stupid since they'd called Al every day and this was the first he'd returned their call. She scrolled through the missed calls. Daisy had called her twice and the other number was one she didn't recognize.

She supposed she should return to the office and get her portion of the interview over. Maybe she could take a nap afterward. They'd need every ounce of energy they could muster in a little more than twenty-four hours.

Two cars were now parked in the lot in front of the office. She didn't spend too much time thinking as she opened the office door. Daisy's laugh filtered through and she forced her best smile on her face and entered.

Except the only faces she saw were familiar ones. Al and, God forbid, Jace. He didn't acknowledge her. His eyes were blank and his expression grim. She wondered what that meant, hoping Violet hadn't found a way to get her hands on the campground after all.

Al smiled broadly and hugged her and it was all she could do to return his embrace.

"You sure like to keep things on your own terms, don't you?" She hadn't meant to sound rude.

Luckily, Al just laughed. "I know you're mad at me. I would be, too, but I didn't want to talk to you until I had all the information. I asked Jace to join us because he has a right to know the truth." Al motioned for them to sit.

Sydney dumbly followed orders even though she had a million questions

"Violet did have a child when she was a teenager. A girl. Her parents shipped her off to a home for girls to give birth. She was supposed to give the child up for adoption." Al took a drink from the coffee cup in his hand. Sydney had to stop herself from telling him to get on with it.

"The baby was stillborn. A girl. Violet was distraught. She maintained that the baby was Del's even though there was much talk over who fathered the child. Apparently she wasn't a one-man type gal. Her parents refused her requests to come home. They didn't believe Del was good enough for her and they figured she'd just get into trouble again so they sent her to a private school and moved away from the area."

Sydney really wanted to tell him to get to the point, but Al appeared to need them to know everything so she stayed silent.

"I didn't know any of that. That's much different than what she told me. Are you sure your sources have the right information?" Why did the sound of Jace's voice cause that razor-sharp pain to slice through the remnants of her heart?

"Absolutely correct. No doubt at all. That's what took me so long to call this meeting. I triple-checked my facts and more." Al stopped in front of Jace and still Sydney couldn't look at him.

"So, the baby Gramps fathered died at birth?" Daisy asked.

"Yes. If that child was even his. A year later, Violet got pregnant again. There's no way that child was Del's. She refused to give the baby up for adoption as her parents insisted. She had another girl. The child died at age two from the whooping cough."

"Kay said Violet claimed that baby was Del's daughter." Sydney finally found her voice.

"That's what she told him. It wasn't true. A year later, she again found herself unwed and pregnant and married the baby's father. A guy she met while bussing tables at the diner in the town where she lived. Remember this was a long time ago. Unmarried mothers were considered an embarrassment." Al leaned against the desk and grabbed his coffee cup.

"Was that my grandfather, or whatever he was to me?" Jace asked.

"No. Her first husband was a truck driver. He was killed when his truck caught fire about three weeks after they wed. That baby died as well, before birth."

Sydney felt a pang of sympathy for Violet. Three dead babies was a lot to consider.

"A few years later, she met and married your grandfather," he told Jace. "They had three more miscarriages and one baby that died at three months before finally having a healthy daughter, your mother. She apparently inherited Violet's childbearing difficulties and hemorrhaged after you were born. She was very young, not quite eighteen. Your father was only a little older. He shipped out for boot camp without even knowing your mother was pregnant and was killed by an artillery accident a few months later."

"Grandmother said they died in a skiing accident." Jace's voice was quiet.

"In collaboration with the DNA results, I'd sign my life on this as fact. None of you are related in any way." Al sat in the oversized chair.

Sydney waited. Her heart alternately swelled and deflated. She wasn't related to Jace. But he thought she'd forgotten how she felt for him. His comments to her when he'd found her and Marshal in the woods came back to haunt her.

Daisy stood. "So why did Violet tell so many different stories?"

"I'm sure Jace isn't even aware, but Violet has been under psychiatric care since shortly before his grandfather died. I could not legally learn the exact diagnosis or anything else, but I think a hard evaluation of her life could give cause. She's dealt with a lot. Remember I went to school with Violet and Del. Violet loved him, but her love twisted to obsession. She tried convinced him the story you were told was true, Jace. He really only pretended to believe you were his grandson because he liked you so much."

"Wait. I thought she said Jace was his son." Daisy stood beside her and Sydney resisted the urge to grab her hand.

"Did she say that? Well, it doesn't matter either way. It's not true. While Violet did come here to see Del while your Gram was away, nothing happened. She told him their daughter had died. Del was polite, even flirted, but he did not cross the line. Your Gram would have skinned him alive. So that story was never told to Del."

"So why did he think Jace was his grandson then?"

"He didn't. He adopted Jace as a grandson. I think because they were so much alike. Del loved Violet. He always did. And I really think he believed he could bring her back. All that pain she went through, I always got the impression Del felt responsible for some of it. Like if he had been with her, he could have prevented some things. I think he realized marrying her was a mistake. It took him a while. She was wonderful to him, just not to anyone else. When she turned that side onto him, he finally understood why his family stayed away."

"That's why he left the money." Daisy covered her mouth as the words spilled out, and Sydney wanted to poke her. They hadn't told a soul about the box of money Gramps had hidden for them.

"So you found it then? I thought so. Good. That's what he wanted. He even had me draw up legal documents that the money was yours if you weren't the ones to find the box. Right before he died, he realized what a terrible situation he'd made. I think he kind of knew that all along. No offense, Jace. Violet is seriously unbalanced."

"None taken. I don't consider the Violet you've all seen as my grandmother. She definitely wasn't perfect, but she loved me and I knew that." Jace sounded sad, and it was all Sydney could do not to reach out to him.

"There is something you need to know." Al stood and stood in front of Daisy. "According to the DNA tests, you and Sydney aren't even related. I had them done a second time and each result matches. You and Sydney aren't even cousins. And you are not Nadine's daughter."

Daisy faltered, and Sydney reached over and put her arm around her shoulder.

"What do you mean?" Sydney stared at Jace.

"There is no record of your birth. I did the best I could searching medical records, but that's a dead end without a court order. I talked to a few people who knew Nadine and they don't ever remember her being pregnant."

"What are you saying?" Daisy's voice was so quiet, Sydney had to strain to hear.

"Nadine is not your biological mother." Al dropped a stack of papers onto the desk. "I checked for kidnappings, but haven't had much luck. This is the information I found. It's yours. Do with it what you want but take some time to recover from this shock first."

Desperation covered Daisy's face and Sydney gathered her into her arms. "It doesn't change anything. You have always and will always be my sister. I'll help you with whatever you decide to do."

Sydney's heart broke for her sister who had been through so much already. Now to find out the woman who abandoned her as a young child hadn't even birthed her would be a blow almost too big to deal with.

Over Daisy's head, Jace caught her eye and shook his head in a sad gesture of commiseration.

Daisy sniffed. "I'm okay. Really. This is actually good news. It means I don't have that terrible woman's blood in my veins. I always knew something was wrong there. Now I know what." Daisy smiled, tears leaking from the corners of her eyes.

"Good girl. You're going to be okay." Al hugged Daisy. "When you're ready I'll go over some of your options."

"I'm ready now. Tell me what I need to know." Daisy squeezed Sydney before seating herself back at her desk and facing Al with a bright smile.

Jace's phone rang and he turned to answer the call. Sydney felt the information press down on her. Sure, she and Jace weren't related, but that still didn't mean he really wanted her now.

Sydney opened the front door and slipped out, heading for the pond via the trail behind the office. She listened for the sounds that would indicate Jace followed. Instead, a ghostly figure passed, oblivious to Sydney's pain or presence. The soft noises of the woods soon covered the sounds of the real world and she dropped onto a bench, staring at the pond without really seeing the ducks that glided on the smooth surface.

"Mind if I join you?"

Sydney jumped, turning to Jace's handsome face.

"It's a free country." It didn't come out as sarcastic as she'd intended. Dang. She wanted him to know how much he'd hurt her the last time he'd had anything to say to her.

"So you're mad at me?" Jace didn't sound mocking so she turned to him and poked him in the chest.

"How dare you? How could you believe that I would run right into Marshal's arms after finding out that we could never be together?" She couldn't help the anger.

"I didn't mean that. You have to know I didn't mean that." Jace put his hands up.

"How? You make snide comments and then disappear until today. How was I supposed to know?"

"I'm sorry. I guess you wouldn't. I was angry, as angry as you were. I followed you so I could talk to you and then found you and Marshal hugging. I was jealous, even though I knew there was nothing between you two." Sydney wanted to launch herself into his arms, but she forced herself to wait. "Being related to you was the worst thing that has ever happened to me. I couldn't eat, couldn't sleep, and couldn't stop thinking about you even though I knew I had to let you go. I just couldn't. I was angry with the world for the blood that supposedly ran through our veins. Every time I closed my eyes I saw you. Every time I slept I dreamt of you." Jace reached out and grabbed her hand and she finally eased against him.

"I know. I think I went a little bit crazy there for a while. I just kept thinking about how unfair it was that after all we've been through that there was no way we could even be friends. I not only lost the love of my heart, I lost my best friend." Sydney let the tears fall.

"I love you, Sydney. I think I have since the first time you yelled at me when you thought I was in cahoots with Grandmother."

"What did Gramps leave you in his will?"

"His fishing gear and the cabin on the river." Jace wiped her tears away.

Only they fell harder. Gramps leaving Jace his beloved fishing equipment only cemented what she already knew. If

Gramps felt Jace was worthy of them, he'd also felt he could be trusted with her heart. She shook her head, the long ago conversation she'd had with Gramps about the right man for her replaying in vivid detail. Gramps had said any man who loved her had better be worthy of his fishing gear.

"I love you, too." She kissed him, loving the way it felt to be close to him again. "You really going to be okay with me being able to see and talk to the spirits around here?"

She wasn't going to lose him by not telling him everything.

"Gramps tried to hide it from me, too, but he managed about as well as you do. Yes. I love you, weird supernatural abilities and all. Nothing is ever going to change that." He hugged her tight and her worries dissipated.

Well, all but one.

"What's your grandmother going to say about us?"

"I don't know. I really don't care, but I can't be like that. Her opinion isn't going to change how I feel and I'm never going to let her hurt you." Jace held her close, and the planets finally aligned for Sydney.

She wasn't going to be a crazy old cat collector after all.

Now she had the cats and the man.

CHAPTER 26

Fourteen weeks later . . .

Sydney smiled as Daisy hung the sign officially closing the campground for the season. "As fun as this summer was, I'm glad it's over."

"You and me both. We did good. People are already booking next season. I think Gramps would be proud." Sydney hugged her before they went to the office.

"And you are getting married in the morning. I'm so happy." Sydney knew that Daisy was sincere but it still made her sad. Daisy's happily-ever-after hadn't happened yet.

Tucker hadn't come around or called all summer. He'd sent his crews to do the maintenance, but never showed himself. Sydney had even bitched him out on a cell phone message for the way he tramped on her sister's heart and left her alone when she really needed a friend.

Graham's mother had passed away the day after he left. Marshal said he was in a deep abyss, but was writing again while helping his sister's clear out the house and settle the estate.

Daisy's search for her true parents continued. Nadine insisted Daisy was her daughter, even though further DNA testing proved that as a lie. She vehemently denied taking her as a newborn. Nadine would never bother her again. The doctors had deemed her unfit for trial and she would spend the rest of her days in a maximum security mental hospital.

Sydney fought with what had compelled Nadine to steal someone's child. She could only imagine what Daisy went through. Daisy didn't speak of it though, except in matter-of-fact terms and Internet searches. When her search found no kidnapped or abandoned babies, Daisy ended up starting from scratch.

What bothered Sydney the most was the fact that Daisy seemed changed by everything. Most of the changes were good. She'd matured much since they started this renovation and reopened the campground. Though Daisy seemed oblivious to men now. Several times she'd been asked out or flirted with by guests and contractors and from Sydney's standpoint she'd never even acted like she'd noticed. That couldn't be good.

Daisy wasn't healing.

"Your house is finished. Mine is, too." Daisy grabbed her arm and pointed to the new house next door to Gramps house. The house Daisy insisted she build because she didn't want to live with newlyweds. She said she and Jace would gross her out on a daily basis and she didn't think she could handle that kind of stuff. The whole thing had been discussed as a joke, but there was a lot of truth behind Daisy's statements.

"Where are my cats?"

"*Our* cats are at *my* house. I will think about loaning you a few after the honeymoon." Daisy stepped out of arm's reach. "You know for someone who was so dead set against these cats you sure are possessive."

"Those cats helped me see that I was trying too hard. They saved me from being a lonely, bitter woman." It was true. She only wished they'd do the same for Daisy.

"I heard from Marshal. He'll be here for the wedding. He said he wouldn't miss it for anything and he's bringing a woman." Daisy wiggled her eyebrows and Sydney felt nothing but pleased that Marshal had moved on. "And . . ."

"And what?"

"Tucker is coming as my date." Daisy picked a flower. "That's good, right?"

"Yes. I think it's very good. Very good." Daisy winked.

"What happened?"

"I called him and told him to quit acting like a jerk. Told him if he felt anything at all for me, he at least owed me a few conversations. He's obliging. Neither of us know what we want in the future. Even though Nadine isn't my mother, I don't know if I'm cut out for motherhood. Tucker is still reasonably certain he wants children. At least we're talking." Daisy shrugged.

"Good. I'm really glad." Sydney hugged her, wishing for her sister's happy ending.

"Your man is so romantic it's sickening." Daisy waved at Jace.

Jace stood on the stoop of their house, a bouquet of roses in his arms, a goofy smile on his face, and a cheesy welcome mat now under his feet.

Sure, their house had finished a month off schedule. She knew they were getting close, but preparing for the end of season had taken up all of her time lately and she hadn't had the energy to find out the progress. Running, she launched herself into Jace's arms.

"It's really done?" she managed in-between kissing him.

"Yep. All ours." His lips trailed up her neck and she was lucky he held her up or else she'd be a puddle at his feet.

"Hey you two. No one wants to see that. Wait until your honeymoon. In fact, I'm not even sure you are supposed to see each other. Mom will have a cow." Daisy laughed from the bottom steps.

"How are we supposed to have our rehearsal if we can't see each other? I think that's for after the dinner tonight." Sydney motioned her forward, determined to keep her sister involved and away from work and her search for her true parents for the next twenty-four hours.

"Oh. Yeah. I knew that. Kiss your man and let's go. Mom is waiting for us at the bridal shop. We have a list a mile

long. You can fool around with Jace on your honeymoon."
Daisy hugged them both.

"Fool around with Jace on your honeymoon. I like that."
Jace kissed her, bringing her as close to him as she could get
without losing her clothing.

"Me, too. Two weeks at the beach. With a sexy man
by my side. With my sexy husband by my side. I don't
think it could get any better." She spoke against his mouth,
wondering if they could sneak inside and christen the master
bedroom before Daisy reminded her of what time it was.

A horn honked and she had to dismiss that idea.

"You're taking your boyfriend and your husband to the
beach? Wow. That's bold." Jace kissed her again.

"You are such a fruitcake. But I love you anyway. You
said you wanted to tell me something? Do it quick before
Daisy has a coronary."

"I had a long talk with Grandmother. She's been
faithfully taking her medication and seeing her therapist. Her
prognosis is good though she'll need support for the rest of
her life. Support she should have had ages ago. I think she's
finally come to terms with us and is starting to put her own
life into perspective. She's going to come to the wedding."

Nervousness spread through her. Violet had tried to
cause many problems over the past few months. She'd
restated her claim that she and Jace were related, coming
up with a totally new and twisted story that threatened their
foundation and Gramps' character. Though they knew the
story was false, the resulting cleanup had taken a while to
wade through. For the past month, she'd tried nothing. Jace
might believe her, but Sydney had her doubts.

"It'll be okay. Al has promised to keep her in line. She's
only coming to the ceremony, not the reception. Her doctor
doesn't want her having to face her alcohol problem. He
doesn't think she's far enough along to be able to make the
right decision. She is apologizing for everything now."

"Okay. I trust your judgment." She kissed him.

How no one had known about Violet's alcohol abuse still baffled them. The woman had spent the past few years constantly drunk. No wonder she'd done some crazy things. She hadn't truly dried up until after Al found her passed out in the front seat of her car and called an ambulance. Sydney's heart broke for Gramps. He'd tried so hard to help her.

Sydney was doing everything she could to keep her emotions soft toward the woman. That task was difficult at times, but she owed Jace and Gramps that much. Both had seen the good in Violet and the least she could do was try, despite what she'd put them through.

More horn honking and Sydney finally broke the promising kiss. "We'll continue this when I'm your wife."

"My wife. I like the sound of that. Are you really okay with Grandmother coming to the wedding?" He kissed her neck and made it hard for her to think. "I know she hasn't exactly been easy for you the whole time you've known her."

"I am. She needs to make her peace with us. Al won't let her cause trouble. It's all good. We'll sit her with the ghosts and the cats. I'm kidding." She kissed his nose and wiggled out of his arms. "Be here at six for rehearsal. Don't be late."

"Eleven for rehearsal. Be late. Got it." Jace laughed.

"I love you." She wrinkled her nose at him. "Even though you are a butthead."

"You called me that the first time we talked." He laughed. "I love you too. I always will. Don't ever forget that."

"I don't intend to."

CPSIA information can be obtained at www.ICGtesting.com
Printed in the USA
BVOW06s2010260516

448843BV00008B/19/P